CW00521156

WHAT IF BOWIE WERE A WOMAN?

BY KITTY RIGGS

AUTHOR NOTE

'What If Bowie Were A Woman,' is entirely fictional. Real musicians, real people and places appear from time to time, but everything else is utterly fictional. What the characters do, say and how they act, are all products of my imagination. The book is based upon David Bowie's life, and the music remains unchanged because I would never (*ever*) erase or change, *even for fiction*, his music. Please understand I admired David, and would never do anything to damage or harm his image. The purpose of David's influence is to highlight the struggle women face in the music industry. Having an already famed androgynous figure, like Bowie, makes Penny's story that bit easier to swallow and believe.

The story of *Julian Hows'* working for London Transport is real, although the story of him stealing the bus is fictional (as far as I know). I want you to know that. I love his story, and I think more people need to know about him and what he stood for.

PLEASE TAKE THIS BOOK
WITH A PINCH OF SALT. MR
DAVID BOWIE IS WORSHIPPED
IN MY LIFE AS A GOD FIGURE:
I WOULD NEVER INTENTIONALLY
DAMAGE OR POTENTIALLY
HARM HIS IMAGE.
THIS IS JUST SOMETHING
OF A POLITICAL STATEMENT
TO HIGHLIGHT THE CHALLENGES
WOMEN FACE- OH, AND ALSO
TO SAY THAT THE PATRIARCHY
CAN GO FUCK ITSELF.

FOR
MUM
& DAD

CHAPTER ONE
A PROPER
KID

In the small hours of a Tuesday in 1974, I'm blind pissed, stoned, and stark bollock naked, wailing about cross dressing pigeons. I'm shooting up in between Keith Moon and Molly Jagger, who jerks off Rod Stewart while unsuccessfully injecting heroin into her forearm. It drips out down her arm to her fingers, which she licks clean from her skin; it's like watching the cutting of diamonds, so pure and originated. There are three men with eight fingers in one girl; seven speakers stacked in the wardrobe; piss at my feet; a fire in the corner, and I'm pretty sure there's a python sneaking about the place.

Chelsea Hotel, New York, 1974.

It's my twenty- seventh birthday, and I've made it. I'm overwhelmed by the fact I've survived.

I haven't surrendered to drugs. I haven't drowned myself in wine.

I haven't jumped off a cliff or got a mate to shoot me.

Yet, I add to my conscience; I haven't got a mate to shoot me *yet.*

Marc Bolan makes the bathtub a punch bowl; plugging the bath and pouring in: six bottles of vodka, one bottle of brandy, a bottle of fine whiskey, a child's carton of apple juice, three bottles of champagne, and about three-quarters of a bottle of absinthe. The sink is also plugged and filled with wine: *'for the younguns,'* Marc says. There's a lot of *'younguns'* about the place tonight, not at my doing, I hate groupies; I am notoriously known for hating groupies. However, where there are men and rock n roll, there are underage girls and their alluring midnight fantasies. We've all been there.

I blame Michael Hutchence.

The corridors are littered with grown men pissing up the walls and into the lift. Women are passed out on top of foodservice trolley's. A couple shag on the windowsill with the curtains drawn around them, their love playing like a zoetrope on the ceiling. A guy tells me the lights are bust in the orgy room for *'atmospheric purposes.'* But I saw him swinging on the lampshade earlier after he'd just taken a hit of smack. The orgy room is littered in threesomes and couples, sprinkled lavishly across the floor like sugar dusted on a cake. The smell of sex clogs my nostrils, it's hard to think about anything else. An awakening of the senses and soul. Fucking, fucking, fucking: until the sun gets tired, but we don't. Some people arrive bare and leave clothed; others arrive clothed and leave stark bollock naked. It usually depends on how many orgy's you get caught up in during the night.

Music blares from every crack and under every crevasse. It's hard to tell where the music comes from, it remains the same volume wherever I go, ringing divinely in my ears. The music slides between each ear and through every vein in my head like cheap pegs slide along a slack washing line in the spring wind. The music performs an exorcism inside of me, penetrating my every sense. Piercing my every thought and feeling. I'm influenced by sound, liberated by souls, heightened with love.

Music is more than the noise drowning out the groans of love and the grumbles of drugs. Music is beyond the soundtrack of the night: deeper than noise, more sensual than direct sound, more poignant than living. When the music is reverberating between souls together in the small hours of a morning, music becomes everything. *Beyond everything.* Every single soul on that hotel floor believes it all means nothing without the music. And so, music becomes the sex and the drugs and the rock n roll you talk of. Music fucks you and fucks your friend. Music gets you high, gets you jumpy, irate, makes you want to fly and soar and fall from heights in glory.

I don't remember how much or what drugs I took; I remember the music.

I remember *'Little Richard, Tutti Frutti'* coming on as I'm leaving the orgy room feeling satisfied yet disheveled. *I went back for more.* I can taste the whiskey when I hear *Jimi Hendrix's: Voodoo Child.'* I can taste a certain someone when I hear *'Elton John's, Don't let the sun go down on me.'*

I believe there were fire breathers, and that wasn't a hallucination induced by a mixture of sweet things, and I'm almost convinced there were naked clowns. There's never much point in bringing clothes, as they're only torn off an hour or so and a bottle or two into the party. I looked astonishing that night. I wore Tommy's fur coat he stole from Molly and nothing else.

Molly typically goes silent when she shoots heroin, which was not the case that night. Some call it a bad batch, others know it's a mixture of a lot of bad things inside *one* good thing. Molly doesn't remember ripping the bedside cupboard off the wall and throwing it (including half a stash of weed) outside the window and onto the streets of New York. Keith spent the night babysitting Molly to stop her jumping out of the smashed window, and chasing after the stash we were all reminding her she'd given to New York for free, eight flights down.

It's unusual that I remember one of Marc's parties; it's, in fact, the only party I have any recollection of. *Ever*. Which is irritating, because I'm told of much more extravagant and exciting parties than my 27th birthday.

Like the time me and my band stole a boat and woke up in Calais' security headquarters after a gig in Stoke. Or the time Molly and I supposedly interrupted a Broadway performance of Les Miserables by swinging on the safety curtain and landing on Cosette's head. Or the memory, I do sincerely wish I had, of climbing onto a hotel roof and pissing successfully onto the street below and directly into Marc Bolan's poor top hat.

I remember my childhood more vividly than some of the (*supposed, allegedly, apparently*) best nights of my life. Who invented that cruel dose of amnesia? I remember being a big, blue baby and being carried home; the sensation of the wind wrapping its punishing fingers around me seeming like witchcraft.

I was born on 40 Stansfield Road, Brixton; to two London parents named: Peggy and John. Titled Penelope (it's always been Penny) Jones, I had dull, hinting red hair and chubby cheeks, like every other baby. Babies are so dull, soulless, naked creatures lacking personality and grace as they fall out a woman's vagina: like a rag in the wind. I'm determined I was never a spiritless baby or a baby at all. I was born with a personality, with *disposition.* In all accounts, I most certainly did not come out of the womb wearing a cowboy hat and blood red stepsons. But in my memory, I unquestionably arrived, *wherever from,* with at least a little glitter in my hair.

My childhood was as lukewarm as a cooling apple strudel. Never any fuss, unless I was fussing, never much calm either. Just a lukewarm, fuss-less existence, in a quiet neighbourhood in South London. My childhood was the last few inches of dirty, pube riddled, lukewarm bathwater desperately trying to escape to the join the shit in the sewers. *A perfectly standard British family trying not to succumb to insanity.* My mother was infested with the foolish termites of absurdity, something I thought all mothers caught in the maternity ward. It's only as I've aged, have I come to understand that a mother who buries her plates if the family has eaten fish, is occupied with such termites. And unparalleled, with such termites. Most of her actions were to *'ward off unwanted spirits;'* like going to church. She couldn't put a face or a name to these *'spirits,'* she could only give you a list; of all the idiotic things, you should do to keep them out your house and lives.

- Make a sponge cake with vinegar
- Line your drawers with salt
- Place a page of the bible in every photo frame
- Remain silent after eleven o'clock
- Bury plates that have touched fish
- Keep a monthly sample of your urine in an outdoor shed.

The list goes on and on, and it doesn't get any better.

My mother was born and raised in an army camp and dumped in the city after her mother died. She struggled to evolve past the war. A clock would chime, or a dinner plate would smash, and she'd visibly cower like the wind come spring. She struggled, like a drowning duck, to evolve to the ever-changing and fast paced London in the 1950s. Her roots were firmly embedded in being the loving wife, she was raised to be, and cleaning the house ready for her husband's arrival, as I shunned her from upstairs.

Her husband, John, was not the father I think he hoped to be. He worked for the children's charity: 'Barnardo's' and was incredibly devoted to his job. Our time together was spent at the dinner table, talking of sick children prevailing despite their arduous circumstances. It seemed his own child just wasn't riveting enough, or perhaps not amply damaged, to be discussed at the dinner table.

Yet, we'd run through fields together on weekends, maybe even catch a few fireflies as the cliché goes.

It was not a loving relationship, in the traditional sense, but rest assured it was not a relationship without love. He liked a lot of the innocent things I did as a kid, like baking with my mother, hopscotching outside, and sleeping with a small doll next to my head. He just didn't like it when I outgrew these things and started smoking cigarettes on his front step; instead of sweetly drawing flowers in chalk. My father was suckered into the idea that fathers are fathers of *children*, not adults or teenagers, or *'adolescent scum'* as he'd call my friends.

If he couldn't silence me with a lollipop, he didn't want to talk to me.

As a kid, I used to think love was dirty. I'd wash my cheeks of wet, sloppy kisses from distant Aunts and long dead Great Grandads. I'd itch if I were hugged. I never kissed my mother or father, nor returned the favour of polite greeting kisses. I would shiver and run to the nearest bathroom to wash myself in horror. Not out of embarrassment or adolescent shame.

No. It was rather hard to embarrass me as a child. I still don't find much embarrassing now. I thought love was dirty because love was not passed around the dinner table in comforting, *although indisputably patronising*, dishes of affection.

Muddy shoes, dirty hands, dirty fingernails; were strictly not allowed at the dinner table. Therefore, *love was dirty*. Love was the steaming hot mud pie I so desperately wanted to bring to my parents at the kitchen table.

It was a hideous, monstrous, obtuse, filthily looking thing that had no seat at our table and no space in our living room. Or in our lives, *at all*, for that matter. I couldn't fraternise with love, or dare get dirt on my skin. I distinctively remember hearing the phrase: *'the mud of love is too tough for your average corner shop soap, and we're just too poor for 'owt else.'* Because love wasn't just dirty in our house, it had its own *class hierarchy* too.

Yet, it seemed my family weren't poor for much else other than love and potential love removing remedies. *'Best to stay clear of a sticky situation,'* my mother would say to almost everything, including love. *'Some things just aren't worth the heartache,'* she'd add, most commonly in response to my terrible baking. My mum was right. Some things just aren't worth the heartache: *but love is.*

Indisputably love is worth the heartache. You learn if you spent your childhood believing love was dirty, unethical, and a nuisance; that love is worth every single emotion: good or otherwise.

For love ain't dirty, it couldn't be sullied if it tried. It is probably the purest thing, the complete opposite of filth. Love is the antidote to dirt. *Love washes all the muck away.*

I watched how to fall in love and out of it in equal measure. I watched poets die in the name of it; I watched the trees sprout from the Earth because of it; I watched strangers steal glances in parks feeling it.

Mothers tell you all sorts of things that just aren't true, like getting curly hair if you eat the crusts.

Love is dirty, being a prime example. Parents, on the other hand, can be a whole landfill of filth, at least in my experience anyway. My mother and father tried to rid me of one of the greatest feelings on Earth.

Love.

The child in me yearned for their attention, although I seemingly didn't care if they loved me or not, because I knew the stars loved me. They wrote me love letters in the sky, sent me creatures of the night, and became the candlelight of which I wrote under.

The stars have always been my *true* guardians.

I was an annoying child, as children always are. I would dip my mother's bras in the Sunday roast gravy and leave them hanging outside on our garden gate, for pure amusement. I'd hide the coffee mugs around the house obsessively when I was eight years old. I'd turn the pictures hung in the wall, upside down, even when I was smaller than the frame, and it took a considerable amount of difficulty for me to do so. The neighbour had a young boy, of whom I would tell the old woman across the road was an alien that was sent to watch little boys like himself; in case they kissed girls, who were the spawn of the devil. I had a nasty habit of emptying the bins in the middle of the street. I was the kid who threw paint on the walls. I made teddy bears out of socks and doily's and sold them in my garden over the fence to a lady that had dementia and would get lost. I sent multiple letters to prisons across the South, with no idea if they got anywhere, that read:

'Dear prison, let them go now, you've had your fun, how would you like it? Huh? It's a bloody bisquit (how I spelt and said biscuit). Love always, Pen.'

My morals and awareness of the criminal system and, indeed, criminal behaviour was hardly that finely tuned at the young age of eight. I thought prisoners were strictly only people who stole biscuits from the biscuit factory; after hearing my dad say, the biscuit factory had been robbed. I thought it was a bit harsh to lock up a few people who wanted a few free biscuits when the church handed them out for free. I know now, they stole money and machinery and not cookies. But I thought they might've been gay men wanting a free biscuit like their heterosexual friends from the church they weren't welcomed into!

I was the kid digging in the soft ground, hoping to reach China by the time the lunch bell rang. I was an introvert by the book. I kept to myself, did weird shit, freaked my parents out a little bit, made my grandparents hate me, and dyed my hair black by the time my parents had contacted an asylum.

My parents would've happily sent me off to a school for badly behaved children; if they had it in blood, I wouldn't cause a fuss being dragged to the car. They knew full well I'd only alarm the neighbours, and families in the 60s *strictly did not alarm the neighbours.* Especially, if they wanted to upkeep the *'sane family'* facade, it seemed the entirety of London were insistent on up keeping.

Instead, I went to a *'normal'* school for *'normal'* children where boys repeatedly picked their noses, and little girls threw up their school dinner on top of their school dinner. The girls would waddle around with their thick grey tights slipping down to their ankles, and the boys would whip out their tiny cocks at any given moment for the patriotism of juvenescence.

I was in a zoo of unknown and untameable species that seemed a whole lot more peculiar than I was. My habit of colouring in my father's beard while he slept; seemed mediocrely guileless and somewhat sweet. Compared to the nit infested barbarians, who would run around the playground demanding I kiss them. Before being chasing into a wasp infiltrated corner that the teachers couldn't see, by a young boy named 'Phillip' who'd get his cock out and piss up the wall!

School was unforgiving towards a young girl who wanted to educate herself. It ran on the ethos that any dose of power for a child is too much power, and knowledge is the ultimate source of said power. Meaning we were often taught how to count and to smile in equal measure, as though to devalue mathematics in the hopes girls wouldn't forget the importance of obeying the patriarchy. I'd steal books from the local library and read them behind the greenhouse to appease my appetite for knowledge the school just didn't attain. I got caught copying a diagram of a vagina in my last year and told: *'I wouldn't need to know about that nuisance,'* by my RE teacher. I told her I had a spot on my vulva, to which she visibly gagged before escorting me to the headteacher who slapped me.

For a young woman, I was unusually aware, unusually inquisitive, and extraordinarily annoying. Or simply, *unusual*, to others. I genuinely think they were fearful of a girl schooling herself enough to learn that the world is, and always has been a shit place for women.

I'd read of it in a hundred novels, all citing the same inequality. Every love affair, kidnap; divorce; loveless marriage; damsel in distress and every mother of 500. It was the same old story. Same blonde, weak armed slag who gets up the duff before her dreams are due. Same brunette receptionist who shags the vicar for a chance to run the bake sale. Same mother of three who puts her head in the oven for the romance of it. I wasn't supposed to be reading such revealing novels at such a fertile age. I wasn't supposed to be reacting in disgust and believing it was all trite; that there was another world for women who weren't the generic mould I was gagged by. I was supposed to be *conforming*. Supposed to be playing along. Supposed to be another blonde, weak armed slag. Only, I wasn't blonde, or weak, or a slag (*just yet*); so, I didn't fit the commercial mould of 'woman.' That's probably why people started thinking, and in turn, partially treating me like a man. Or maybe a man with a vagina. Definitely the latter, I was still completely ignored, disrespected, molested and paid less; so, they couldn't have thought I was wholly a man. A stinking, spotty arsed, boring man who could recite every Austen novel backwards. What a sight I was.

I was that much of a freak, the school practically registered me a tourist destination; without the extortionate gift shop.

It's safe to say; I was what they'd call a nuisance. I was the rat you couldn't catch; the infection you couldn't clear; the nostalgia you couldn't forget.

I see now my behaviour, *for a child,* must have seemed strange to other children. I spent a lot of my childhood outdoors, predominantly barefoot and chested like a tribesman, searching for creatures and howling at the sun. Our neighbours at Stansfield thought I was a boy. They'd buy me toy guns for Christmas and small suit jackets for my birthday.

I would always play dress-up, raiding my father's wardrobe and dressing my whole frame into one trouser leg, or wrapping his shirts twice around me or my head. I loved the boys' uniform at school, I didn't understand why I had to wear the black, pinafore dresses. I once quite literally tore the clothes off an unsuspecting boys' back and made him switch clobber with me for two sticks of liquorice and a gobstopper.

It lasted some whole glorious ten minutes before I was curtly slapped on both my knuckles with a ruler, five times for a week. My parents did the same at home with an iron cooking spatula and locked me in my room at night after school. Being locked in my room and bluntly punished happened rather frequently as a child. I got caught stealing the neighbours garden wind chime because I was intrigued by the sound, and my father showed me the cane.

I'd just sit on my bed and read for hours on end when they locked me in my room. It was no bother, in fact I preferred the peace and quiet. The first book I remember intensely devouring is *'William Golding's: Lord of the flies.'* I was that hooked, I demanded my mother call me 'Ralph' for a month. I would bring sticks into school and encourage my classmates to read the book and join me in avenging war against the teachers. I was suspended for the first time, when a girl, who always had snot on her jumper, named *Julia,* told the headteacher I was trying to kill him. When he found my bookbag was overflowing with sharpened sticks I'd gathered from my garden, it must've looked suspicious to be fair to him. I tried to explain that the sticks were just for throwing at the windows because I liked the noise and wanted to annoy him, not to bloody kill him! But he dutifully told me that's just as bad and suspended me, showing me out the door shaking in unjustified fear. For that, I was forced to kneel on rice for half an hour and read the bible, which did nothing but make me laugh. The tales of the bible always amused me as a kid. They were as lavished in fantasy as a Tolkien novel.

Despite my dad working for a charity supporting disadvantaged and often abused children, it did not make him more lenient with punishment. Like every child in the 50s, corporal punishment was an unfortunate aftershock of the war; now considered a humorous topic of conversation at the dinner table as we discuss *the good 'ole days*. It was not comical at the time.

The worst tale I ever heard was that of a boy named Ruben Shipp, who was locked in the broom cupboard for the entire weekend for digging up a worm and teasing his sister with it at the kitchen table. He appeared red eyed, as thin as a rake, begging every kid on the street for a gobstopper or a bit of bread, for the starvation. I don't miss the knuckles so raw; picking up your fork felt like a second punishment, and I most certainly don't feel more obedient for it.

The only punishment I would be thankful for was being banished to my room. My mother would lock me in my bedroom from 9 in the morning to 9 in the evening at the weekends and overnight in the week, which gave me plenty of time to myself. She'd either barricade the door with the spare rooms' chest of drawers or eventually invest in a sliding lock that could quite effortlessly be snapped with enough of a kicking.

In the early years of being locked in my room, I'd be alone with a pen and paper: *the perfect punishment.* Although at the time, I would write diary entries begging to be set free. Little scraps of writing asking Gods to forgive me and love from my mother. I'd create these complex lands; insistent on solvable crimes being corporal punishment for badly behaved children. I would write out of complete monotony.

As I grew older, my parents would take my vinyl and record player from me as retribution, so all I had in my room was a bed, clothes, pen, and paper.

Sometimes, I'd make my friends sneak up the drain pipe, and haul them through the window using a pulley system I made out of old bras. That quite bluntly stopped when we'd sit smoking by the window, and mum would walk by and smell the nicotine like a blood hound. She put bars on at one point, but I paid a boy from down the road two shillings to tear them off and share a joint with me. My mother then bought a dog that was trained to bite ankles, and after it completely tore an ex-boyfriend's ankles to shreds, I stopped inviting people around when I was grounded.

Instead, I'd try on every single piece of clothing I owned, in any kind of misshapen order and see what looked the best. I used to plan my weeks' outfits and made it my challenge for them to look as audacious as possible to prove to my mum I was going crazy being locked up like a heart in the ribs. I would eventually get bored, and by the end of the week, I'd be bent over, my eyes stinging red raw for the words I'd poured out. I felt as though I had nothing compelling to write about my life, or where I lived as a young kid; I hadn't quite seen enough of London to fall in love with it yet.

I didn't understand, at that time, the sacrifice you make as a writer. I thought I was in control, which is preposterous. No writer is in control. Your writing is an unconscious product of your being. Writing is more than just the oil to the machinery inside of me. It is every cog, every screw, every bolt, and every nut.

I wouldn't know how to function without it. *It* tells *me* when to sleep. *It* tells *me* when to stop and start. I have no say in the matter, and I'm okay with that. At least, I'm okay with that *now*; it was all very new and intimidating to start with. Writing *music* is a sacrificial thing; you sacrifice your feelings, your memories, and your hurt. It's a *God-like-deal-situ.* You meet the devil, he says: *'I'll give you what you need if you give me all that pain,'* and you can't say no. You just can't, he'll take them anyway. You think it'll be a satisfying release, but it's not. Not really. It's more than vulnerable.

It's like having to meet a new you, without causing any havoc, to keep your deal with the devil a secret and allow the illusion of writing to continue to exist. It's all very soulful; or *soulless*, depending on how you look at it.

My habit of writing blossomed from a state of tedium, so much so, that I now find myself never being bored; for my fingers unknowingly occupy themselves with a pen before I think about the task. That's how the sacrifice works.

That habit is the only thing that's sustained me my career, as I never wrote anything of significance to start with.

I wrote about a pirate at a water park once and his handsome parrot. I penned a distant land called 'Cereal City' where everything was made of cereal boxes, and the hills were orange, and the sky was always a fading black.

I would often write poems about the cat down the road and how fucking annoying it was. Sometimes, I pretended there was a girl at school that I was in love with, mimicking an Elvis song I'd heard the once on the radio.

All the writing I was surrounded with, was written by men about pretty women, so I wrote about the same. There was a Jewish girl two streets down the road, who would sit in front of her blue painted fence, for boys to come and kiss her. Lola was winsome. I kissed her once and wrote my first song that night, imaginatively called: *'Lola.'*

Writers tend to spend their childhood slushing through drafts and manuscripts of senseless sentiments. But it is those fragmentary sentiments that later make sense. Or maybe they don't. Not everything should. Those sentiments that don't make sense though, are building blocks. They enable you to learn. The best way to better your writing is by writing. *And writing and writing and writing,* until your fingers bleed and your wrists ache like that first time you successfully wanked off your boyfriend to a climatic surprise.

You learn. Like when you get your period for the first time, and you learn that white underwear is neither sexy nor practical. You learn from doing. And *failing.* I learnt to never, ever, *ever,* ask a crowd of fifty men in a south London pub what they're doing later that night. I learnt not to do that, by (you guessed it) *doing exactly that,* and receiving, what can only be described; as a plethora of a hundred ways one man can fuck one woman.

24

Writing was a form of escapism that I failed to find in other things. Like crafts or ballet or even reading. Because of this, my childhood was spent in character. My favourite character is indefinitely the scandalous male businessman, *Mr Rex*: my eleven-year-old self for about three weeks. He wore blue shoelaces tied around his forehead, red pants *only*, and spoke in riddles during the week and remained silent at the weekends. I liked the play, the adventure of a character, the tease of innovation. I could be whatever I wanted to be; isn't that what childhood is for?

Experimenting; dressing up; adventures; playing; falling in the mud; swinging in the park; visiting distant imaginary worlds; speaking in make-believe languages.

Expression was to my imagination what courage is to the lion in 'The Wizard of Oz.'

I'd perform to the shampoo in the shower. I'd look it dead in the lid and sing my guts out, dancing hungrily for the array of stolen hotel miniatures. I'd recite stories to the gnomes in the garden, reading poetry to the trees. Shouting at cornfields, dialogue from books I didn't understand, narrating love anecdotes from literature to the birds that flew past my head too fast enough to hear the end. I was debauched in being a kid. In being free and reckless; loving and elementary. In believing in everything and dreaming of it all. Creating as much as possible, for as long as possible.

When I was a kid, the trees did not make a forest; they made a jungle. The birds did not make a noise; they made a song. The flowers did not grow; they boomed from the Earth with vigour and defiance. I was, in my childhood, a *kid*. A proper, dirty, rotten kid, formed from a loveless marriage and nurtured by literature and shrubs, as kids often were back then. *A proper fucking kid.*

CHAPTER TWO
SACRIFICIAL
BLOWJOBS
FOR A SKIFFLE

I'm sure there's a reason I was born in Brixton and raised by London.
I'm sure there's a reason I lived in a city I did not build; on an Earth, I
never discovered. I'm sure there's a reason I stamped my feet on the
soil one day and declared it my own. I'm sure the small things matter.
And I'm confident the intentions will align; but until then, I will always
resent my home. Not Brixton, but the *Earth*: if we must live on this
planet, of all places Brixton ain't the worst to be. I have fond
memories of coming home to Brixton, I've always enjoyed returning
more than staying. The familiar roads coming into view, settling your
rumbling stomach. The streets seem to smoothen, it feels as though
you might be driving to the end of the Earth, but you know your
house is just before the drop. The signs all speak to you, welcoming
you home. Shops open their doors for jam and butter. You know
where the shade is for shelter, the homely sunny spots too. The best
woodland paths; the busiest bars; the happiest of people; the dodgiest
of back streets. You can feel the hive of life bustling underneath the
streets you walk down. You can name the loudest voice that pierces
through the noise; somewhere in the middle of a humming pub.
Home is a strange word for me. The word home doesn't feel like a
home at all. I have three homes now: one house outside of Bromley,
one apartment in New York and a coastal home in the Lake District.

Home was Brixton for a bit; a three-storey Victorian house on a busy
street with plenty of annoying neighbours. Like Daniel the roofer who
smoked two packets of cigarettes a day or Doreen; a care worker with
a limp and six cats.

Then home was Bromley; a small white house that looked as though it belonged to a village about 250 miles North. Bromley was a home for mum and me, Dad wasn't around much when we moved to Bromley. He wasn't having an affair or running a criminal underground; he just kept busy and out of the house to avoid talking to either of us. Mum was getting crazier by the day. She started putting milk on the fire and candles in the fridge for no apparent reason when I started high school.

School was very muchly a place of refuge, I was more than happy to stay after school and get there early. Spending as many possible hours there, reading every textbook I could get my hands on. Or aimlessly walking around the corridors for something to do and to stay out of my parent's hair.

My parents originally sent me to an all-girls school about a mile walk from our home. When I first joined, I didn't have a uniform. I had a black mini skirt, I'd cut from one of mum's funeral dresses and an old white baggy shirt of my dad's. I'd tie the shirt with a bit of ribbon at my stomach and wear pull up tights and low black heels. My math's teacher put me in detention on my first day for violation of the dress code. I ended up having my first kiss in the supply closet; he was called Robert and carried a book on coastal erosion around with him. He was an awful teacher, but an *excellent* kisser.

Word got around that I shagged the teacher (*I didn't*), and he was fired. My mother wasn't best pleased, and I was immediately transferred to Bromley Tech as punishment.

Initially, the switch was tedious. My mother was terrified I'd shag the whole faculty, and since there wasn't a vagina trap, she could buy off the catalogue; she demanded I go on the pill. She also made me look after a doll for a week, which ended in me lobbing it out my bedroom window and a confused old neighbour calling an ambulance. For the first time in my life, my mother took an interest in what I was doing and if I was safe. I think this was because there were several stabbings about two miles down the road, but I wasn't used to having protective parents, so in a word, I did *rebel* and rather *nastily* did I rebel. I burnt my mother's wedding dress; smashed my dad's car window in; threw the toaster in the compos and left a dead rat on their bed. It was a one week rampage I'm hardly proud of. It worked though, my mother never took one interest in my life after that.

School started at 9am, but I was always there at 7:30am with the janitors and the teachers. I'd have my breakfast sat on the work surfaces with the cooks and dinner ladies chatting about the inner gossip. Belinda was having an affair, Tracey hated her mother in law and Jayne was a lesbian on the weekends. I'd sit in registration an hour early, reading whatever book took my fancy; quizzing my science teacher about whatever came to my mind that day. I asked a lot of questions on the physics of motorsport and space. That was my hour and a half of school; the next six hours were always hell. Too many people, too much noise, not enough teaching, too much bickering.

The girls all immediately labelled me a slag after hearing I'd shagged the teacher (*I really didn't shag the teacher*); the boys would only try it on, and the teachers either avoided me entirely or were often a little too close for comfort. So, I was an outcast.

Hanging underneath bleachers is the cliché or eating sandwiches in the toilets. I did both. Mostly I sat reading in the sports equipment shed. I'd sit on a crash mat and take a nap for an hour. I loved learning. I loved having an education and soaking it all in. I just hated sewing, and that seemed to be all my teachers wanted me to do. They didn't care about my interest in physics or how the Earth worked, they only cared if I could sew a zip on a cheap-looking dress. Sewing was one of the sole reasons for burning my mum's wedding dress. They didn't have sewing at my old school.

I would spend my afternoon's sewing with dull minded, boring women, who all obediently chatted away as we knitted and stitched the world in our hands. I must admit; the women were *fine women*. They were the kind of beautiful women who made tough sacrifices, like marrying *men* so other, more *ostentatious* women, could be lesbians. They were the kind of women who'd make sandwiches for the protest. They were the women the world *needed*.

While it brought me anger beyond description to have to sit still and stitch a straight line while listening to the giggling anecdotes of a dozen girls' abysmal sex lives; the women sat in my sewing classes were exactly *those* women.

The women who really do save the world by making sandwiches.

That being said; they were still the most tedious and vain people I'd ever met with too many tiresome tales of chivalrous sex instead of the raucous sagas of storeroom shagging I was accustomed to. When I got my first paycheck from my first big tour, I tracked down all 12 women from my sewing classes and sent them all a hearty, strong vibrator with a pair of stockings and a handmade book on female liberation by a good friend of mine; *Kitty Burkhart.* It was the very least I could do.

One day, I was that bored, I stitched a neat looking blue star into the palm of my hand and was sent to the nurse in horror. I'd stitch thread into my skin or purposefully stab myself quite frequently, just to get out of class. I was the expert on bunking from sewing classes. Sometimes I'd just go for a fag behind the building, unpicking the thread, or other times I'd go for a walk around the school. There was a lovely grass bank at the very end of the school where I'd go rest and read, picking the grass for the hour. This particular time, I wandered through the school and snuck into the empty music room; picking up a recorder for the first time after admiring the boys doing it for weeks.

Something stronger than electricity; sexual gratification and an outer body, drug-fuelled, astronomical, galaxy explosion, happened when I played the recorder for the first time. Something so simple, so sweet-sounding; led to the rock n roll, drug wrought life I went on to lead. I saw my future through the tiny holes stripped down the piece of wood I was spitting into. I saw the headlines; I heard the music; I tasted the victory, and then I listened to the noise a recorder makes and realised I wasn't going to get that life playing that piece of dog shit. Instead, I picked up a ukulele that was casually sitting in the corner, practically begging to be played and I strummed that passionately; I snapped two of the strings, panicked, and ran to the toilet with it tucked under my jumper.

I went about hiding the evidence by jumping on the guiltless instrument in the toilet cubicle until it was horrifically looking up at me in small, tender, heartbroken pieces on the piss-stained floor. I flushed what I could, walking out the toilet humming to myself, thinking; *I can finally answer the stars when they ask me what I'm doing at night.*

I stumbled back to class, witnessing the boys '*dancing*' as part of their 'music and movement' classes. Not a single boy was flawless, they were all poorly nimble and fatally inept at practically *everything*. But I hadn't thought of moving my body in such ways. The teacher combined ballet, jazz and some form of contemporary style dancing into something teachable to young London boys. He got them to stretch upon the benches and the ladder part of the climbing frame attached to the walls. Mostly, the lads ran around pushing each other over, but a few of them took it seriously as I stood outside, peering through the window, trying to mimic what they were doing without getting caught.

I started to make a habit of going to the school nurse most weeks; pricking my finger on the needle or sewing thread directly into my skin; just so I could walk to the gym and watch the boys. I'd try to memorise the movements in my mind, so I could go home and practise in my mirror. I most often forgot by the time I made it back, meaning I'd scramble on my feet for some form of artistic movement. I'd make up my own dances, trying to be as light as possible on my feet so my mother wouldn't hear me downstairs and ask where I learnt such *outrageous* movements from. It wasn't like I was gyrating in front of the mirror; I was simply allowing my body to flow from one motion to the next in whatever order felt right, but I knew my mother would call it a waste of time and ask me to help her with the washing.

I set out to play whatever instrument I could after that. Since school couldn't even offer me a *recorder*, I begged my parents, who relentlessly refused for a couple of years. In the meantime, I would kiss boys for an hour play of their instruments, after snogging the schools' trombone player for a lesson in brass instruments. It seemed a genius idea. I didn't consider the moral complications of my proposition at the time. I'd find the susceptible boys in school corridors, loitering and looking like a Stanley Kubrick character. The spottier and more miserable they looked, the more chance I had of getting them for an instrument. Some of the boys I kissed didn't own an instrument, but were that desperate they'd buy one just to give to me so I would kiss them. I had one boy poorly rob the music store down Brick Street, gaining a permanent criminal record just for a two second snog behind the bins outside the canteen!

Henry Ford was my most frequent acquaintance. I would mostly go around to his house every Wednesday at 6 o'clock when his mum was at the Bingo, and his father would pass out for the alcohol; kiss Henry, and then play his guitar in his room for an hour while he played football against the wall outside. Henry turned out to be gay and used me for seven years, telling his parents I was his girlfriend and that the sound of *my* guitar playing was actually *his* skilful playing; even when I was long out of the house and no longer kissing him. Frank was two years older than me but desperate to tell his mates that he had actually kissed someone; so, I offered my services in exchange for his ukulele, which he simply gave me as permanent payment.

It took me a lot longer than expected to learn all the instruments I could get my hands on, but piano the longest. I couldn't find a girl or boy in town who played the piano and was willing to let me play in exchange for *anything*. I eventually found old Mrs Sampson, who wanted someone to clean her house and look after her cat twice a week for a small amount of money, while she went to visit her granddaughter. She happened to have the most gorgeous grand piano, sitting out of tune in her hallway, unloved since her husband died. I would tidy for a whole 5 minutes, playing for the rest of the day, making sure I at least stroked the cat before I left for peace of mind. I didn't care that the piano was out of tune for a long while, unable to tune it myself; I was simply happy to play, learn and revel in the noises. I came in the house one day, and there was a note on the piano seat reading: *'The neighbour says you're pretty good, but the piano isn't. It's been tuned. Have fun, but please put the bloody cat out.'*

I was touched by the sentiment and started looking after the cat more; to the point where it followed me home and then got ran over by a bus outside my house.

About a year into my lying and scheming, a boy in my class named; George Underwood invited me to a *skiffle* session with another kid in our class called: Peter Frampton. He invited me to the skiffle session via a lovely handwritten note on the back of an intricate class sketch of the view from our maths class. I wholeheartedly went into the music room expecting to kiss both the boys before I would even pick up an instrument, but the pair of them were utterly repulsed when I leant in to kiss them and abruptly told me to never do it again.

I was terribly confused about why these two boys were inviting me to play. As far as I knew, no one knew I played any instruments. There was a silent deal with the boys I'd kiss. I'd kiss them in private, and they could tell their mates as long as the instrument deal was never spoken of and they didn't lie and say I'd fucked them and a pack of wolves while I was at it. The only rumours being spread were those of me kissing different boys and girls. Some of them verifiable; most of them lies- *all* of them hilariously spun and exaggerated versions of what *really* happened.

I later found out that George's girlfriend at the time; '*Suzie*,' was Mrs Sampson's neighbour and was the one who told her of my piano playing. Suzie was one of the girls in my sewing class, so of course, she selflessly acted for the greater good of another woman. And if this isn't the perfect definition of such sacrifices '*those kinds of women*' make; I don't know what is. Suzie felt that passionate about my talent, she told George she'd give him the blowjob he'd been waiting for if he invited me to play. I like to think the fact I kept playing with the boys for a long while was because of my sheer talent, but I can't shake the idea that Suzie's blowjobs are *just that good.* The unelaborated definition for fellow female empowerment is *sacrificial blowjobs for a skiffle session.*

Instantly, something was electrifying about playing in a room with other people. Something incredulous about noise hitting with other noise and being able to look into the eyes of the soul of the sound. I think I surrendered myself that day to music, in fact, I am sure I did. I didn't want to look back, I didn't want to ever stop kissing boys for an hour, a minute, even a *second's* play on *any* instrument. I didn't care what it took, I knew it wasn't going to be easy, but that didn't matter to me. There was a fire raging in my stomach. Scalding my insides to move and dance and sing and create. That is what us humans do. We create, and we invent so intensely and routinely, we're miserable when we don't. We're wretched when we do, but it's a different kind of misery. When we don't create, we're sticking our *head in the oven* kind of miserable; when we do create it's just a *Monday* kind of dolefulness.

I wasn't miserable. I was drowning in euphoria. Flying, falling, cascading, dancing, spinning, swaying, soaring through a feeling of hope and delight.

The fire in my stomach led to a desperate need to write and share my music. A desperation I can't explain but have never felt with anything else; not even my *life*. I've never been as desperate to *live* as I have been to share my *music*. It's more than an itch, more than a necessity, more than a desire- it's always been a *must* that I share my music. As though, if I didn't, there would just be *blackness*. Not nothing, not the world ending; just pure, charcoal *black*.

George and Peter seemed complacent with me playing with them every week, a pleasant surprise since neither of them ever complimented my playing. I'd been thieving and playing instruments for a good few years by this point and had developed a strong sense of my personal playing, that it was a taxing adaptation to get used to playing with others. They were both talented musicians, and I admired their ease, the way they both walked in with their instruments already strapped to them. I craved the simplicity. I would fantasise about owning my own musical instrument, dreaming about the day I could walk into a music store and buy the lot. Romanticising the day, I could waltz into that music room and need not hope and pray the janitor had locked the instruments up just yet.

I once had to lock myself up in the music cupboard with the instruments so I could get the chance to play that week. It wasn't until a few hours in, that I realised to the full extent what I'd done and spent the night performing to my heart's content; pissing in a broken bongo barrel and surviving off the selection of sherbet in my bag. *Music was my sea, and I was prepared to die lost in it.*

Around this time, my half-brother, Terry Burns, was infatuated with Modern Jazz; the likes of 'Charles Mingus' and 'John Coltrane.' He would brag about his 45s collection, at every family party, while my mother would sew my mouth shut with phrases such as; '*and how are the children,*' or '*that's wonderful news Terry, great to see a good man succeed.*'

Before every family birthday party, Christmas, or some form of family gathering where the prospect of me opening my mouth causing World War 3 could occur; she would brief me on the things that I had been doing recently. Things like: private sewing lessons, personal language tutoring, wife training and house cleaning- which were all things I, *of course*, had *not* been doing. She would, with a stern lip, tell me that if I were to upkeep this façade with the family, she would support me (in a *minimal* sense) with whatever I *actually* wanted to do. This simply meant her not turning up her nose every time I told her I wanted to play the saxophone, or her not telling me '*that's for boys,*' when I played Frank's ukulele. My father wanted absolutely no part in any of it.

This particular family occasion cut my piano playing short by four hours, so I was not happy to be there. I was instantly agitated by Terry, who wore his *'second in play'* Cricket medal around his neck as a fashion statement. I had profound fantasies about strangling him and the patriarchy with it; simultaneously killing off the two reasons why being a woman in the 1960s *sucked.*

Completely losing control (as I often did), I raided his beloved vinyl collection and stole all the Mingus and Coltrane records I could slip under my dress. I hobbled out the house with my hand up my skirt, shouting something unsophisticated about feeling *'unwell by the weather.'* No one batted an eye, and as soon as I was on the street, they fell out on to the road, smashing to pieces, leaving me salvaging three of the dozen-odd I'd nicked.

I got caught the next day when Terry himself rang my mother and claimed I'd stolen his *entire* collection. I called him out for being an outright liar *and* wanker, but my mother made me apologise and pay him back over three years; which was the time it took for me to repurchase his entire record collection. It really took the biscuit when I had to spend my hard-earned money on shit vinyl such as the horror film 'Peeping Toms' soundtrack, that he never owned in the first place, but claimed he did to rub salt in the wound. I did get a good night's worth listening to the surviving albums, which was more than enough to make me fall in love.

Love at first play frankly does exist.

I wouldn't shut up about it for months, my mum eventually gave in in late 1961 and bought me my first instrument; a Grafton Saxophone, second hand from Terry (*of course*).

I didn't care that, in my mother's eyes, I wasn't good enough to deserve an instrument to myself. I couldn't give a shit that my mother wholeheartedly thought it was '*just a phase*,' or lucidly to; '*cause attention and make a fuss*,' as she would frequently tell her disapproving friends. I never cared for ownership of an instrument or what other people (mainly my mother and her bridge friends) thought of my playing. When I was playing an instrument, it was *mine*, whether it stayed in my room or not.

When I played *anything*, I *owned* it- otherwise, what's the point in playing it?

For as long as I could touch, breathe, drink in and play an instrument, I was more than happy. I was simply honoured to be in the same room as music, forever grateful to have noise in my life.

That saxophone was as iridescent as a gateway drug, and I was more than hooked.

CHAPTER THREE
I'M SORRY YOU KISSED MY GIRLFRIEND

Suzie Parker was a sweet girl, far too sweet for George. You'd think Suzie grew up in the deepest English countryside you could imagine. You'd take one look at her high collar shirts and thick grey tights she never grew out of, and say: '*Little House on the Prairie.*' But *no.* Suzie was a city girl, through and through. Born and raised in Bromley in a rough part of the neighbourhood; her front step saw two stabbings, and she was robbed four times. The third time; she head-butted the robber, grabbed him by his awful mullet and proceeded to introduce the granite kitchen tops to the robbers' head. The police (who were deeply involved in the community in those days) nicknamed the notorious robber: '*granite head*' and sweet looking Suzie: '*the head-butter.*'

The fourth time she was robbed, she simply called the police and said: '*Yeah, hiya love, sorry to bother you, it's me again, the head-butter. One of Granites mates are here tryna steal my mum's new TV she just got off catalogue. I know, again, they're gonna make a habit out of this; poor dads gonna think they're meals on wheels if they keep turning up this often.*' I was having a fag outside, it was all very pathetic.

You wouldn't know she knew most of London's drug dealers back in the 70s by looking at her bloody awful ballet pumps, rosemary beads and recyclable shopping bag. But that's the perk of drug dealers still being sons and daughters of mothers who want their kids at Sunday church *or else.*

Suzie wouldn't miss church for anything; mostly because she was terrified of her parents, who were somewhat on the cusp of being fraudulent themselves.

Such a sweet girl.

For a brief time, Suzie volunteered as some kind of mentor for the kids in church. This essentially meant she suddenly knew all the words to Roald Dahl, and had to appear more pragmatic than her drug use perceived.

She dragged me, with her church friends, to a committee of 100 anti-war group protest in Trafalgar square. I didn't intend on picking up a placard and shouting: '*no more war,*' for a whole day; but Suzie had attached herself to me like an urchin around that time and I've always struggled with female friendships to say *no.* Earlier on in my bisexual discovery, I just didn't know whether I wanted to be friends with girls, treat them all like sisters or fuck them. I mean, how do you say no to a girl who wrapped her lips around a man's old Johnny so I could play an instrument?

"Why does a war start in the first place, Suzie?"

"Power," She said, adding; "*And money and sex.*"

She saw me laugh and started laughing too, elbowing me in the ribs to grab my attention towards the masses of women holding signs and handing out brown paper bags filled with fruit and sandwiches.

"Notice how there are hardly any men?"

She never added anymore; simply jumped off the wall and made sure George's collar was straight.

For someone so drastically domesticated, she had a head firmly screwed on two sturdy shoulders. She'd be at the frontlines with me whenever I had something to protest after tasting the sweet sensation of my first march. We'd typically protest for female education rights. We'd knock on doors asking for funds for better equipment, tools and teachers for young women at local schools. We were spat on a few times; the door was slammed in our face at every other door, but if we were lucky enough to catch the mothers at the stressful time before tea and just after her husband's elevenses; we'd score a shilling.

A few years after this protest, I invited Suzie to join a secret girl's organisation I had stumbled across. The secret girls' society in question was named: '*The Magnolia Society.*' Initially, the name was to diverge anyone off the legitimate basis of our meetings from female empowerment, to flower-loving women. After a while, the name became somewhat popular as a statement in itself. According to ancient Chinese; Magnolias are considered the '*seamless symbols of womanly beauty and gentleness.*' What better symbol of our dignity and nobility than a fragile flower that dies within a week or two.

I discovered the Magnolias via an advertisement in the 'NME.' It was a *cryptic* message that read: '*Ran by Emmeline, Emily and Christabel, we teach the knowledge on the rise of the Magnolia.*'

The message is hardly cryptic at all if you know anything about the suffragette movement. I've always thought the advertisement might've well have read: '*Women who are fed up of being disregarded, disrespected, disapproved, marginalised, molested and faced with misogyny. You must also like cake!*'

We met in a new location every week. The first time: it was a disused rail line, the second: a storeroom in a chocolate factory and the third; a barista's house, Lottie trusted from her time on the psychiatric ward.

We'd find out about the location via a weekly newsletter that cited where magnolias had been spotted growing. The newsletter was created for keen-eyed husbands who might wonder where their wives are going in the dead of night. We learnt that if you tell a man, a flower has been spotted growing in one of the changing rooms in the local swimming baths; the husband will pack you a torch and remind you to change the batteries if you're watching it grow for longer than six hours! The whole idea of the society was to empower women and for those empowered women to go on to empower *other* women; an entire growth cycle if you will. The group was led by a young and incredibly thin woman, who always teetered on slimline heels, name Kitty Burkhart; correctly named by her mother after the late Suffragette; '*Kitty Marion.*' Kitty wore pantyhose's and garters with linen dinner jackets or corsets and petticoats. Her 9-5 job was at a bank, and her father married her into a well-heeled family with an abusive husband, whom wouldn't let her so much as say the word '*corset,*' never mind wear one; even for his pleasure too.

The meetings would be spent well into the night; amalgamated with masses of pot brownies and cups of Kitty's acclaimed '*Trafalgar Rounds*,' ice, Sambuca, vodka and blackberry juice; '*sprinkled with female masculinity*,' as she would say upon serving.

It was myself, Kitty, Lottie, Samantha, Josie-lee, Olivia, Elspeth, Karen and my Suzie.

We all shared a kindred flame for freedom, and I think most of us suffered from insomnia or drug-induced restlessness at the very least, so it wasn't like we had anything else to do.

Besides that, we were all keen to learn and learn what society couldn't teach or *wouldn't* let us learn. We all also had a marginalised respect for the law, since the law had done nothing to protect us.

Our first raid occurred after a few too many brownies and 'Trafalgar Rounds.'

It resulted in us waiting until sunrise outside the delivery entrance of Bromley's Library and sneaking ourselves into the delivery room via our slim frames fitting into the empty crates left from the previous delivery. We then stole every new book we could find on: health, history, space, DIY, sports, martial arts and a handful of dirty books we discovered just as we were about to leave.

We stuffed as many as we could in our pockets, coats and down our pants; putting the rest in bags and the final few in crates we carried out into the day and to the location that evening: a church still in ruins from the war.

We then spent weeks reading the books back to front, learning absolutely everything we could. A few of the girls tested each other on what they'd learnt, while I would sit quietly next to the record player reading away into the night.

Lottie Banks was a primary school teacher, and therefore our most influential Magnolia. We ripped out the front pages, ridding the evidence of our theft, and donated the books once read to the primary school where Lottie started a book club for ten-year-olds; who were read the '*history of women in war*,' and paragraphs on how to put up a shelf. Lottie gathered a whole army of ten-year-old girls, who could simultaneously reel off a list of female veterans while knocking in a nine-inch nail in their mothers living room. One of the kids is now a supreme court judge who sued her father for abusing her younger sister. Another is a field marshal for the British army.

We taught ourselves martial arts from the books and a lot of handy work to the point where the wives had to suppress their skills from their husbands, so to not make them feel inferior when it came to flat pack furniture. We had to raid sheds across the gardens of London for power tools since the hardware store manager had a strict: 'no women in the store, only in the *storeroom*, behind the door shagging', *policy.*

The Magnolias were the closest thing to family I had at that time. I felt more than a part of a team, I felt a part of something much more monumental and significant. We were single-handedly shaping the future, which was rather impressive for a group of 9 women pissed off too much Sambuca. We all went into cafés and schools, sewing classes and dance halls and made conversation with women.

We targeted what we called; '*the lone woman.*'

You can find out if you're '*the lone woman,*' by asking yourself one simple question: How many times a function do you roll your eyes? If the answer is between 8-15, you're a '*lone woman,*' and we'd have likely targeted you for recruitment or education because you're the most bored, most fed up and therefore the most likely to actually listen.

We rarely recruited new members except for Elsie who joined about a year after I did. Elsie Smith worked selling popcorn at the cinema, and we were interested in displaying archival footage to the women we were educating; as proof to accompany our point like milk accompanies cookies. Elsie managed to grab the keys every now and then, blaming either her dizziness (which didn't exist) or the man selling the tickets who was fired routinely for negligence and theft. We then had access to the archives and screens to do as we wished. We only got away with the viewings twice and Elsie was eventually fired and left the society since she blamed us for being penniless and divorced because of it. Some women just aren't prepared to make the unyielding and gallant sacrifices needed for the future of females.

Some women just like cock too much.

The magnolias started to wilt after a good few years when half of us got pregnant or married and couldn't sneak out of the house at night. We now reminisce the days where we'd be chucked out of café's if men heard us speak of history in such a way that didn't glorify the existence of men.

It was a sweet time, and it was nice to share such a sizeable part of my intelligence growth with the woman who inspired me to think in the first place. *Suzie*, by merely being Suzie, unknowingly provoked me to educate myself so that I could fulfil my potential in whatever I wanted to do. Be that: reinvent my character, own a house, write a song, build a boat- I believed I could do it all.

As a society, we went on to protest countless times over the years. Mostly to no end or development, but the mere act of women protesting for their right and future *together;* is an act of power in itself. I want girls to feel they can pick up a placard and be heard. I don't want them to feel disheartened by inequality, I want girls to be motivated by.

We're all products of what we see; the images we consume, the words we hear. Protesting is an image of resilience and hope that every woman needs to see. Other women who believe in the same as you are out there. You'll find them howling at men in suits or shagging the receptionist for intel on the gender pay gap in the London Stock Exchange.

50

I was just a kid at my first rally; only fifteen years old. The committee of 100 protest was just the beginning for me. The start of a lifetime of screaming at cloth-eared folk.

That protest, I was supposed to be back for curfew which was around 9pm at that time, not that I ever abided by it.

However, it was late by the time I realised it was late, and I could already feel the soreness of my knuckles from the beating for being tardy. Knowing I was going to be greeted with a punishment, regardless of how late I would be; I went to a pub down Carlton street with George, Suzie and Peter. I first got served when I was 11 years old. When I was asked what I wanted, I nervously said: '*whatever he's having,*' pointing to a man with one eye talking to the wall about the war. He was on neat whiskey.

George became insistent on getting the most hammered, on proving to Suzie, he was a '*real man.*' It wasn't an issue, because it didn't take long. Suzie was far too dainty for alcohol and knew her mother would send her to Church school if she even so much as smelt a drop on her clothes. Peter and I sat comfortably watching Suzie lose her little mind watching her boyfriend in all his drunken glory, making a complete *tit* out of himself.

At one point, he put his money in the cigarette machine, trying to play 'Elvis' Hound Dog' through the packet. The bar stopped serving him eventually, which was the point where Suzie stormed out into the night. I obediently followed her, comforting the girl for a good half hour before kissing her.

She was the one who questioned her sexuality, I merely told her I could answer her questions.

George chose that unruly moment to stumble out onto the street where he saw me; dressed in my father's hand-me-downs, looking more manly than ever with my boisterous tongue down his girls' throat.

He blindly grabbed me by my shoulders and turned my lights out. The next thing I remember is the hospital lights. Bright, blindingly bright, through absolute nothingness. I could tell it was daylight outside, I could feel the sun through my eyes, but I couldn't see a thing. There was a lot of noise around me, I wanted them to shut up, but my mouth was too dry to tell them.

I could hear George shouting in the distance.

'I didn't know, I couldn't fucking see her, it's her own fault, she shouldn't have had her tongue down my fucking girl's throat.'

I think it was Peter that told him to; *'get over it, or piss off.'*

Suzie told me I smiled a lot while I was unconscious and being wheeled about the place. She described me as having; *'a smile in the clouds, a heart in the ground.'* I never got to know what she meant by that, but I've always liked the imagery.

When I came to, my mother was talking to the doctor with a bible in her hand. The doctor was quite stern when he told her, 'she could very well look like one of them *freaks*,' to which my mother was very much distraught.

All anyone could say to me was: '*it's not pretty.*'

My mother brought face powder and some form of industrial, drama school, face paint the following day to hide the bruising and as much of my face as possible. I didn't wear makeup back then; seeing my face as pale and soulless as a bedsheet, was more traumatising than seeing my bloodied and bruised eye. That's the disturbing tale of how I got the illusion of two differently coloured eyes.

Despite already taking what I considered enough of a bruising, my dad still hit me across the knuckles five times a day for a week; some for my lateness but more for my homosexual sinning. They were the least bit impressed or humoured at the tale.

George came to visit later in the week with a timid looking Suzie; both carrying flowers they took from a roadside and sherbet they stole from the corner shop. Suzie spent the whole hour laughing, while George tried to apologise for something he didn't feel guilty for.

'*I'm sorry you kissed my girlfriend, and I'm sorry I thought you were a man, but I probably would have punched you anyway, because you did kiss my girlfriend. But I am sorry you're in the hospital, and I guess I shouldn't have done it, but you did kiss my girlfriend!*'

There was a long conversation about whether I liked kissing boys or girls and we were all very immature about it. I guess I didn't really have all the answers myself. I couldn't exactly be the messiah of bisexuality George wanted to hear from when I was still partially confused about *who* I wanted to kiss and *why* I wanted to kiss them myself.

"So, you'd kiss my mum?" George bellowed.

"No, she's not my type."

"Oh, so now you're fussed about what chick you want? What's wrong with my mum?"

"She's got a moustache!"

"Men have moustaches!"

"That's different, George. They're kinda supposed to." Suzie replied for me, angering George even more.

My bisexuality sprouted from an abundance of curiosity and slack relationship with conformity. I've never seen my sexuality as a talking point, it's just a part of me. I'm part bisexual in the way I'm part woman, part musician, part daughter, part failure. A fraction of me is bisexual, in the way a part of me is water. I answer to my heart in the same way a heterosexual woman, or a homosexual man or a pansexual woman would too.

With passion in the face of blind direction.

It's *universal love.*

Of all the fascinating things about me, being bisexual ain't one of them. I once had an extensive collection of newspaper clippings with the word: '*horror*,' in the headline; which is much more fascinating. 456 excerpts over two years. *Gripping stuff.*

George couldn't get his head around the fact I didn't care who it was; what sex, what genitals, what clothes they wore or looked like, who they shagged, what the fuck they did- if I liked them, I'd kiss them. Or if they had an instrument, I could play, or something I *wanted*- I'd *also* kiss them. It wasn't called being bisexual back then, it was called being a *freak,* and I was quite content with that.

Suzie found the whole conversation enlightening and apparently broke up with George on the bus back home. George didn't speak to me for two weeks, which I thought was pretty childish since he landed me in hospital. Regardless, I recovered, and eventually, we all got along again as though nothing had ever happened.

Suzie went on a two-week lesbian binge, before kissing her neighbour's girlfriend, who was sick on her new Biba shoes; encouraging her to revert back to being a heterosexual.

George had already moved on, and by the time I was back at school, there was this ginger-haired, big-boobed, bat of a girl named 'Francis;' who kept telling me to shave off my hair or stop looking at her.

CHAPTER FOUR
BUSKING PROBABLY WASN'T WORTH THE TIT ACHE

When I went back to school, after a four month hospital vacation, I overheard George talking to Peter one time about him being in this band called: 'The Konrads'. When I asked him if I could join, the first time, he said: '*we've no room for a sax.*' The second time he said: '*we've no room for a girl*,' and the third time a simple; '*no.*'

I told my mother I was going to the sewing clubs' (*that I was not a part of*) yearly summer party (*that didn't exist*) and headed to Bromley youth club, where the band were performing. Knowing I wouldn't be able to get in, I squeezed my spryly thin frame into one of the equipment boxes (pioneering the Magnolia library trick) and was unknowingly carried in by George himself. I later got out of the box and was caught by the current saxophonist, that I advised should leave the band because he was way better than the rest of them and far too good looking to associate with such childish boys. The egotistic prick agreed and quit that night. It was all too convenient for me to step in, which I consistently proposed as a '*pro*' in the situation. But George refused to have a girl play in his band, telling the booker that '*they'd rather not play at all than play with a girl*,' to which the booker shrugged and agreed with an unnerving amount of disposition. George has later told me he was still pissed about the kiss, and that was the only reason he wouldn't let me play that night.

At the time, I was more than outraged, and outright prepared to return Georges' kind favour of landing me in hospital for four months, but was rushed out of the venue before I could say another word.

Walking home that night, I kicked every stone there was, at every cat; bawling at every star I could see, for answers I didn't want. The simple act of getting people together in a room to play music was not as simple as I first, *naively*, thought, and it frustrated me tremendously. I assumed people wanted to play with me, or at the very least were just as happy as me to be playing with *anyone*. I didn't know you could *choose* who you played music with. I thought everyone got what they got.

I didn't know the roll of the dice was always landing against my favour. I felt like a little girl; mute by mutilation of my hands, unable to strum a guitar; without the knowledge of words to speak; with my severed head bouncing against my kneecaps.

Always the melodrama in my mind.

I felt like a broken kettle boiling on a gas hob, but I didn't know why. I was angry all the time, relentlessly vexed, for reasons I just couldn't explain.

I think I gave Calpol a headache at the time.

I'd ask the boys I'd met through the skiffle sessions if they wanted to play, and they'd all produce terrible lies to get out of it. One boy told me his mother had said to him that he'd catch diarrhoea if he played the guitar with a girl. Another asked me to wait a second, left through the door, which had a Perspex slit in, so I could watch him quite comically punch himself in the nose and re-enter bleeding, flustered and with a terrible excuse for not playing with me. I tried paying a girl in my class to play with me. She'd never played an instrument before in her life, but I paid her about a shilling a time to learn guitar. I quickly realised I was paying someone of whom I was personally teaching each week, and figured I'd have to cut my losses before I made an even bigger tit of myself.

Despite knowing the answer, I couldn't understand why it was so difficult for me to do the same as George and Peter. No one would even play with me, never mind make a band. I was sure there must be other girls out there who wanted to do the same thing as me, who wanted to perform and play music. I was convinced that they'd be looking at the same stars wondering '*why them*,' too.
I had work to do.

George recalls me lobbing the door off its hinges, but he's always been melodramatic, and I most certainly did *not* pull the door off its hinges. The only damage I did to the music room that day was: utterly abolish the drums by throwing each piece at George; break four recorders by snapping them over my knee and persistently try to stab him, and roughly around two cymbals, three shakers and the nape of a guitar. All in an attempt to release the rage I was feeling.
It worked.
The mess was *outstanding*.
I felt equally as proud and humbled staring at the mess I made that day, then I did the day I finished my first album. I'd successfully lived my '*Lord of the flies'* fantasy.

George was stood cowering in the corner, blood dripping from the gash on his forehead and a piece of recorder poking out from his thigh. Peter had long gone. I do believe he made a swift exit the first time a cymbal was thrown. It was just a heaving George and me timidly seething with confused wrath and astonishment.

He said something about it being payback for the punching, which I noted was part to blame, alongside the fact he wouldn't let me play music.

George was positively shocked and outraged that I'd made such a fuss over something so *trivial* in his eyes.

'*You really that bloody desperate to fucking play a saxophone, you mad cow,*' he said, cackling as though any part of the situation (other than the recorder sticking out his leg) were funny.

I sternly told him *yes* and explained how hard it was for me to play or get involved as a woman and educated him on the trifles of a woman's life.

He didn't seem the slightest bit interested and much more concerned for the hole in his leg as he hobbled for the door. He just about accepted my request to join the band under the promise that I would *one;* never cause such a scene again and *two;* try to look boyish on stage.

It was just the scene causing that was an issue.

On our eighth practice; the guitarist, Neville, thought it would be funny to stick tampons up the nape of my Saxophone.

The next practice, I pulled my bloody tampon straight out of my vagina in front of the band and shoved it in Neville's shocked, open mouth.

I was suspended from the band until further notice, but by this point, we were all finishing high school, and they weren't dreaming big enough for me anyway.

I'd made it crystal clear to everyone I knew, the life I wanted to live. Despite my mother desperately pushing me down the '*wife*' route, by inviting random schoolboys over for dinner each week; I would take them upstairs and bore them all with my sax playing or singing before fucking them. I swiftly noticed how unimpressed men were at a woman doing '*their job.*' The boys of the Konrads, were no different and the old saxophonist replaced me swiftly after the tampon incident; meaning I was back to square one, and seemingly worse off now I was coming towards the end of school and wasn't participating in the skiffle sessions.

In my final year, I tried talking to the headteacher about allowing women to participate in music classes. I got on my knees and begged, to be laughed at, and told to: '*stop being such a girl*,' which didn't offend me much.

"I am a girl. Why would I stop being *such a one?*"

"Because you're annoying me. Now leave." That was a pretty standard response. Our headteacher had zero originality when it came to being anything other than a mansplaining monstrosity.

So, I left and stole a mug as restitution. Then I went outside and smashed the headteacher's window in with it. I got suspended for that, and received a hand-written letter from the stubby man himself, telling me: *'I regretfully cannot remember the purpose of our conversation, or indeed what we conversed, but I absolutely know it did not warrant your violent and idiotic response, as nothing warrants such behaviour. You are hereby suspended until the end of term where you will be reinstated on a behavioural watch system.'*

When I returned, I protested. I didn't know very many people, even fewer girls, yet I camped out in the girl's toilet for a week and sat in the sinks passing out handwritten notes about feminism on scraps of paper from the headteachers recycling bin.

I wasn't educated as such. I read an awful lot and could write. I wasn't the best speller, but I also made sense, which I knew a lot of people my age didn't. They were either dropouts, stoners or just plain dumb. I had a lucky streak in me. I was all three of those, but I also had a back catalogue of books to find words from.

I'd write sentences like:

'Do you know men hate you?'

'God hates women, rock n roll loves you.'

'You'll get paid less, even if you wear less.'

It was mostly to shock. I was under the belief that the girls knew how oppressed they were but didn't see hope for a revolution. However, most of the girls would either dry their hands with the flyers, use them as makeshift sanitary pads or hand it back to me.

I abandoned the sink and advertised myself as a clairvoyant in the 6th toilet on the second floor. I'd go through a pack of cigs each day as something to do while I waited for the rush of customers during lunch. I'd sit on top of the cistern, feet on the seat, chatting utter bollocks about high school romances and sloppy blowjob techniques. Then I'd pretend to get a feeling from the toilet spirits that it was of the utmost importance they'd go to the school field at 12 next Friday. They all bought it, and I had fifty or so confused, cautious, girls gathered in a circle on the field.

I spent the week before making protest signs out of loo roll, sanitary pads and cardboard on the toilet floor. I handed them out and made a speech that the spirits had spoken to me too, and ensured I oversaw the running of the vital event or they'd curse us all with barren wombs. That was more than enough to encourage the girls. They all picked up the signs and shouted whatever the hell I did. They weren't very loud. In their defence, they understood their volume didn't matter to the spirits, but only me; and I was the one who took a pound off 'em for the pleasure of sharing a fag in a shit-filled toilet as we discussed the economics of kissing their girl best friend.

We chanted:

'You make me wanna put a firecracker up your arse,

when you leave me out,

leave us out again

we'll do more than just shout!'

The headteacher sent his secretary out to deal with us. She was a northern chain smoker who wore men's trainers and had a wasted psychology degree. I loved her.

"Get inside Pen. I'll have to deal with this paperwork, and Barry's promised me a weekend of rather expressive sex, and my vagina feels like a frozen pea that's been left out in the sun for a fucking year."

"Let us join the music class Mrs, and then we'll leave."

"He won't even let me drink coffee in his office 'cos he thinks my hands are that lubed up I'll drop it on the printer. You've got no fucking chance Penny. In fact, you've got more chance of me sucking him off for a pay rise than you have of hooting a recorder any time soon Pen, and I'll tell you right now, *I'd rather suck off my dad.*"

She told the girls to fuck off (which they did) and passed me a cig to say sorry.

"Why d'ya want to share spit with a man anyway? You do know those recorders aren't so much as felt up with a damp cloth."

"I just want to feel and breathe and listen and make music. I don't know why being a woman stops me. I don't have a vagina blocking my earholes. And if I did, that would be fan-fucking-tastic; I could block out all the shit coming from men in the charts. I just wanna be heard, Mrs Kendrick. *I just wanna make music.*"

I tried busking for a bit after that. I'd play my sax or ukulele at the end of the high street on Fulham Road, twice a week and then random streets in Bromley for the rest.

Suzie lent me a collection basket from her church, but I ended up throwing that at a man who spat on my tits. I used a fancy dress fedora my dad had for a bit to collect the non-existent money I earnt for playing non-stop for six hours, five days a week. School didn't exist for the last year unless I wanted to see George, Peter or Suzie; I had an exam or my science teacher threatened to personally dismantle my sax with a Bunsen burner. In which case, I'd reluctantly sit writing lyrics under the desk.

I'd play on the street to middle-aged women trying to do their shopping in peace or irritated business men hopping from one client meeting to another. Neither audiences were the kind likely to give me a record contract or actually stop and listen in the first place.

I'd get the odd youngun who'd skipped school too, but they were usually lads with anger management issues who'd nick my change or aggressively tell me my tits looked like wilting sugar plums.

I had one lad start a promising conversation about the Beatles, which I was mildly interested in, before he scooped up my fedora, *money in tow*, and pelted it down the high street.

I'd already had one man slap my arse and call me a 'finely tuned monkey;' my favourite jeans had ripped that morning, and I'd read in the newspaper that there'd been another senseless shooting in America.

He'd picked the wrong girl to steal from.

I chased him, with my sax on my back, down the high street and down every avenue, backstreet and shop he tried to escape into. He wriggled his way between bins and up fire escapes. I threw myself down a laundry shoot after him, nearly losing him in the hotel, until I heard the distinctive clatter of a scrawny boy running on top of tables embellished with the upper classes esteemed afternoon tea.

He finally escaped through the doors of Harrods, running the wrong way up the escalator and rampaging through the children's floor. I eventually tackled him, knocking over a 7-foot giraffe and a dozen or so stuffed sheep teddies.

"Fucking 'ell, you put up a chase don't ya?"

"It's my fucking money. I earnt it you tosser. Piss off."

He didn't so much as hand over the money. I had to pry the hat from his nicotine-stained fingers and punch him in the bollocks before he offered me my money back.

In all accounts, a fifteen minute sprint; lifetime ban from Harrods and a bruised tit from the tackle was hardly worth the two shillings I earnt from busking that day. However, the satisfaction of catching the little shit and watch him be chucked into the back of a police van was definitely worth it.

When I retraced my steps through the city of London, I found a penny and a half full pack of cigarettes that I claimed as remuneration. I smoked the whole pack on the bus home, deciding that busking probably wasn't worth the tit ache.

Suzie suggested I join her church choir instead, which I did reluctantly, hoping to meet someone keen to play with me. Turns out, Vicars don't like you trying to hotbox the confession booth or smoking marijuana underneath the organ during the ceremony. He thought the organ was on fire and called the fire brigade, bless him. The vicar did graciously forgive me, allowing me to continue playing at the following week service, which ended in me arguing with a churchgoer over the technicalities of sexism within the religion. According to the churchgoer, *it didn't exist*, to which I picked up a page of the bible at random, and was intricately able to explain the ridicule of shame placed on Mary for being the mysterious virgin, and town slag in one sentence.

They gave me one note to play in the entire two-hour ceremony, and not a single other musician would talk to me, *for assumedly fear of combusting into hell fire.*

Suzie would sit at the back, putting her thumbs up every five minutes for encouragement.

I was eventually, *officially* kicked out of the church for baking pot brownies and selling them on their fundraiser day. They clearly must've had bad trips, because, by all standards, I was only helping.

After that, I focused my attention on starting a band, figuring I might have more luck the more people I had fighting my corner or stopping me making terrible decisions.

I put an ad up in a record store on Charing Cross Road and saved up to put one in the local paper.

I wanted other women to make music with since I'd tried dealing with men and they were hardly worth the headache.

The ad read:

'A chick wanting another chick to start a band. Men will be ostracised. I want women with spunk, there are enough men with that.'

Two separate men called me wanking down the phone, another man found my address and sent me an envelope full of his spunk. Two women enquired, and three mothers called to complain.

I met the two women, who were sisters; *Ardelle and Samantha Jackson.* They lived with three drag queens above a watch repair shop near Soho. I liked women with spunk and a sense of disobedience, but these sisters were a bit too bat-shit, even for me!

I knew I'd need people I could rely on. Girls I could trust would at the very least turn up to rehearsal, late or not, I didn't care, but I knew these girls would struggle to commit to *breathing* for a year, never mind making music.

When I was first welcomed into their room, there were two men unconscious on the bed, seven stale sandwiches on plates on the floor and one of the drag queens was handcuffed to the radiator. Ardelle could play the guitar fairly basically, and Samantha could just about squawk out a note.

They started fighting, real violent, within five minutes of me being there. Ardelle broke Samantha's wrist by jumping on it in 6-inch heels, and Samantha stapled gunned Ardelle's head to the floor.

I left not long after the drag queen, handcuffed to the radiator sighed: '*there goes this week's rent,*' in response to the entire bed being tossed out of the smashed window.

They called me later that week to tell me they thought my lips looked like '*a prawn falling into melted butter,*' because if there's one thing you can rely on a girl to do, its comment on another girl's appearance for the fun of it.

I didn't know whether I was misbehaving and ruining the few chances I'd been given or whether I was alluded into thinking these chances existed in the first place. There weren't any opportunities for women like me. George had six offers to join six different bands in our final year of school. He was offered a place at Oxford university to study music, and I'd watched him sit and chat with a dozen or so guys about their love for music at pub tables, a dozen times. He wasn't even that fucking good.

I joined him at the pub one time and offered a comment on my love for Little Richards, and one guy asked for another pint as though the pubs were hiring underage girls in their father's boxer shorts over stolen fishnet tights.

Another said: '*I know you've heard him through your dads' radio, but trust me little one, you know nothing about music unless you've got a cock and know exactly what they mean when the Beatles say: 'you know you twist, little girl, you know you twist so fine, come on and twist a little closer now and let me know that you're mine.'*

To which the entire table erupted into an impromptu and shit, *might I add*, rendition of The Beatles 'Twist n Shout,' thrusting their cocks at me in a tango of patriarchal saluting.

I couldn't swallow the comment as '*men being men.*' I threw a pint on the lad, to which he obnoxiously grabbed my vagina, and synchronised the assault with the dead eyes of the dripping bastard staring into mine. I'll never forget those black bastard eyes, as vulgar as a child's doll submerging into wet, setting tarmac.

George escorted me outside, but I shrugged him off me for not helping and watching me be ridiculed. Struggling to process the incident, I headed to a late-night pharmacy, nicking three packs of laxatives. I stormed back into the pub, my best apologetic, innocent little girl face on; offering peace by buying the lad and his two closest accomplices a pint. You know I spiked their pint with enough laxative to make 'em wish they didn't have an arsehole to be fucked.

I left before the explosion, waiting eagerly at home for the inevitable phone call from George.

"Danny, Tomo and Spike shat themselves tonight. Know anything about that?"

"You see, little one, you need a *vagina* to know *exactly* what Little Richards means when he says; '*Woo baby, havin' me some fun tonight, yeah!*"

CHAPTER FIVE
GIRLS SLIPPING
ON PIGS TESTICLES
ALL ACROSS THE
DANCEFLOOR

Myself, George, Suzie and Peter were the most unlikely of friends. We were the outcasts strung together on a ship heading to an Enid Blyton novel. We were confused about why exactly we were friends, but it seemed to never stop us from spending time together. I liked them because they all brought something different. George was slightly arrogant, and I liked that. His father was his role model, and he had the swiftest backhand I've ever received; it was mostly naturally uncouth of him to be the way he was via inheritance.

He had an extensive vinyl collection and was bloody good at art, it almost made me jealous; in fact, *it most certainly did*. Peter was quiet for a man, which meant that me and Suzie could be loud for women; so, we had to thank him for our hurried moments of liberation. He was also great at a lot of things so, it made him a convenient friend to have as inspiration.

Just before the three of us were to brace the executioner's table, under the law of high school friendships expiring; Suzie begged me to go prom dress shopping with her, which I obediently did in return for sherbet. I would've done anything for a bag of sherbet back then. Genuine sweetie sherbet you get at the sweet shop before you jump to conclusions; I wasn't on crack cocaine at my prom night.

Suzie was real feminine and girly and liked every single pink dress she saw. Her only problem was deciding between a *fuchsia* pink or a *coral* pink. I couldn't exactly relate.

I'd already told her that I wouldn't be wearing a dress, but my father's wedding suit; which she agreed to get down from the attic with me.

This particular dress Suzie chose for me was very classic of its time; a bright red laced sweetheart neckline with a billowing tulle skirt. I looked like a very flamboyant bloody tampon, and the woman told me it was very on-trend, which made me hate it even more. The first problem was that I couldn't get it off. Arguably the second, more pressing issue, was how much I hated it and wailed and cried about just how much I hated it and wanted it off my skin so badly. I hollered Suzie into the very conservative and upmarket dress shop changing room she'd dragged me in and asked her for help, to get *none*.

Suzie had recently made a vow to her church to not touch a fellow human being in any kind of sexual way since her little lesbian binge and debacle with ex, George. I emphasised the fact the dress was cutting off my circulation, and there was absolutely nothing sexual about her prying off cotton from my wilting breasts, but she left me and said she'd meet me at the pub with the lads.

I had no choice but to nick the dress.

You might wonder how I stole the dress, and the answer is rather simple: I ran like the wind.

The ladies in the boutique were thin-framed, delicately refined ladies, but I knew from experience that they're the worst. The moment the bell of the door rang, I was out onto the cobbled street pelting it in my cowboy boots and a handful of clothes. I heard the chime of heels on concrete and threw my clothes in their face at an attempt to distract them, as I ran into the pub and straight into the gents' toilets where I hid in a cubicle.

We had a few pints and then left into the night with the dress still suffocating me. I remember waking up hours later at Suzie's ankles, my chest that heavy I thought George might be laying on top of me since I couldn't see a thing. I thought to myself, this is it, I'm *dead*. George has fucking flattened me. Death by George's arse cheeks; *what a way to go.*

Turns out, I was still a little drunk and most defiantly hungover, and as soon as I tried to rise from the dead, my hat fell from over my eyes, and I could see the dress still choking me like string around sausages. I got the scissors to it and made a point of getting my dad's wedding suit out of the attic that day to show a disapproving Suzie.

I was dragged to Prom and kicked in the back entrance as I refused to pay for a ticket. A mate hot-wired a car and drove it around Bromley, picking up ex-school mates to crash the Prom. Suzie drank too much vodka and was sick in the boot where we left her while we got food. The start of the night is somewhat 'Clangers' on crack compared to what was to come.

George and Peter oversaw the task of arranging mediocre pranks since they seemed adamant on being the best pranksters Bromley Tech had ever seen. Their previous pranks included: plenty of trouser pulling, hide n seek in the school gym, truancy and brownie stealing; which they were very adamant was a prank since they were brownies for the *church* and not the canteen.

The boys had planned to throw cut off meats from the butchers into the staff room and the odd bit on the dance floor and if they could manage a few girls' purses too. I thought that was just a horrific idea. Let the children boogie for Christ sake! *Girls were slipping on pig's testicles all across the dance floor.* While the boys pranced around, I dragged Suzie to the maintenance room to spike the entire water system with a mixture of Viagra and marijuana. Suzie was mortified, but I've never seen a Christian drink so much unholy water in one night.

The teachers, the pupils, even the band; were all full of erections and paranoid thoughts about the legitimacy of our government and it was *remarkable.*

We made a swift exit when the teachers started groping each other, and the students were being sick on each other's shoes and left for town. Lightweight George and his leftover grub made a beeline for the strip club where his meat was flung on stage to a rowdy crowd of strippers; who made it clear they prefer payment in cash. We headed to a pub where Peter broke the jukebox by playing 'Tutti Frutti' too many times the jukebox gave in, and the landlord called us all; '*a bunch of fucking futuristic hippie twats.*' Which was very prolific and correct for a man with one eye and a driving ban.

By this point, Suzie was crying every other minute when she remembered (and then simultaneously forgot) George ripped her dress when he begged her to go on stage at the strip club. Peter was sick around every corner, pushing his luck when he chundered on a policeman's shoes after already being sick on the police headquarters front step because he couldn't make it to the bin in time. That was just the start of the cat and mouse chase.

We hid in shopping trolleys; garages; living rooms of strangers' homes; pubs; clubs; bakeries that were just opening; strip joints that were just closing; back alleys; underneath cars and in the back of cars. Until finally, the garden of a mental asylum; where we were found by a cluster of guard dogs and six panting police officers with handcuffs and receding sweaty hairlines.

I learnt three things that eventful night: Suzie crying sounds very much like a scratched vinyl that refuses to stop playing; Peter's sick smells like stale milk and the inside of a prison cell looked awfully like my childhood bedroom.

Suzie didn't speak to all of us for a good few months after we were released a couple of days later. We all thought she was stubborn, but her parents had sent her off to a church camp in America in a desperate attempt to cleanse her of her sins. Suzie wrote to me inciting how crazy she was going and how badly she wanted me to get on a plane and come save her.

She even sent a cheque.

Who in their right mind would say no to a scared Christian girl lost in the big apple, willing to pay you to come save her? *Not me.* I was more than desperate to get out, I was frantic at leaving my parents in a bid for freedom. I've never quite understood the dire need to escape everything you've known, even if everything you've ever known is quite nice; but I was riddled with the disorder.

It's almost as if, sitting in your childhood bedroom you used to wet the bed in; you can hear your entire town wailing and shrieking at the crippling weight of who you could be and the lives you could have lived.

I packed a rucksack and hitchhiked a lift to the airport where I used most of the cheque bar about £10 on a return flight to New York. It was very responsible of me to get a return ticket, and I wish I could accept responsibility for the deed; but in truth, it was the check-in woman who told me I wouldn't like New York and should book a return flight, *just in case.*

She was right, I was home within a week.

I've had much, *much* better experiences of America since my first trip. At the time, you realise arriving in New York to rescue a Christian, is the least bit fun and restricts certain *pleasurable activities;* like drinking or smoking or snorting or basically *anything* not cited in the bible. Suzie was adamant on remaining intact with her spirituality and keeping her celibacy to sex and drugs intact. It took one night and a bag of marijuana to crack her.

78

Before I could ask her what a *Clam Chowder* was and what the fuck it was doing in a Tupperware box in my lap; she was kneeling at the holy graces of our Lord: the illegal high and *thriving* off it.

We spent our days recovering from the nights we slept in hotel rooms we didn't pay for and the drugs we'd consumed stolen from unsuspecting pockets. We watched the local theatre and stared at books in bookstore windows before finally boarding a plane back home. We weren't ready for America and America wasn't quite prepared for us.

Plus, I turned up to Christian camp in a Led Zeppelin shirt; demanding they release my daughter as her father had just passed away of shock at the death of pirate radio and we had a funeral to go crash.

I figured that either the Christian camp or Suzie's real mother and father would be on our tails pretty quickly, and we both wanted to be on common ground when we were being chased back into conformity.

America had given me a sense of reality. Flying in that rattling plane, I understood the feasibility of it combusting into nothing. Despite that trip to America seeming somewhat senseless and lacklustre, I did arrive home feeling a little more desperate to write. I spent a lot of time watching people in America. Watching little kids with holes in their shoes staring at punks smashing in windows. Old men sharing cigars on porches. Women running together in cheap spandex.

Groups of kids, with their flares dragging in the mud, talking about the charts in the sun. Amongst all the clamour of New York, I could hear *noise*. Sounds: small, soft, subtle sounds amongst it all. The rolling of dice; dealing of cards; tuning of a radio; shutting of a barn door; the bell of a shop; the shuffling of tired feet. The screeching of tyre on tarmac; the creak of a tree; the rustling of a burger wrapper; the chink of metal as a bike is chained up.

Sound being and *meaning* more than sound. Ordinary noise, creating extraordinary sensations. Like the moment I picked up the recorder for the first time or the first time playing with George and Peter and hearing noise hitting with other noise. The feeling of it charging through me, I am *crucifi*ed. And *words*. Beautiful words strung together in books, poems, songs, plays. I heard remarkably beautiful words spoken between two elderly women in New York.

"My Tony, last night, well he took a while to get up the stairs, you know his hip still ain't great after the operation. But he brought me a nice cup of cocoa in my favourite mug, I said: 'thank you very much, darling,' and he gave me a kiss."

"Well, that's lovely Marge."

"I said to him, you know, 'I could've left you on that ship front and our baby Caroline and Jimmy, wouldn't be, and we wouldn't be drinking cocoa together, and I'd have died an unhappy woman.' Oh, he does make me happy, Linda."

"I can tell my love."

"I think I'll shoot myself with Jimmy's gun if he goes first."

"The guns a good idea Marge. *Swift.*"

"Yeah, *swift.* I think I'll do that, Linda. Indeed, *indeed.*"

Such beautiful words, hurried and rushed words, but charming none the less.

Those words amalgamated with the bike chain clanging and the deck of cards dealing; the rubbing of spandex and the clogged breathing of five smokers on a porch. The bike chain and haggard breath, a soundtrack to Marge and Linda's words, sounding so perfect. So unintentionally and inexplicably beautiful. When those small sounds and beautiful words are looped together, well there is nothing much else I need. America seemed superior at convoluting noise and words together. London never quite so beautifully amalgamated the sound of a beer bottle smashing on a bald man's head with the script of Shakespeare ringing out from the theatre's back door smoking area. But London was my *home.*

I brashly told my parents at the kitchen table, when I arrived home, of my intentions of being a rock star. My father's initial reaction was to spit out his dry roasted chicken, and my mother's response was to cry *'at the death of her precious baby girl.'* She told me that she'd *'seen me derailing and spiralling for months now and had feared I would turn to drugs.'* As most irrational parents fear the worst, I was hardly surprised and positively underwhelmed at the reaction. I relentlessly informed them about my love for performing and my passion and ability at playing the saxophone. My father stayed silent while my mother announced she'd managed to get me an incredible opportunity working part-time at the sewing factory a few miles away.

I chose that unruly moment to inform my mother that I had in fact, never successfully sewn anything in my life; to which the gravy boat went flying and I realised where my poor temper came from.

I worked part-time at that factory for the money and the money alone. It was purely coincidental that I got the job in the first place. A fire alarm went off, right before I was due to show the manager my sewing skills I didn't have. He shrugged and told me to be here, '*8 o'clock tomorrow morning.*' My mother was ecstatic, could hardly contain herself with pride. The whole bridge club sent congratulation cards and cake that I ate alone, in my room, *crying*. My mother's dedication of me becoming a seamstress was paradoxical. She would spend her small wage on sewing books and neatly wrap them, leaving them on my bed. At one point, I had a pile of unwrapped sewing books in the corner of my room, so high, I used it as a ladder to the top shelf of my wardrobe where I hid my instruments. Being torn between loving your mother and wanting to make her proud; answering to the voice in your head nagging you day in and day out to share your music with the world; is a prosecution I wouldn't wish on anyone. I think it's a side effect of being young. Obeying your mother to appease her, sacrificing your happiness. It's something I grew out of rather quickly.

The factory girls were not my kind of girls; lovely, sweet-hearted girls with absolutely no backbone whatsoever. No humour, unless it was at the expense of a freshly wed wife or cheating husband. No small talk, unless it was about the weather. Nothing but 'hello's,' 'wanna brew' and a short 'goodbye.' I needed a bit more from people.

I found the job tedious and monotonous and even at the time, I failed miserably at hiding my disgust. I tried to focus on the money, but that barely existed either.

I also seriously couldn't sew. I kept trying to learn discreetly so I could keep the job, but that was much harder than I anticipated. I ended up sweeping around the machines and asking the cleaner to do my job of sewing instead.

I would only bring my sax to the factory, nothing else, sometimes not even shoes. I would walk the four miles' barefoot, playing my sax down the country road at five in the morning, wishing I was heading elsewhere. Fantasising I was walking to the beach. A white sand beach, the kind that you find sand in your knickers for months. Dreaming I was heading to the city. Not London, not New York; a different type of city, an *undiscovered* city. A metropolis of girl rockers, with a transvestite for president. Cake shops open until 3am, libraries for vinyl, concerts for the millions in a cosmic paddock of sunflowers. A city full of lovers, dreamers and freaks with the map of space on the back of their leather jackets; stars for eyes, glasses to match, red leather pants, *OH man what a catch*!

I'd dream I was running towards the end of the Earth, preparing myself to run, skip and jump into the oblivion; the *sweet-smelling* abyss.

It was always rather disappointing to see the rhombus chimney of the factory above the treeline as I crossed the road.

I'd hope a car would run my toes over, *but of course*, it never did.

I did not take lightly to the routine of work. My mother would always say; '*you've a sane mind for such a lion*,' but I wasn't that at work. I wasn't sane at all.

I was a barefoot imposter failing miserably to sew a straight line while staring off into the distance dreaming about prostitutes taking over the world.

On my one month anniversary of sticking at the factory (by the sheer skin of my knees), I staged a protest; mostly because I was bored, to be frank. I didn't have much else to do, and I enjoyed protesting. It was my '*go to*' solution around that time.

No one will listen to me, maybe they'll listen to a hundred of me.

I told everyone a week before, that all the women should walk out at noon and stand in the smoking area, bras to the wind, demanding we gain a reasonable pay rise; *because we could.* At the time, I genuinely didn't know there was such a thing as a '*gender pay gap.*' I knew our boss, Mr Kraken, and all the delivery men earned more, but they also did different jobs, so I believed it was normal. Regardless, I just direly wanted more money so I could buy a guitar or leave the country or do anything but stay at the factory with numb fingers. I figured the more people that supported me, the higher chance of me getting more money.

The boss did not take likely to a measly 15 of his hundred or so workers, stripping naked outside his office window for what seemed like absolutely no reason whatsoever.
It was my last strike.
I'd already broken two machines by kicking them off their tables when I performed in the factory for Jenny Harding's birthday. The first straw was a complete accident; I wholeheartedly did not mean to set the thread on fire.

I figured quickly, that as much as I wanted and *needed* the money I wasn't going to get it at the factory because I simply couldn't keep the job down. Not only was it mind-numbingly soulless, but the part of my mind that whirrs and whizzes 24 hours a day; creating lands, drawing up worlds, singing melodies; cannot be caged up in a factory.
A day later, I turned up at work dressed in just my underwear and fathers suit jacket, completely open with my green cowboy boots and hat. Apparently, it wasn't '*work appropriate,*' and I was sacked with immediate effect.

To say I wasn't arsed is a mild understatement. I grabbed my wage packet and blew it all straight away on a deposit for a guitar. I had absolutely no idea how I was going to get the rest of the money for in a week, but something told me I would be fine. I shed no worry for the money, and kept leaving the house early morning with my sax; playing in the woods near my house for hours on end, until the hunger would get too much and I'd go home for half a sandwich. My mother didn't find out for a whole two months before a friend from bridge club, whose daughter worked three machines from me, ratted me out and I was done for.

She didn't take it lightly. I slept outside for three nights before Suzie took me in for a fortnight while my mother calmed down.

Seeing what I've achieved and who I've become was not easy for my mum. I'm not sure whether watching your child refine their passion into a career that becomes; drugs, drink, tabloids, girls, boys, sex, scandals; amongst chart hits, album releases, arduous tours, nights in Japan, record contracts- is an easy thing to do. While being supportive, she was always wary, *as every mother would be*, of the paths I was choosing.

When I chose to commit myself to music, she, of course, worried tirelessly about the reality and long term impact it would have. Mothers have that sixth sense of reality, don't they?

She knew there'd be bad; nastier than the bad in a factory job. She knew there'd be trouble, much, *much* worse than any kind of trouble that could come from working in a factory.

There's a particular life we choose to live and a specific person we decide to become, and I chose very early on in life to take the trouble, to take the bad and to sew it into the most audacious outfit I could imagine.

Mum just worried *as all mums do.*

I just about managed to get together the money for the rest of the guitar deposit. I sold some old clothes and bric-a-brac at a car boot but spent all the money I made on a white, frilled cowboy jacket. Since I only had three days left to pay the deposit, I fucked for cash. Laying in a stranger's bed, next to an alien I'd just *fucked,* and the only face in my mind was my *mothers.* My damn mothers face that I'd never seen in my dreams before; not once in a trance of fairgrounds and candyfloss or a nightmare about her hate for everything I did. It made me miss her. I wanted her so badly, it *hurt.* I'd never felt the sensation of throbbing before I fucked for money.

Surprisingly, it was Suzie that suggested I do it since she'd done it a couple of times for spare money to help the house. Her sweet, cute, innocent little Christian face assured me it could be easy and quick and decent money, and that was exactly what I wanted. I figured if she (a woman who still cut the crusts off her sandwiches) could do it; *I could too.*

Sex was always clinical back then, since the first time.
Boys were always being invited around to my house for dinner they didn't want, by mothers they didn't like. I almost felt bad. In hindsight, I definitely felt guilty for these boys who'd put on their

father's suit under their mother's orders and had to eat my mother's terrible cooking *just in case* I could be their wife. I know now that fucking them as an apology is most defiantly, *not* the way I should have reacted; maybe I felt it was how a '*good wife*' would respond. Either way, it meant that sex was clinical. Sex was always a favour; to say sorry, to say thank you, to say: '*I think this is what real women do.*' Utterly oblivious to the fact a tiny *apology* child could soon be running about the place; I kept sleeping with men after dinner until my mother postponed the search for a *husband* with the search for a *job* instead. Maybe it was natural for me to fill the void of 'husband search,' to 'job search,' with the same thing; *sex*. Perhaps I was too stuck in my routine of fucking every week that I couldn't get out of it and saw a window of opportunity.

Maybe I was a highly sexual being but didn't know it yet.

Whatever I was back then, I fucked for money, three nights in one week and earned just enough for the deposit and a week in town.

I spent the week completely out of my mind. In fact, I don't remember much of the week at all. On the first night, I went to a part of town I hadn't been down before. I'd heard so much about the place from George and Peter; tales of vicious brawls and one-legged prostitutes. There was something familiar about how George would talk about these '*freaks*,' that made me want to go.

The street is residential now, but at the time it was commonly nicknamed '*Cunt Corner*,' for the number of girls who'd walk down the road ready for guys to drive by and pick up whoever they fancied. There was a time when London was rancorous with its residents,

'New York kinda vicious' I'd call it. London might've been smeared in royal undertones and china mugs; but beneath the tea party were streets like 'Cunt Corner,' that prostituted its soul to the damned youth for a gram of what said youth were high on. To be blunt: London was drowning in drugs and 'Cunt Corner' was the outcome of it.

I met a slim looking man, disproportioned by all accounts, with acid white hair, dressed head to toe in denim with red heels. He was stood outside a strip club smoking a cigarette and looking at women in a way he shouldn't have been doing.

"Hello."

"*We say Howdy here.*"

"What's your name?"

"Tell the paramedics it's *Baby.*"

Baby was so stick thin you could see his ribs. Me and Peter made a pact to buy every packet of nuts behind the bar to fill him up to try and put some weight on him. But Baby was indefinably bulimic and probably had undiagnosed body dysmorphia; which wasn't a thing back then. Back then, you were just skinny or *ignored.*

Baby was the model: 'Twiggy's,' biggest fan and was the same tiny size as her; which he believed was his first step to becoming Britain's best male model. Turns out a skinny man doesn't sell as well as a skinny woman. A man must look healthy to be a model; a woman's ribs are sexualised. Baby was told '*he wouldn't sell much old spice,*' and promptly gave up modelling.

Baby escorted me inside the strip club that night, and the next thing I remember is having a tequila shot poured down my throat as I'm frenziedly trying not to throw up the previous one.

Then I'm in a bedroom in God knows what part of London shooting heroin.

Shooting heroin in a stranger's bedroom aged 16 is not something to romanticise, but I'm gonna. I'm gonna romanticise heroin, because, like every love story; at first, it's *fucking beautiful.*

It's the most incredible thing. You'd do anything for it, *absolutely anything.* Nothing is too far; nothing is too little; everything is for that *one* thing you love.

The moment I saw it, smiling on the most glorious spoon I had ever lay my eyes upon, I knew it would be the love of my life. There wasn't a thing I wanted to change about it. I loved the way it looked at me, teasing me, telling me it was the best thing for me. I loved the way it said my name in my sleep, calling me out of my stupor. I loved the way it got along with my friends and just made every party that *little bit more sufferable.* I was never late to the party if I was late with it. I was never alone if I was alone with it and I was never gonna die if I died with it.

We were the most beautiful love story. Unfeigned, undeniable, intolerable, crushing, freeing, fucking *love.*

I loved its name. I loved its friends too.

I loved its brownish colour, the way it changed when heated, but the thing I loved the most; *it inside of me.*

Oh, we were strictly sexual from the word go. I fucked it, it fucked me.

Until the day it *kept* fucking me, *wouldn't* stop fucking me, *couldn't* stop fucking me until I was *fucked.*

I must praise that first night together, I can't tarnish that. No matter the outcome of our relationship, I cannot and *will not* deny our love; as disastrous, as stupid and as horrific as it ended- it once was as sharp as a scissors blade, and as astronomical as the planets I dreamed of. The part I can't romanticise is the *end.* All stories come to an end, even when you don't want them to; they end at *some* point, in *some* way.

Ours ended with the kiss of death nuzzling my breasts, as I try my hardest to revive my breath.

An *overdose*, to you dear.

CHAPTER SIX
A CLEAN
SURFACE
FOR DRUGS

As soon as me and Suzie came back from America, we started putting on these awful American accents when we spoke to men we'd meet out shopping or at the pub with George and Peter. We did it for years. I had a pretty good way of standing like an American, and if you tell a London boy, you're more exotic than you actually are; they believe it out of pure boredom. I told this one guy I was America's hottest model at the moment and his sweet little face took a photograph of me, asked me to dinner and gave me his mother's address and told me to write sometime. I went to dinner in nothing but an American flag with a belt tied at my waist and spoke about how radical air travel is. He outright told me I was far too flamboyant for him and gave me the sturdy piece of advice to; '*speak a little less and look a little more,*' when going on another date. He chivalrously didn't kiss me; '*out of respect to America.*'

Suzie was a little luckier with her American accent. She found the man she'd eventually go on to marry; once they'd broken up when she exposed the news of her English accent and then got back together after a year of realising they didn't like anyone else as much.
It was during this American accent fad that I met Freddie Anton, who needed back-up singers for a wedding. We met at an unfortunate police raid in a pint-sized pub around Cunt Corner. He was flushing a stash down a toilet I was about to piss in.
"D'ya mind?"
"Raid. Gotta do what I gotta do."
"You're wasting it. Snort it."

"Halves? Reckon full is gonna send me hospital and I got a really cute date tomorrow."

We snorted a quick couple of lines off the toilets tank, and Freddie did a little extra off the seat. We heard the police heading our way and instinctively dropped our trousers and pretended to be incredibly irate when they interrupted our sham shagging.

After that, we left together and somehow ended up passing out on a barge we seemingly borrowed for the night. Freddie awoke next to me, wide-eyed and positively chirpy which only agitated my hangover, cooking eggs on the dirty stove. At some point during the night, he must've asked whether I wanted to be back up for his band, or knowing me, I likely performed an entire rendition of Little Richards back catalogue (stage and costumes provided), because by the morning the band were outside the temporarily stolen barge and ready to go.

I was reluctant to join them. Not just because of my drug-induced fever, piss-stained pants and developing scabies; but because I didn't want to be back up.

I don't know any performer who'd *want* to be back up. Yet I knew my chances, and they were bleak. I wasn't a part of anything; I wasn't in a band, I wasn't doing skiffle sessions or busking, and I only owned a couple of instruments. I understood that I needed to swallow my pride and do what I needed to do, to further my career.

94

You have to do your time in creative jail to appreciate the freedom of life in a band. My creative jail was singing back up.

I said *yes* to singing back up and went on tour with Freddie's band exploring the UK, singing to drunk and loved up couples.

I thought I was the best backup singer the world had ever seen and it was clear I thought so. *Arrogant*, would be too kind; I was an absolute *cock* about it.

I was happy, I guess that was it.

I was *finally* content; *elated*, even. I felt productive. It wasn't what I wanted to do, but it was *something*, and it was getting me closer to where I wanted to be, so I had to appreciate the journey.

My days were spent driving in a van full of people who loved and talked about music with as much passion as me. My nights were spent singing with those people to a room full of drunk, happy and loved up folks wanting shit music to see the night through.

And my mornings were spent by myself, writing or dreaming and sometimes *both*.

One night we all took the van to a bowling alley shy of civilisation, like some American dustbowl kind of thing. The lights were bust, one man ran the whole thing, the food gave half of us the shits and the bowling balls would break if you attempted to go full strike. But we were too high and happy to care. Dolly Daydream was back up with me, while Freddie and his brother Greg with John Andrews consisted of the rest of the band.

Andrews was a good contact if you wanted a lawyer. He knew every lawyer in South London; from criminal to marriage. I thought John was a con man until we dared him to steal a bottle of whiskey and he buckled at the last minute; throwing our entire pay from the previous nights' gig to a delighted shop owner. Turns out he went to Kingston University and studied law, then got in a car accident and said, '*I saw the end, and it wasn't pretty*,' so joined a band instead. *Music arises when a crisis sinks.*

Freddie was practically the opposite. He couldn't obey the law if he tried. There were occasions where I felt deep within a criminal underground by merely standing next to Freddie. But if you'd had a few too many and needed to count sheep, Freddie was always the one to carry you to safety and tuck you in, staying with you while the sickness subsided.

Greg was always AWOL, but you'd only worry if a guy like him was present.

And Dolly Daydream was precisely that. A pepper haired rocket of a woman who loved cigarettes and was obsessed with wearing odd shoes and matching gloves. She had an unnerving amount of leg and a worryingly amount of hair for one person. Boys loved her, girls loved her, animals loved her, and it seemed the Earth did too.

There was never a person in the room that wouldn't tell her she was being wasted as back up. While I did nothing but blend into the reason why parents hated the youth; Dolly restored faith in both humanity and *boys*. They really could have a woman who looked like those they ejaculated over in their father's magazines. They weren't a *myth*, after all.

We most certainly were polar opposites, and so were our voices, but I think that's why we sounded good.

The weddings were never anything extravagant, always in a youth club or community hall. I never played Edinburgh castle or Kensington Palace. I sang love songs, and then I ate cake with the groom who would most often cry and ask if he'd made the worst mistake of his life.

I spent more time comforting the public than I did singing; but if I could score beforehand, I was more than happy with that. It was an easy time, a gentle life, a solid peaceful six or so months where I could just about afford to live and survive doing it.

That was before the groom shagged me.

You might be surprised to hear the most daring thing about raping someone at a wedding, is *not* the chance of someone catching you. *No.* The most daring thing about raping someone at a wedding, is doing it behind the ceremony's curtain and letting your victim run to the bride in shock to be told; '*it's a wedding darling, what did you expect?*'

I quit the wedding scene not long after that and the band too. Freddie was pretty hurt as I lied to him. I told him I couldn't stand being backup anymore and he called me a '*narcissistic bitch.*' I agreed and went back home to Bromley and got so high I lost a week and my favourite red mules. I *loved* a good spiral back then.

That hot desire in the bottom of my tummy was still as ever-present and roaring as it was the first time I picked up the recorder. The need to fulfil; the requisite to supply; the whole world just out of reach. Nothing had changed, except now I had been raped, I'd sold myself for cheap money, I'd started taking drugs, and I hadn't done anything but write nonsensical songs and wear zany clothes in the process.
I was still so young, so furtive and innocent; but I didn't feel it. I felt dirty all the time. I always wanted to wash and empty everything I owned from my room and life. There were still toys on the shelf, next to the music box I was given as a child; most recently used to store my stash.

I was a big-boobed adult lavished in childlike demeanours. I still lived with my mother and father. I slept in the room next to them. I ate their cooking, they paid for my baths, I drank their wine, they booked my dentist appointments. On occasion, they'd still warn me of the monsters running loose on the streets. Monsters, I was *friends* with. I was still a kid. Children weren't children for very long in the 60s. They were adults often before they were teenagers.

I was starting to think I'd confused the desire in my stomach for a disease and I was beginning to think I was severely *sick*.
It made more sense than the truth.

98

I couldn't stomach the thought I was merely *failing*. That my stars knew exactly what they wanted from me and I was flying in the opposite direction. To think I could be letting the universe down. To accept that I was what mothers try their best to avoid raising.

I made myself sick, or the drugs made me sick, or the rape made me sick; I didn't know what made me sick; except I was sick every morning for two weeks straight.

I spent the entire two weeks in bed, staring at my ceiling, which was covered in the stars' constellations from an activity book when I was a kid. I wasn't taking drugs because my body couldn't keep them inside of me, so I was delirious and now slightly dope sick too. I trembled and tremored, and I wept, and I sobbed. I wet the bed, I shat the bed. I was sick on myself, I was sick on my mother. I passed out six times, I swear to God I only woke up five.

One hysterical night, I saw my face in the stars on the ceiling, and I pulled out my eyes. I put them back in backwards so I could see the back of my mind. It was shelves full of dinky jars with all the things I'd done and still had to do, and I couldn't make sense of the order. I scavenged for the best one, smashing a few in the process. I ripped open a dozen to try and find the first moment it all got this bad, and when I couldn't find it, I went back to the stars; found my lips with my wet fingers, tore the skin off and knitted the flesh into a piece of paper for me to bleed out onto.

I woke with ulcers, and bloodshot eyes, screaming about Nancy; who was the first girl I accidentally kissed in a school play back in primary school.

For the first time in months, I had a clear mind and what felt like a clean slate. Only with the power of hindsight, I didn't keep my head clear for music at all, I unintentionally kept my head a clean surface for drugs. Regardless, I wrote more in those two weeks than I had ever before in my life at that point. It's worth noting, none of it made sense. There were scribbles of figures I had called '*God*,' armless scribbles with black curly hair and what I described as '*ginger lips with cola noses.*' There were stories and sweet little nothings on the pages. None of it amounted to much at the time, as I couldn't read a lot of it for the blood or occasional sick stain.

I was a teahead (stoner), who did the occasional line of Charly and had just been introduced to the damnable temptations of heroin. Weed can be good for you, but it can also make you crazy. Cocaine is somewhat amicable unless you take too much it makes you lose your horn. Cocaine is only suitable for sex and staying awake, and that's what should be on t-shirts.
And then there was one; *heroin.* Junk. H. Smack. Horse. Gear. There are a million synonyms for heroin, and not one of them describes innately the degree of its horror. I once heard is referred to as the '*Devil Spunk*,' and think that's the closest.

I was a fresh face to the complexion of smack. I found its eyes as tempting as the churning cerulean seas of the ocean. Its lips were damn kissable, and I found a resemblance to my father amidst the face of heroin. It was comforting. It was as familiar as a foreign substance could be, and yet it felt a whole lot more like home than the bricks I slept amongst.

There was something I adored about the process; from buying to injecting, it was a routine I enjoyed. I found no joy or even sombre indebtedness in the habit of a working day; it positively poured concrete between my bones, jarring my soul into a callous confinement.

To begin, I'd joy bang with anyone who offered. I often put myself in some stupid positions to do this. Pushers are sceptical of women trying to score. They'll mostly only sell to a man or the woman of a John.

I eventually met a pusher who'd sell me two caps every other day for around the equivalent of ten pounds, and a handwritten love note to keep his mother happy.

We'd meet in a café on Burroughs street called 'Crosbies,' which did egg on toast and a pot of coffee for a pound.

'*Bounce*' would drop them in the sugar pot and eat my eggs. Bounce was a slender, precipitous man who annoyed the hell out of me. His eyes were as sloe and hollow as the needle welts up his arms.

I would run my fingers over his needle welts if ever he caught me after a line of Charly. There's something profoundly arousing about needle welts on others skin.

On your own, they're just physical reminders of a mental problem. They're not like tyre marks, citing on roads where cars have been. *Needle welts are postcodes for dependencies.*

I was not addicted. Addicts say this and non-addicts roll their eyes and say; '*sure,*' with all the enthusiasm of a jockey riding a legless horse in the grand national. But I was not addicted, and that's important.

At the time, however, I'd been joy banging for six months or so and a teahead for well over two years. I assumed it'd finally caught up with me. I wasn't too far off the kid who'd stolen six bags of maxi sized Haribo's and was now lying in bed, yoshing into the family sick bowl. Only I wasn't throwing up heart-shaped confectionery, but pill-shaped sentiments; and it was the least bit appealing. While it's easy for me to romanticise the consumption of drugs and incite the ethereal sex or the initial rush that compares to nothing else. Not climaxing, not exercising or even the lull of temporary unconsciousness that quiets the mind.

Nothing.

The beginnings of an addiction and the physical wear and tear it bestows on one's body is simply grim. The diarrhoea churning your stomach feels like a baseball bat embellished with nails stirring your stomach at the pace one stirs a crockpot of stew. You can vomit enough fluorescent acid to fill a bath, and it is not uncommon for an addict to do precisely that while pulling rotting teeth from spinning down the plughole.

The lack of hunger seems convenient until your legs stop working. Until your feet stiffen like a man's Johnny and your knees kiss the floor with the reverence of an army wife. You're dazed and woozy like a young chick just out of the tree.

Your heart beats with the clout of a thousand fists performing justice on a rapists' face. It is silent in its duty to keep you alive, you are permanently awake in search of affirmation. It is that search that sends your head chasing itself. It is that expedition that desires the smack to sustain the cat and mouse chase of mind vs mind and keep yourself alive. Because suddenly you've experienced a heightened sense of reality and stayed alive. So, it seems borderline stupid to revert back to the dull existence of reality where staying alive seems much harder. But for every hit, every electric sexual encounter, every high and every trip; there is a low and a comedown and a week of the shits. There's 10 missed calls from a mate that saw you picking bus tokens from bins; four rancid pints of milk in the fridge. A lover left strewn on the same bed you shag your partner. A dry purse, a black eye and a pending sexual assault case from a lush worker who tried to earn his living in your pockets.

But at this point in time, the sickness I was enduring was not at the hands of addiction like I thought. But an entirely different form of illness.

A *mental* one. Probably called depression or anxiety or even PTSD. Nicknamed in my mind as: '*The Buggar.*'

'The Buggar' made me feel worthless beyond belief; it made me irrational, fearful, and incomprehensively shy. I could not stand the thought of much. Even the thought of my own thoughts sent me into a fit of anxiety. 'The Buggar,' socialising with Charly is a party you don't want to host. Or attend, or watch, or even think about missing out on. I became incomprehensively riddled with distress and anxiety overnight. Suddenly the world terrified me when it had never so much as made me jump before.

'The Buggar,' would call me names. Vile names, not to be repeated. She'd spit on my memories, taint them with bile so sticky, they'd hug my skull like a well-fitting pair of slacks.

And I swore all the fucking time because I was an entity of filth. A complete 5ft6 landmark of rotting nappies and clogged drain pipes. One singular thought could not find its way to the surface. It would panic and drown, its maggot riddled corpse lying next to the memory of running barefoot through a field I have as a child.

Both quite poetically disintegrating into my bones, the way they entered.

CHAPTER SEVEN
FAT GIRLS
GO TO HELL

I met Molly Jagger in a toilet on Eel Pie Island. Eel pie was a notorious place for culture off the River Thames at Twickenham. It was only accessible by boat, a rickety footbridge on the north side of the bank, or if you were feeling brave enough: a quick swim with the eels.

You wouldn't go to Eel Pie unless it called you. It was a dank, dark place full of piss and cig butts; if the music did not call you; you'd visit Eel Pie: call it the abyss and smite rock n roll on t-shirts at rallies and we'd have no choice but to call you a pussy.

In the light of day, every crack it had was exposed, but everyone knew to scarper by then if they wanted to keep their clothes dry. George and I would go, just the two of us, because the music called us. It was a primitive noise that came from Eel pie, it blared out of souls we recognised; souls we were familiar with, could relate to. I'd go to the island to get hard, the music was utterly seductive to me; I'd had no sex like it. They prostituted the music on that island, and I bought it every time.

I'd pay the bridge keeper (a 90-year-old woman with a bag on her head) a tuppence; buy myself and George a beer and disappear. Kids would climb up rafters, hooking their legs around the beams, hanging down to get a glimpse of the band. You always had to check above you at Eel Pie, to see if a lad with a spliff in his mouth was gonna jump on top of you. George was knocked unconscious by a lovely girl in overalls, who lost her grip and fell on top of him once; we learnt the hard way after that.

Eel Pie Island was sinking into the Thames; when you jumped, bog water practically seeped into your platforms and made your toes wet. When you lit a cigarette, the smoke joined the mist upon the lake. It was a place for the blues to ripen amongst the weeds of British bog water and boy did it ripen. The place was always bursting at the seams with kids dancing and singing and drinking. The lawn was littered in couples shagging, the boats usually too. The toilets were a hot spot for dealing; it was a heavenly hotel that smelt of the 60s and didn't apologise for making each and every one of us hard. The smell of damp and cigs has never smelt so sweet to me.

Molly was in the toilets with blood dripping down her nose and into her toothy smile when I met her at Eel Pie. She'd just jumped from the rafters. She was wearing a ripped man's shirt and a tartan skirt with the tallest black leather boots, right up to her vagina. We spent the night dancing and ended up swimming the Thames to the other side, with a bottle of champagne we nicked on my head and two glasses on hers.

Molly Jagger would eventually go on to front one of Britain's best rock bands: '*The Rolling Stones.*' However, when I met Molly, she was a university graduate with herpes and a vast shoe collection. I didn't know we shared the same dream when I first met her. Not much about the way she slurred her words and kept asking me where her cat was; told me she wanted to be a rock star too. That was kind of the *thing* about Molly Jagger; you never really knew what she was thinking, even when she was supposedly telling you exactly that; you couldn't rely on it being the truth.

'The simple element of just being an oppressed woman is not enough to make you interesting. All women are oppressed in some way and what's interesting about oppression anyway?' Molly taught me that. It was one of the first things she told me that night at Eel Pie, alongside a quiet plea to be saved from the man awaiting in the next cubicle. She caused a family feud by hating her sister, simply because Molly found her utterly uninteresting.

Molly's sister, Janie, thought that being a woman was enough to make her stimulating; in a climate where being a woman was not even enough to be *respected*. In Molly's eyes, her sister was plain bloody *stupid*, and she had no shame in telling the whole town.

Molly had no time for arduous chit chat. She never spoke about the weather or her family; other than perhaps an update on how much she hated her sister. She'd dive in head first about the decaying process of a body on a Sunday morning. People say she needed drugs to talk, or talk *good* at least, but that's a lie.

She spoke to me, on many occasions, about what she loved and hated- entirely stone-cold sober. She was better sober. She told me of how she particularly liked it when the vinyl cracked between each song. She loved the crusts of her toast. She loved the way northern boys said; *'mornin',* likening it to her father. She loved the zoo and shopping and her mother's cooking. She enjoyed a lot of other things besides sex, drugs and alcohol. I guess sometimes she did love them the best; but ultimately, she was just a girl who loved, laughed, cried, lived and died: *the female epitaph.*

There's no hiding Molly Jagger threw herself around town like the paperboy. There's also no hiding how shamed she was for it. At the time, the notion of a woman plainly having a *life* was audacious, never mind having a *sex* life.

The press used her as the poster girl for anti-depressants, since she practically funded the early days of mental health pharmaceuticals. Amongst her fans, she was the female rebel with a cause; although no one knew exactly *what* that cause was.

It shouldn't have come as a shock that the woman who was so severely addicted to drugs she'd take them in the shower; would ultimately turn to drugs when her head went sideways to fix the problem. But it was a shock. It was a proper fucking shock.

You get so wrapped up in the entire rock n roll world; drugs are habitual. Utterly ordinary, it's like sharing a bed, it's a generous thing to offer someone; or like sharing your birthday cake. It's easy, it's regular and if it's not on the table; someone will be running to your door to make sure it is within seconds if that's what you want. Or if that's what you *think* you want.

I'd hoped she was sane enough to realise that fighting drugs with drugs was not going to work. But I was naive of her state.

She scored, she shagged, she slept, she did it all over again. She hated herself, I can tell you that. I get asked so frequently why she shot herself in the head, as though it weren't transparent. I don't know what answer you want to hear, but she fucking hated herself, that's why she put a bullet through her brain. People don't want to listen to it, but she wouldn't want me to lie and say it was the stars or some outer body feeling; it was her head, and it was *fucked*.

Society made her hate herself. Society told her she was the worst woman in the world because she had sex. And not only *had* sex but had *a lot* of it, making her *worse* than worse.

While she was drowning herself in all the drugs, sex and alcohol, she could get her hands on; the world was advertising, she was a monster for it. While she watched the men in her life do the very same; they weren't shamed for it. They were praised and glorified on posters and TV shows. She had church groups protesting outside venues of her Jesus hating behaviour and deadly sinning. She had feminist parties either preaching or protesting against her. Men throwing themselves at her in whatever violent manner they saw fit solely because they *could*. News companies named her; '*Molly Jagger, woman dagger,*' while the press wrote nonsensical articles about her every single week. Photographs of her leaving different homes; footage of her in bed sold by desperate men trying to make a quick quid; pictures of her in the comfort of her own home *crying*.

Inside men had black books just for her. Venues would often empty a store cupboard and tell her; '*if you're gonna do anything, do it in there. We don't want the press.*'

Molly shagged for the exact same reason as me- she just wanted to sing. Or, at least that's how it all started. That's the only reason she ever fucked anyone in the start; in the hopes, one of them would let her sing that night. She lost her virginity at thirteen to a tour manager who promised her a record contract by the time they reached the next state for fucks sake!

It's a terrible weight, a weight I know all too well that she carried through her career. You wouldn't quite believe it, considering the career she ended up living and the success she went onto achieve. Yet, that crippling weight never leaves you. That desperation for a chance. The knowledge that a *good* way to get a man's attention is to show him how smart or talented you are; a *quick* way is to take your clothes off.

After a while, it becomes a habit or an *expectation*. Molly thought she'd be kicked out the band if she didn't fulfil some needs every now and then.

She was that desperate to sing and stay in the band, why is it a surprise she was that desperate she killed herself?

"You know Molly, the world ain't gonna change, *and I'm not saying you should*. But bookers already got a black book just for *you*, does that not make you wanna take a break for a little while? Get your head down in Paris for a year?"

"I don't care about my reputation."

"Mol, you know men can get away with not caring about their reputation because it's their *dicks* that get them their career. It's your reputation that'll get you yours."

"Fuck my reputation Pen."

"I just don't wanna see my best mate end up a patriarchal fatality, alright? I don't wanna see your face on the front of newspapers 'cos you took too many drugs, 'cos your reputation was sold for a gram of coke and a bagful of smack. *Alright, Mol?*"

"*Fuck the patriarchy Pen.* I can't make it clearer than that. I like sex, I like drugs, I just so happen to like to sing too. Damn my reputation, I ain't my mother's daughter. I don't belong to anyone."

That was a pretty standard manuscript for the kind of conversations we'd have. That one, in particular, was in the shower, that we'd share together to save money on the water bill when we briefly shared a house for a couple of months or so. I told her to fuck off so I could have a wank, and she went on a reasonably average binge; I didn't see her until the police found her passed out in a park a week later.

I don't know if it was a tremendous shame, like all the papers plastered on their front pages. They were partly to blame for the bullet in Molly's head. Ain't it funny how charming people are when you're dead?

It's absolutely a shame and a waste of talent, but her suffering was tremendous; death was the kindest anyone had ever been to her: including myself.

She'd scream in her sleep for Christ sake; it was *solemn.*

I hold a small amount of regret for not trying to pull her to the good side sooner. I knew she was struggling, but I didn't quite know how bad it was. We were all struggling. If you weren't half in the rock n roll business and half in the depths of depression back then; you weren't really doing it right. People need insanity for art; *we pioneered that.*

The worst part is, she became her sister. In the months before her death, all she was, was an oppressed, suffering, disaster wrought addict; who couldn't piss in a toilet or talk in sentences. All she had making her interesting was the fact she was an *oppressed woman.* When she realised she'd utterly fucked it, she took too many pills and shot herself in the head. There's nothing else to it.

Shame can kill a woman if society makes you choke on it enough.

In the beginning, she was at my house most days, most weeks; unless she fell off the grid for a while, then she'd come back with a new stolen wardrobe; a dozen or so more scars and a few even deeper hangovers than before. She was good at being a woman and even better at being an addict. She hid her addiction so well. She hid it in her bra, she hid it in her knickers; but my favourite place she hid her habit, was in her bum length hair. Even when her hair went drastically out of fashion, it became too practical, and too notoriously '*Molly,*' to get rid of it.

Her voice was gnarly and angelic, the perfect tone for a man; meaning a lot of the boys would ask for advice, still unwilling to let her on stage. Her heart was too big, she'd offer support to anyone who asked; getting nothing in return; in a business that flourishes off favours and friends. Like me, she was scouring for a chance. We spent countless nights begging the stars on our hands and knees; rising when the sun came up to do the same thing all over again on our backs.
Together we tried to sing and perform, but two women together made our chances even slighter. Nobody wanted *one* woman, why would they want *two?*

I was pretty fat back then. My mother once told me that if I ate the biscuits in the Christmas tin, she'd kick me out the house. I could only dream of being kicked out the house because of cookies; so, I saw it as a challenge and kept eating all the biscuits she'd buy throughout the year, saved '*for special occasions only.*' I was unfortunately never kicked out and bluntly slapped instead.

Molly Jagger was quite the opposite, and she looked even better when I was her accessory. Molly once told me: '*fat girls go to hell,*' to which I was delighted since I already knew whores went to hell!

I genuinely didn't care about my weight. I was eventually made to care about my weight when I entered the glamorous world of the media: in which the schoolyard bullies were a hell of a lot worse.

I only cared about whether I could fit into my red flares; that was my only care in the world at that time. I wasn't even fat, looking back. My body was just changing and growing, and that unsettled me to believe I was bigger than I was.

It's straightforward, as a woman, to label yourself *fat* when the world sexualises bones. At the time, I thought it was better to be bullied for being fat, then sexualised for being skinny. I was tired of being sexualised all the time for just being a girl; it was almost a relief to be hated.

Which is an extraordinary situation to be in at that age, yet no stranger than the kind of things girls go through nowadays. Thigh gaps, rib cage flexing, and whatever the hell those lips are; were not a thing when I was young and I'm very, *very* glad.

My biggest body worry was whether my hair was long enough for all these trends that were coming out of America.

It never was.

The last time a stranger called me fat and ugly in front of Molly; she used her knickers to choke the man, ripped a chunk of flesh from his arm with her teeth and savagely spat his own blood in his eyes. I could've done with Molly earlier on in my life.

I don't remember any of the words said to me, but I remember the *feeling* of being bullied quite strongly. The only words I do remember happened when I skipped an exam because I knew Little Richard was in town. I simply walked out of the school gates and went straight to Walker Grove where I sat on an industrial bin and watched Little Richard, and his band set up. Suzie refused to flunk with me, but she, George and Peter joined me eventually and watched with similar amazement in their eyes at the mechanics of the backstage.

"I'm gonna go ask him if I can touch his guitar!" I declared to a sea of worried exclamations.

"No, you're gonna get us kicked out tonight."

"No, he's cool, it'll be fine."

I carried myself with a lot of whit and confidence for a fat fifteen year old wearing her stepbrother's hand-me-downs; right up to Little Richard and his band, who huddled around me like I was a chip on the seafront and they were all hungry and keen-eyed seagulls.

"Can, can, can I please touch your, your guitar?" I stuttered.

"Can, can, can you please leave us alone you *fat fuck*."

It wasn't Little Richard who called me a '*fat fuck*,' I think it was one of the security guards, but I was still crushed that an acquaintance of my hero thought I was fat. I was mostly bummed that I didn't get to touch his guitar, it would've been the best brag in the playground.

Still, I got to see him perform later that night, and it was as magical as I had expected. In fact, I had my first orgasm watching him that night.

My next *real* orgasm was a year later after meeting Johnny for the first time.

He was balls deep in a cowgirl from Kansas. There were no socks on the door handle or a stream of clothes from the door; so, I wasn't to know he was busy and the show had already started.

'The Three Pencils' were the hottest and newest band in town. Well, in hindsight, they were most definitely not mainstream or well known at all. I liked both under and overground stuff, and I forget the difference, but me and Molly were both infatuated with them at the time.

I'd been tipped off that they might be a way into the industry as they were looking for a support band.

I'd heard lovely things about Johnny Wilder. Everyone that spoke of 'The Three Pencils' said he was '*the gentleman of rock n roll.*' It was a nickname that appealed to me for plenty of reasons.

Which is why I felt somewhat guilty showing a cowgirl out of his dressing room for a chat with the '*the gentleman of rock n roll,*' who was the least bit impressed that I'd interrupted his shagging. I nearly dropped my knickers straight away out of guilt! The pitiful look on his face at my lousy timing.

It was the reasonable part in me that stopped me from offering my body before my talent. Even though sex was just sex- just a side effect of rock n roll. *I* was not a side effect of rock n roll.

I *was* rock n roll.

And I was fucking good at it.

He's since told me that he thought I was the worst woman he'd ever met and called me the one word my mother hates beginning with C. I don't think I asked to talk to him, I seem to remember just sitting myself down on the sofa and staring at his bare chest. He was exceedingly good looking, not really my type, far too '*singer*' for me, but I liked the way he held himself. He was quick to tell me I was a bitch, I remember that and thinking; *I've blown it, how on Earth am I going to swing this one around.*

I handed him a vail of cocaine I nicked from Molly, and he snorted it quicker than I'd seen anyone take any drug before.

I could talk to him then. Johnny was like every single man in a band I'd ever met: *unapproachable if not under the influence.* It gets to a certain point in a man's career, where they can't go on without something easing the long nights, constant heartbreak and the daily act of leaving your soul on a stage in front of hundreds for 10 of the 12 months a year.

Some need heroin, there's no other way to ease the blow. Some men just *need* heroin. Others are better with cocaine and Johnny's one of them.

"I want a gig," I told him.

"And you're telling me, *because?*"

"I want a gig, and you're a singer. Get me a gig, introduce me to your bookie, agent, anyone."

He damn nearly pissed his pants at that. I wasn't prepared for him to find the suggestion funny, I thought he might just say no and show me the door like most frontmen.

I must give it to Johnny; if there's one thing he was good at, it was understanding. There was an absolute compassion with him that I've not seen in any other frontman.

"My cousin needs back up singers."

It was my turn to nearly piss myself laughing. I was not going back there.

"I'm a frontwoman, I think you know that," I told him and he nodded in agreement.

He told me I could sing a set with him the next night, as it was too late for that night. I hadn't even opened my mouth to sing or given him my name. I was instantly impressed with how trusting he was; or *stupid*. Either way, it was nice to simply be considered and not have to fuck for consideration. It was the first time I felt like enough.

"Everyone likes a bit of impromptu," I remember telling him, pushing my luck.

"Our Luke doesn't."

Fucking drummers.

If I had a penny every time a drummer fucked up a band, I wouldn't have needed a career.

"We're singing 'I'm a believer.'" I told him and gave him no time to argue.

If I remember rightly, it was the bassist, Danny Moran that told me to: '*fuck right off*.' I think I've told people since that it was Luke Marco because we all hated Luke, but I should be honest and admit it was Danny. Although I had the attitude of; '*you can't stop me coming on stage, grabbing the mic and singing*,' reality was: I was *fucked*. Johnny was (in hindsight) most definitely too stoned to make sense out of anything. Danny was always the sensible one, and the guitarist simply agreed to whatever Danny said; as long as it wasn't sharing a woman. Luke was a dick.

I did tell them all separately that I was a singer and a good one and an even better performer, but they all showed their arses to me that night. I felt like burning the place down. I was tempted to ruin the show by pulling the mic, and I very nearly stamped all over the drum kit before Molly suggested we steal Danny's bass.

It never felt like a good idea. I do want to stress that we both said at the time; *this is the most stupid thing we've ever done*. It was the pure white rage, it was *uncontrollable*.

The men were unreasonable. I'd met boys who had no talent whatsoever, proper beggar boys, who looked the part but had a voice as good as fingernails down a chalkboard. They were everywhere, you couldn't walk through London without stepping on one or go into a teenage girls' bedroom without seeing a poster of one.

It was as though the idea of a woman on stage was audacious. Simply *outrageous* that a woman *could* be rock n roll. That a woman could be the *group* and not a *groupie*.

Stealing Danny's bass felt like the most obvious *fuck you* at the time. It was the simplest heist in the world. We quite literally picked it up and walked out the main door and into the night with it strapped to my back.

Molly said I looked like I'd just had the best shag of my life that night. I told her I had; *'I'd just fucked the best band in town,'* and she split her lip laughing.

Danny still hasn't forgiven me. It was his father's bass, a priceless sentimental piece that I'd flogged two nights later for a new pair of cowboy boots. I've assured him the boots were absolutely beautiful and absolutely worth it, but he still argues that the bass of his dead father would be much better.

Getting a booked gig the conventional way a *man* got a booked gig, was looking near impossible or exceptionally difficult to say the least. It was nonsensical the things I tried. I shagged a few more frontmen and guitarists for a chance of singing, being on the bill that night, or even just getting my name out in the industry. I quite suddenly realised that sleeping with the band is a great way to get your name known, but getting your name known for the *right* reasons is something I learnt is easier said than done. If there's one thing men are good at, it's talking about women. You can count on a man you've shagged to tell his mate all about it, more than you can count on our Earth to keep spinning for all eternity. I was comfortably being talked about at dirty pub tables across the country and quite content with the idea that maybe *one* of them would take a chance on me.

Until I was introduced as '*that girl*,' to an older man who wasn't part of the band. You quite swiftly learn how dangerous plainly *being a woman* can be. I drew a line that night. I said no more sleeping with men I'd just met.

It lasted a week.

I met Tommy by accident. I was supposed to be meeting some big named, industry yobbo who was going to put me in touch with an even bigger named, industry yobbo; but he didn't turn up. I wasn't hopeful that a man I'd slept with after a substantial amount of cocaine would be good for his word about a man named '*Steve*' he knew from '*way back*,' but I took every chance I could get back then, including the *stupid* ones.

Tommy was robbing purses on the bus.

I caught him as soon as I stepped foot on the bus.

He had his whole arm in an old lady's bag, who was none the wiser that a scruffy looking, black-haired boy was earning his living right in her handbag.

I sat next to him, trapping him between me and the window, to which he looked out of with utter disarray.

"You gonna take my purse too?" I asked him, whispering real low under my breath.

I don't remember being scared of him; I instantly knew his eyes would be the sweetest eyes I'd ever see.

He didn't act sheepish about being caught out, and I remember being tied in thinking whether he was an arsehole or a genius. I'm attracted to arrogance, in the same way, we're all partially attracted to criminals. It's the blazon. The pure egotism for the law. It's a quality we all wish we had, but are disciplinary brought up not to. Tommy was quite clearly a boy who'd never been brought up *at all*.

"Not unless you got me something worth stealing," Tommy told me in not a word less.

I gave him about one pound, kissed him on the cheek and moved to the seat opposite, freeing him of me.

He seemed strangely thankful for a thief. I admired the fellowship about him. I could see he was a commodore of artistry pilfering, but his ability to embezzle me was next to magic.

He scooted next to me, smiling, his hand out, he told me his name, and we shared a conversation about mothers and shopping and then the seasons and before we knew it we'd both missed our stops and were stuck at the bus station with five stolen purses and a whole lot of love for the other.

It's not often I get distracted with men. I was still clinical in those days. Meet, sex, leave. Tommy was a real surprise and not part of my plan.

I slept with him at the bus station that night. It was loving and real and ridiculously cold. He struggled to get hard, and we laughed at how the cold had bitten him nearly clean off.

Then we got some food and sat on some London bench talking more about mothers and shopping and the seasons before he suggested we go for a drink. I was dreading any suggestion of his about where we should go. It makes or breaks it when a man suggests somewhere to dance.

You can imagine my surprise when he suggests a bar I hadn't heard of: *Mary's.*

It feels stupid now that there was a time in my life that I didn't spend wasting someone else's money getting paralytic in the place. It quite swiftly became my regular joint for a good time.

That first night there, I was introduced to Bev; still the best barmaid I've ever known.

She was dressed like a pirate, eye patch and all, with ripped, laced stockings wrapped around her legs.

She poured me free drinks in exchange for stories about men she'd never met. I made most of them up. I ran out of audacious men pretty quickly. It was eye-opening; I suddenly realised how boring men are when they're not inside of you, and even then, it's the same old story.

Tommy yanked me up on tables, and we danced all night long until my feet quite literally bled into my cowboy boots. I then sang some karaoke, awfully, *probably*, but by chance, a local booker was in town, and he caught my attention by the jukebox not long after.

He was a sleaze from a distance, so you can imagine how hideous he was up close. He stank of beer to the point where after five minutes, I felt as though I'd drank five pints and whiskey chasers, by second-hand passive smelling. He was very hands on, nothing I wasn't accustomed too, but there was a rugged, unnerving deception about him: as though the man was bred with a *sewer rat*.

By this point, I'd only ever sang back up, for Molly and a bunch of men who couldn't care less and just wanted a quick shag. I was utterly desperate to make it. Making music, writing, singing, performing *music*- simply sharing the euphoria that is a good piece of music; was what I wanted my days and nights to be consumed by. I didn't want to breathe if it meant not sharing the pure magic that is *music*.

I mean, what's the fucking point to life if music didn't exist?

More so, what would be the point to *my* life if I couldn't write and perform music?

I learnt, not that long ago, when in conversation with another female performer, that I can't be ashamed of doing what I did. I'm not the only one, and as much as it pains me, I doubt I'll be the last woman to agree to a sex act for a *chance*. I've been shackled by the objectification of my body for years.

Hypersexualizsd and based on the bias of my body; on the *value* placed on my body by men. Why can't I use the very same sexual power men use over me, to get what *I* want?

Why is that deemed more morally wrong than men treating women the way they do?

He said he'd give me the job if I gave him a blowjob, but he ended up raping me afterwards, despite how hard I tried to crawl out from underneath him.

At the time, I didn't see any other way. And trust me, if there was a way for me to get a booked gig *without* performing sexual favours on anyone- I would have known about it and done it. But I wasn't a man, so I didn't have the privilege of being heard, or respected, or regarded, or considered. Being a female performer means I am seen as just a woman and not considered for my talent. I'd rather be an *invisible* performer- at least that way people would *hear* my voice.

I was a *woman*, who dressed like a man; who liked girls and boys; who sang about things people didn't understand; who thought highly of myself; in an unforgiving city that seemed to hate women with that exact description. I don't want to say; '*it felt like the world hated me*,' but the bookers certainly did.

In fact, after the booker raped me, he black named me, and every booker I met after that would only talk to me about sex and try it on with me.

I never got that shitty gig, it was a lie that hurt Tommy and me.

He was drastically pained by the decision to let me leave him for the booker that night. I could see in his eyes the last thing he wanted to do was allow a nice young girl, he'd just met, leave with a horrible looking grown man.

The apologetic words on behalf of the entire male species towards the unyielding life of a woman didn't leave his lips that night.

He's since cried and told me he's sorry. He wished he were a tougher man and put his foot down, outright *refused*. He wished he could've aided me in making better decisions. I told him; 'there was nothing, anyone could have said that would have stopped me from leaving with him; you could've told me how it would've ended up and I still would have done it, *just in case.*'

Desperation is the strongest drug I've ever injected.

That booker had the smallest cock I've ever seen.

CHAPTER EIGHT
AN IMPOVERISHED
PHOTOGRAPH
OF JESUS CHRIST

I was pregnant. The bastard booker had got me pregnant.

It was not part of the plan, *to say the least.* Pregnancy was something that seemed so distant and almost incomprehensible, it pretty much landed like a dad *joke* in my brain when I found out.

I was 19 years old.

I'd been around enough bands and enough people in the industry to know that having a kid around your ankles is *not* how you make it. I'd met enough musicians to know that the life of a rock star was *not* for children. The prying eyes of a child watching a routine overdose of half their parental supervisions? *No.* Even if I wanted that kid, it was gone before I could think twice.

It's a strange feeling, knowing your child is inside you; resting, getting ready for the world. All the while, I was pretty fresh out the womb myself and still resting; getting ready for the world. There was so much I didn't know or understand. So much I hadn't done and always wanted to do. If being a woman hindered my chances of a career, I was petrified to discover what being a *mother* would do.

I went to the bus station and spent an entire day getting on and off buses in the hopes I might find Tommy. It got to about midday, and it seemed utterly naïve of me to think I'd ever see him again. I was more than accustomed to one night stands and the look of love, just being the look of *sex.* But something different told me he'd understand. He was the only one who knew how much of a sleaze the booker was, and it wasn't like I could go with Molly; she knew the nurses a little too well for me.

I found him on the bus route from Brixton to Westminster. He was still thieving, and I was the least bit surprised. He was wearing the exact same clothes as a few weeks earlier, that's when I figured he was homeless.

I'm not a pity person, I don't pity people, not on *this* Earth. We're all entitled to fresh air, and that's it. Anyone else who walks about thinking the Earth owes them anything more than air to breath is an arsehole- including myself.

The world doesn't owe you *anything*.

Tommy, a homeless, teenage boy from London, understood that and made me realise I couldn't even pity myself.

Even though Tommy was downtrodden, positively poor and sleeping rough in a bus shelter; he knew, like no one else seemed to know, how little the world offers those who *believe*.

I think that's why he knew I had to be a *different* kind of mother.

The fact women had to risk their own lives by going to backstreet abortion clinics because *some people* disagreed was terrifying. I hadn't given much thought to the ordeal before I fell pregnant. Abortions were illegal and unspoken, but *common*. Neighbours, dressmakers, friends; would die unexpectedly and you'd have to attend the funeral, knowing full well you were mourning not one, but *two* deaths.

Supposedly, the criminalisation of abortions was to *protect* life; but it did more natural un-good than nature itself. The illegal abortion clinics were precisely how you'd imagine an underground, backstreet abortion clinic to look like. Most often, they were spare rooms of residential homes or the back storeroom of a bakers or butchers. Unhygienic, uncomfortable and unethical.

I attended one on Clarke Lane. It was a room above a newsagent. I only went there because Molly had been before and *survived*- which was the best I could've hoped from the situation.

It was freezing. My bare legs were riddled with goosebumps that shuddered by themselves. I was scared. *So very terrified.* I could hardly keep my heart in my chest. It bounced around and rattled my ribs like a pinball machine. I was afraid of dying above a shop that sold 'The Daily Mail' and out of date gumballs for half a tuppence. Petrified of dying a mother without mine. So uncontrollably terrified and alone. Lonely like time; accompanied by motion, but unmoved by it. Alone with my youthful terror trying to convince me I'm irrational to worry about dying, despite the face of death staring down on me; smiling, *smirking* in my blue face. I could feel my own death washing over me like a tide strokes the shore. I was so afraid to die so young, for such a senseless reason.

I didn't want youth to be the death of me. *I was so afraid.*

The floor was filthy. The kind of ground where the filth stands up by itself and walks around the gaff demanding squatter's rights. Coaxed in layers of dust and mud from the comings and goings of boots and slim heels in the back alley. You have to pass a squalor of bins and a family of mice, to get up the stairs.

A square, small space. An impoverished photograph of Jesus Christ hung next to an old and yellowing photograph of Buckingham Palace. It felt like a shrine to the taboos of our country, and I didn't feel comfortable or welcome, *to say the least.*

One of the women hung a gold cross around her neck and made, what felt like, a conscious effort to persistently hit me in the face with it during the procedure. She'd say things like: '*offer salvation to our Lord,*' and '*forgive me, forgive her,*' every time she touched me as though I were a plague.

I asked her why she was doing this as a practising catholic, and all she said were the words:

'*God is with you.*'

Lying on a heap of boxes for a makeshift bed, with a shroud of judgment keeping me stilled; whimpering in pain at the impoverishes of my situation: I laughed at the crisis.

"What you laughing at?"

"If I die, it's because I'm poor. If I survive; I'll be the richest woman alive. *Rich of life.*"

"God is with you."

"I hope *luck* is too."

I was not all that well after the termination, but I had survived with only a short period of panic I may bleed to death.

I was one of the lucky ones.

I couldn't spare the hundreds, or in some cases, *thousands* of pounds that was needed to have a semi-legal and semi-safe procedure. I was one of the lucky *poor* ones. Most of the poor women died because they were poor, and the women with a chequebook survived for that fact alone.

"On your feet. We have another woman in now and six after that."

I was mildly astounded, hobbling off the makeshift bed lathered in my still-warm blood. The woman folded up the sheets, covering her worn hands in my blood and remains of what they terminated. She spoke to the other woman about what they were having for tea that night.

Of all the things that terrified me, it was the *normalcy*.

The routine washing of the needles and instruments in a bucket of soapy water; red from a previous woman's blood. The pile of blood-stained sheets, toppling over in the corner; a stack of bibles on a shelf above my head. A piece of cloth used as a gag for every woman. I can still taste it. Black coffee, salt for the tears and pain: the anti-potion of womanhood.

We were all gagged with pain, *every single one of us.*

A part of me found solace in the fact I had not and would not be the only woman to experience the ordeal in that room. Although I was all too aware of the reality that I may be one of only a few that would leave the room again.

I was sick on the catholic woman's shoes when I saw the next woman enter the room; a protruding, visible bump, bulging from her stomach. I knew the complications of her termination would be immense, and I begged her to leave for fear she'd definitely bleed to death due to how far into the pregnancy she was.

"She's made her choice." The catholic woman stated, shoving me out the door, still bleeding, where two other women waited patiently and silently.

It was a Friday. *Payday.* Their busiest day of the week.

Women should have a choice and control over their body.

In most cases of abortion, the mother makes the decision on count she wouldn't be financially or emotionally ready to fund and protect the child. Women make the tough decision for the benefit of their unborn child because it's irresponsible to bring a child into a potentially dangerous or maybe unloving situation if another option is available.

I didn't want a child formed from being raped; to be raised by a single, 19-year-old mother who had a developing drug addiction and was practically penniless.

I was rather honest and abrupt with myself. I had a life inside of me, I couldn't be in denial about myself and my environment now. There was no chance I wanted my child growing up in those circumstances. I knew I would be shamed for my decision. The stigma and controversy around abortion was rife in the 60s/70s and arguably still is today.

Women can't put the washing out without being scrutinised for the way they peg their husband's briefs.

Having an abortion was buying a one-way ticket to hell.

I wasn't a *real* woman if I didn't just hush and deal with the consequences of being a woman. But pregnancy is not a consequence of being a woman. Pregnancy is a consequence of *sex*, and I was *raped*.

I didn't consent to the sex, and therefore I didn't consent to the consequence of pregnancy. And there should've been a safe and legal option for termination. But there wasn't.

Women drank bleach to increase the chance of miscarriage. Women ran boiling hot baths or used a crochet hook to carry out the procedure themselves. Women went to extraordinary lengths to hide the shame they felt of unwanted pregnancy. And for what?

Women need to be cared for. There must be safe and unbiased options for women, else you're just going to create unsafe and unloving environments for *children*.

I rather cruelly didn't tell Tommy where we were going once I found him.

I know *now* that dragging a stranger to a backstreet abortion clinic and giggling a nervous '*surprise*,' is borderline cruel; at the time, though, I was too confused to care.

Tommy was more upset than me and spent a good while kicking the bins outside.

While I admire men for the hurt they feel on *behalf* of women, it is utterly useless, and you should tell the men in your life that fact. *I appreciate you're upset that a disgusting man got me pregnant while tricking me into a booked gig. But, maybe if you didn't nourish the breeding ground of misogyny, we wouldn't be sat in an abortion clinic asking ourselves where the hell we went wrong.*

It wasn't much of a painful procedure (thanks to the narcotics I'd taken earlier that morning), but I ached relentlessly for weeks and cried obstinately too. I simply felt consumed with how lucky I was to have *survived*.

It felt like a part of me had been taken, even though I didn't want that part of me in the first place. I learnt how cruel it is to be a woman. To give birth to life, but not hold the right to be equal to it.

I figured that if I had birthed a son, he would've had no problem achieving the career I would've surrendered on his behalf. I would dream and wake up in hysteria; a brutal concoction of tears, sweat and belly ache laughs at the thought of me at forty years old and a mediocre musician and my son; a fresh-faced teenager hailed as the hottest musician in town.

Those days were confusing. I'd wake up with regret, but fall asleep somberly happy and most often high. There's truth in numbness.

I knew, as hard as it was to know; that it was kinder for me to carry the pain of losing a child than my child to bear the pain of losing a mother. I wouldn't have been able to be the mother I would've wanted, or the child needed. It hurt. Hurt like a bitch. Still does. I think about what my child would've been like. I think about what my life would've been like.

I don't regret my decision. I harbour my pain; like I once harboured my child. Right there, *beside my heart.*

Pain reminds me I'm a woman, and there's no greater pain than losing a child. If it weren't for that pain, there wouldn't be a doubt in my mind I'd think I was a man.

Those weeks in pain was the most '*woman*' I'd ever felt, and I hated it. It was excruciating. The weight of life upon me and my stomach as it was wrenching for something that'd just been torn from its innards as nonchalantly as ripping open an envelope.

The weight of expectation, the requisite of womanhood and all that goes with it. It was a dull pain. A constant, aggravating, dismal pain, that was relentless and unforgiving. In the end, the drugs were numbing enough to question whether womanhood even existed, until the morning when I was sick, and the cycle started all over again.

That bus journey home with Tommy was long and tiring. I remember choosing to sit next to an open window and sticking my hand out so the cold wind would numb and freeze my fingers enough; I'd put them on my face to wake me up.

Tommy sat quietly and patiently by my side, never speaking unless spoken to. He sat in his own solace; I've never seen pain like it.

Two stops before the end, he opens his mouth to speak, and I stop him before he can.

He wanted to know if it was his child or the bookers. I slept with them both within hours of each other, both without protection other than the pill. It could've been either.

Truthfully, I didn't want to know. I told myself, and Tommy, that it was the Bookers'. Believing it was his made it easier to trust the abortion was the right decision. I never allowed myself to consider it could be Tommy's. It hurt to imagine losing Tommy's baby. Still does.

I told Tommy I knew it was the bookers because it moved too much. I could feel that it wanted to get out, as though it knew it'd be fucked. I don't think it brought any comfort to Tommy, but he respected my decision, and I owe him a lot for that.

I didn't see Tommy for weeks after that. You could say I scared him with an unborn foetus, but I also called him a twat that day while under the influence of my own hormones, and I think it upset him.

I never intended to keep a hold of Tommy. If I'd had my way, I would have got rid of him after that, but shit sticks and Tommy is the best diarrhoea I've ever had.

CHAPTER NINE
MUSIC IS MY DIRTY
SPOON

Molly went missing two weeks after my abortion.

I got a call at my house from some random man, saying that he was concerned about Molly Jagger, as she hadn't come home in a few days. I quite literally howled laughing down the phone, told him he was nothing special and that Molly Jagger doesn't come home for anybody.

I put the phone down and went about my business before it rang again and he was on the other end of the line all in a flurry.

'You don't understand, she owed someone some money, and now they're here and the last time I saw her she was sick,' the guy told me. I was strangely calm and couldn't find the energy to be worried. I was tired of dealing with Molly and her many merry men at that point; I selfishly had my own men to deal with. Molly thought it was funny to give the guys she slept with, my home phone number instead of her own; so, I had a random man calling me every single day asking for Molly Jagger. This one was no more desperate than the others.

'She'll be back, she's like a homing pigeon, don't worry yourself.' I told him and went straight upstairs to write.

Turned out the man that called, acting concerned, was Molly's father. I hadn't met him before; Molly's house was more than out of bounds- it was a *nuclear zone*. I'd met her mother at her hairdresser's. Molly was always determined for me to cut or dye my hair.

'Will you let her dye your hair. It's ginger.'

'It's red.'

'It's *shit.*'

Molly hated that my hair was never brushed, always a mess and a whole lot manlier for her womanly eyes at that time. I think she was just jealous: her blonde locks would never have looked good cut short, and she knew it.

Molly was in genuine trouble this time. Some man from some band framed Molly for a drugs debt. Even though the dealers wholly knew that Molly would never have been allowed to buy that number of drugs in the first place because of the *vagina* between her legs; they held her accountable none the less, and she owed an amount of money way out of both our wages. To say she was fucked was an understatement, but I don't remember any of us being in a panic as such about it. The drugs truly were numbing enough back then.

I conveniently thought of Tommy. Initially, I'd decided it was an awful idea to ask a thief to steal a whole lot of money; then I quickly realised it was the *only* idea I had. The bastards beat Molly's dad up, landed him in hospital, and her mother couldn't cope. Molly was AWOL during all of this, but I couldn't blame her. Tommy was more than keen to help in exchange for a bed for a couple of weeks. Those two weeks were bliss, *pure bliss.* Even with random men circling our house like hawks and the constant threat of them beating us to a pulp. Together, we discovered Tommy was adequately good with a guitar; so, we'd spend our evenings driving my mum crazy, jamming until the early hours of the morning, where we'd do it all over again.

It was bus, thief, food, home, jam: *repeat.*

Two weeks solid of making over £10 a day (which was a lot for us, back then); which in the end, was nowhere near the amount they asked for, but I think they got bored of listening to us playing each night and gave in; clearing Molly's debt, with only a few small busts up in between.

Molly came back into the scene not long after with a fresh pair of red boots, a gorgeous new two-piece orange and green tartan suit and three new hats from above and beyond. Everything fell back into a routine, with the addition of Tommy.

Me and Molly set back onto the scene, attending every gig we could, begging everyone we could see for a slot on the bill that night. That's all we did for years. Begged, shagged, asked politely and asked *not so* politely; for a chance, a slot, or a phone number of someone else we could solicit. We never gave up. We were sure someone would take a chance someday. It was Tommy who suggested he get involved by conning bookers into thinking they were booking Tommy, and sneaking me in disguise as a man. The theory was to test what about me they didn't like. There was a lot of potential ideas on the list. The fact I was a woman; my voice; my appearance; my clothes; my songs. The concept of being Tommy didn't faze me at all, in fact, I was simply annoyed I hadn't done it earlier; although I swiftly realised it wouldn't have worked with anyone else. Tommy had no genuine interest in being a musician. He didn't want the light, the people, the audience; he just wanted to see me on stage and stay busy. There was no other man on this Earth that would have surrendered that for me.

Tommy was a good sell. He was instantly likeable and annoyingly competent at not sounding arrogant when he was basically shagging his own arsehole.

The bookers listened to him, and I don't just mean, *heard what he had to say through their ears*; I mean they *actually listened*, they *really cared* for what he had to say.

And what he was saying was genuinely impressive.

Tommy would pull out all these little anecdotes; surfing in Greece, carving wood in Canada, climbing mountains left right and centre.

For a long while, I never knew, nor asked, if the stories were true. They were a fundamental part of getting a gig. The bookers liked the character about him; they liked that he'd seen the world and been places, done things. In their eyes, they were looking at a travelled, tanned star in the making. They never asked him to play or sing; simply trusted that face of his.

I can't say I blamed them, his face is *gorgeous*.

Without Tommy, I'd be in a stranger's bed, begging for the booker to listen, as I sang my guts away; by the time Tommy had got a booked gig secured by batting his eyelashes, with no hassle whatsoever.

I didn't know how to thank Tommy. He was staying with me in my house during it all, and I'd split the bill if we got paid. My mother and father put food on the table for him, and I made sure he was still okay doing it.

It was *his* name on the bill. *His* name on the posters, *his* name on the list, on the door- on *everything*.

While I couldn't care less what name I was singing under; I was fully aware that he might care about how I was *using* his name.

Traction was made instantly.

A small local newspaper covered one of the first gigs I ever did in London, assuming access to backstage by informing the techies they were old friends from school. Back then, security wasn't tight, and anyone could walk in and out. I was careful, always on guard backstage.

Usually, me and Tommy would lock ourselves in a room until it was time to go onstage and then Tommy would hide, and I'd leave the place looking the spitting image of him.

It wasn't hard.

I had to wear a wig, dying my hair eventually. We had a very similar haircut, so it didn't bother me, and Tommy chivalrously grew it longer, so it was around the same length as mine.

The more we got into the routine of things, the more I experimented, and he started wearing makeup meeting the bookers so I could get away with it on stage.

I wore one blue contact lens in my left eye to match Tommy's colouring or sometimes just kept glasses on until everyone seemed too far gone to notice what colour eyes I had.

I'd strap my tits down with as much sports tape I could find. One gig would typically cost me one roll of tape for two shows; money was not great back then, but that was never the point.

I wasn't waiting for someone to come along, grab my empty and drying up purse and say; '*I'm gonna change that if you listen to me.*' I was searching for people to fill up the empty seats in the audience. Acceptance, if you read between the lines. I was searching for an audience. For a receptor, recipient and reject to consume my music. Money was just another easy step to drugs back then.

Tommy had to share my wardrobe; since he didn't own much more than one suit when we first met and a lot of my clothes were tailored towards men anyway, it wasn't a problem. I mostly wore baggy suits and big trench coats back then. As much as Tommy was prepared to sacrifice for me, he wasn't quite ready to start wearing dresses to London pubs to get a gig. He made a valid point of reminding me how toxically masculine these bookers were, and how disgusted they would be at a man in a dress wanting a gig from them. As soon as he finished speaking, he knew what I was going to say and came straight downstairs in a green dress.

If it was going to cause a reaction, *I had to do it.* Not because I wanted attention or in fact a reaction for expressing who I was, but to play the *game.*

To be seen as a woman, you have to be a man.

Tommy understood that and started wearing dresses to Sunday church, simply to outrage the disapproving Christians.

This particular gig, I was wearing a fluorescent, studded orange skirt with a pale blue suit jacket; buttoned over my flat, taped chest. My hair was dyed then, and I'd painted red stars from my eyes upwards. I was just sat talking to Tommy, who was looking particularly gorgeous in what was becoming his most notorious backstage look; denim flares and an old fur coat of Molly's.

In walks, the two suited and booted journalists and we're fucked. They were young; an adolescent girl and boy, about the same age as myself; specks for eyes, bleeding hands as they ferociously scribbled down a story. In the panic of it all, I'd done absolutely *nothing*. I quickly discovered how calm I am in a crisis. There was nothing I could do; it wasn't like I could suddenly hide and we could all go back in time, or they'd disappear and *forget*.

We bartered with them for money or drugs, but they weren't interested. In hindsight, locking them in the room with us probably was a bit extreme, but that was Tommy's addition to the panic. They sat, quite smugly and happily on our sofa, looking at us identical twins, bar the clothes. They smoked a cigarette with us and got high with us. At first, I think we believed we could get them high or pissed enough they would forget, or the story wouldn't sound feasible. Then they started asking questions, all of them with a '*why*' in.

Why do you look like him?

Why do you look like her?

Why have you got so much sports tape?

Why have you got different coloured eyes?

They were taking notes, despite Tommy setting fire to the poor boy's notebook at one point, the girl was inexplicably insistent (and *good*) at keeping hers out of the flames.

We'd tried everything borderline *legal* and neither of us was exactly in the mood to adopt these two kids and keep them away from a newspaper for the rest of their lives.

And it wasn't that dramatic. It was a girl being a boy in an East London pub.

I simply told the pair to write what they wanted. Tommy wasn't happy and didn't say a single word for the rest of the night, but I realised there was nothing else we could do and it wasn't like either of us *could*, or in fact, *wanted*, to upkeep the façade for our entire lives.

At one point, we would want the story to break. In our naïve minds, it would be outrageous, audacious, *groundbreaking*. And then it would be even more significant when people realised the boy in the dress was, in fact, a *girl* and the girl in the suit was in fact *me.*

It didn't happen anyway.

The pair wrote a tearful piece about how dedicated '*Tommy*' was to music and exactly just how far he would go to perform on stage. It was a beautiful piece about the brutalities of the London music scene and how sad it was that a perfectly normal man like Tommy felt the need to paint his face, dress like a woman and do outrageous things just to be noticed.

The irony was laughable. The piece was incredible.

They sold 40 copies and gave away 50 to the local nursing home.

Even if my secret was exposed that night, I think the façade would've been my life for just a *little* longer.

And it was. We were more careful, but also somewhat more relaxed. I was arrogantly big-headed about the whole thing; thinking I was the best and I would be making national television if I so much as exposed a nipple.
The truth was, nobody cared, and the whole buzz of '*Tommy*' quickly dwindled. A man dressing as a woman wasn't cool, nor was the makeup or the hair. Nothing about me was pleasing. *I* didn't want to fuck me, the way I looked on stage. It was kind of the point, but they weren't to know that. I was tired of looking like a woman- looking fuckable 24/7 no matter what I wore or did. I wanted to be looked at as a *performer.* I wanted to be taken seriously and considered for my talents. But I was also a '*man*' on stage, and I often forgot that.

People came in search of a fight. To most men in the audience, I was a '*faggot,*' and a '*freak*,' amongst other, *not so* kind, words. I was what they feared- I was free of the masculine irons, of the '*should follows*' and the '*should be's.*' I was exactly who and *what* I wanted to be on stage and of course people didn't like it. They never often do. Especially if you're displaying liberation.
I went outside, down a back alley next to some bins behind a venue one night for a fag. I'd just come off stage, I was still dressed and looked the same except I'd taken my contact lens out.

It was dark, except for my cigarette and out of nowhere I was on the ground being kicked and punched to a pulp by three lads calling me every name under the sun and not one of them was *polite, or accurate*, for that matter.

Being on stage wasn't the safest of places either. I'd get a constant stream of things thrown at me. A lad threw a biker boot at me once, whacking me in the face and splitting my eyebrow. Every one of us gathered like an irate mob outside the venue, waiting like hawks, trying to spot a lad hobbling out with one shoe on so we could batter him.

Another time, I had a knife pulled on me backstage by a naval boy dressed in the most hideous pair of trousers my eyes had ever seen. Trouble swiftly followed me. I noticed, as a woman, it's a different kind of trouble that follows you; you're followed by *men*, who are the objectification of trouble. They're not looking for trouble, they just cause it *instinctively*.

Men are followed by *other men*. Other men *looking* for trouble.

I was getting punched and kicked every other week at one point, after applause-less gigs for next to nothing money.

You might think I was at my wit's end and ready to throw in the towel but, despite everyone advising me to jack it in; I was more motivated than ever.

I'd been at a low point. I'd sold myself, I'd been raped, I'd got pregnant; I'd experienced all of that from trying to make it myself as a *woman*. I could take the punches; I could take the hate if it meant I could get on that stage of a night and perform.

I could be a man at night because being beaten to a pulp every other week is a whole lot less painful than being a woman *every single day*. Then Tommy got caught in the crossfire, diving in a fight, getting stabbed in the stomach three times and suddenly performing on stage didn't seem important when lives were at risk. It took nearly losing Tommy's life, to realise how many times I'd almost lost mine.

It's strange what clouds your judgement; for what and *why*.

I didn't lose sight of what was important exactly; I knew that my music was more important than my life and still is. But I'd lost sight of the people around me. I was putting Tommy at risk, and that simply wasn't a risk I was going to take.

I quit- or '*Tommy'* quit. No one cared.

The friction had long sparked out, and we were swiftly both back to stealing purses on London buses, after our five minutes of fame.

Music is everything.

It makes me hard, even makes me cum. Gives me goosebumps, makes every hair stand on edge. My breath flutters, I can hardly control it. I'm almost at cardiac arrest, and I allow it. It ain't a rush, it's more than a sensation; it's like a fucking awakening. I'm alive. Really, genuinely fucking *alive*. Feeling everything; big and small kind of *alive*.

Feeling money spiders on your shins as you're fucking in the mud, kind of *alive*. Feeling hate and love- but mostly love, sort of *alive*. Love that makes you smile at a cenotaph because he was once a soldier. Love that makes a lobotomy seem cheap. Love that equals death in sense and religion.

And I'm reminded exactly why I breath, as though I were taught to sync my heart with music as a child. As though I died and were given CPR with a radio. Its radio waves and electronic beats zapping my heart like a bee sting. A bee from Manchester, no doubt; the kind with extra swagger, extra mean and meaty. Persistent in its job to keep me alive; keep me singing, toe-tapping, head bobbing and dancing. Keep me dreaming and believing and knowing music saved my life; so, I must live by it. Swear on it like a bible. Owe to it. Commit to it, abide and love it, like a God or a child of a loving mother. Never speak ill of it. Recruit members for it. Bake fucking cakes for a village fete in its name.

Above all; cease to forget what saved my life; what will always save my life and what exactly I live my life for.

Music.

Rock n roll, the Blues, Jazz. No hit; no amount of smack; no fucking bottle; injection; drag: has ever been as good or kind to me as *music*. *Music is my dirty spoon.*

It's my obsession. My life. What I get out of bed for; why I open my eyes; what I live for.

It's not hard for me to lay my soul at its feet and *surrender*.

Surrender all I am; all I've got and known and loved: for it.

For a second, a moment with *it*. With it inside of me; crucifying my light; slicing my soul with a riff.

I will be defined by nothing but music. Die a music box of secrets, with nothing much to hide. Jewellery bits and bric-a-brac sales stuffed into this box. A ballerina spinning, her skirt skimming past the mirror. Some tune her mother will forget. The box will pass to sale at a charity shop; car boot; tabletop sale at a poorly Ofsted reviewed secondary school in Chorley. The ballerina won't move.

Won't fair a bit.

But the music still plays.

The music will never die.

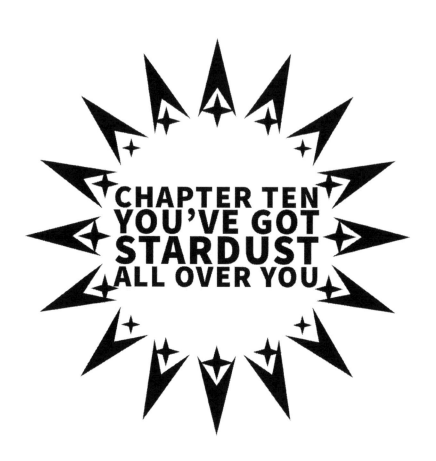

CHAPTER TEN
YOU'VE GOT
STARDUST
ALL OVER YOU

I can't quite tell you, other than a fascination and desire to be someone or something else; what gave me the need to feel as though I must reinvent myself. Yet I did. And I did so, so vulgarly and so consistently; I most probably lost a lot of good things and people for doing so. Things change all the time; it feels only natural to me that people do too. And what would be of life if you died not knowing who you were? It was and still is, a thought I can't bear to carry. I hope the one thing I can do: is die knowing exactly who my family will bury.

An idea grabbed me. I could live in any house of brick and mortar I could possibly afford or steal. I had tried (until I got lice and scabies) living amongst the wild, in between the grass and underneath the stars. I had not tried life on water. I immediately asked around every pub for a sailor or a pirate; or anyone related to life on the water. The only name I was passed; was a woman named Magda, who was a lifeguard at the local swimming baths. Then chance would have it; a stocky man named Barry, with a lot of facial hair and a low, gruff voice; came in to use the pub's toilet because his toilet on his *barge* had temporarily broken.

My ears pricked up like a dog, and within two days, I was living on the barge with Barry. The barge was bright blue when I first met it; a thin, streamlined piece of utter shit that was fraying at the edges and unravelling in every way. It was named 'The Loud Cannon,' after his mate's death in the war; which I frequently told him is a rather

depressing reminder, but he refused to change it to 'The Spaceships' Cabin Garden,' as I wanted to name it.

A few days in, we moored up and bought some cheap paint at a hardware store. Barry took forever looking at the different colours and types of paint; so much so, I got frustrated and stole three tubs in the meantime, buying one paintbrush as compensation. He bought one tub of brown overcoat, for motives he later couldn't reason. When we got back to the barge, and I opened the tins of paint, he got increasingly nervous at the sight of the colours I'd chosen; yellow, red and a bizarre aqua green.

Barry told me he was that anxious, he couldn't watch and sat inside reading a war novel he'd been on the same page reading since I stepped foot on the barge. I started painting, and by painting, I mean: I threw the tins on the boat. I don't know if you've ever tried to paint a barge, but it's fucking difficult. There's the whole problem of the water living right there and the entire moving water under a somewhat unstable barge thing, that made painting a bitch.

I threw all the colours on until you couldn't see the name or the windows and I ran out of paint and realised I hadn't and couldn't do the other side until we moored up elsewhere. It then started to rain, and it ran like I've never seen paint run before. Barry cried.

If he wasn't so desperately alone and didn't still hear his best mates drowning in his sleep; he most certainly would've kicked me off or put me in jail. He forgot about the paint job by not leaving the barge for a good week, in which time he'd read the one page of his book and was onto the next one.

It was an idyllic time. Living on the water didn't bother me much, living with *Barry* was the hard part. I asked him for stories about the war because it helped him sleep at night, therefore allowing me to sleep too. I also asked him if he'd ever met a pirate and he refused to answer for weeks on end, saying; *'not tonight sunshine.'* I eventually got him that stoned he couldn't tell day from night, and that excuse was transparent. He told me the tale of his crew having no option but to give way and obey an oncoming ship, its crew coming on board utterly outnumbered and outgunned in every kind of way. They were pirates and unforgiving ones. Barry told me he was confused as to why pirates were in the middle of the Atlantic sea, but then he was also confused at his order in the first place. I didn't let him conspire too much, too giddy for the pirate story to care.

Like a child, I listened on tenterhooks, for the squash buckling tales of plank walking and sword fighting. The child in me wanted the fantasies to be real, so desperately real. I wanted black-haired, dreadlocked souls, inked to their toes with swords and daggers and guns and grenades- the lot on their belts.

I wanted eyepatches and cut, jagged-edged trousers. I wanted treasure maps and treasure chests. Colossal vessels with levels and levels of buried treasure from the depths of the ocean. Sword fights for the fun of it with parrots and sharks. Mythological creatures stored under the floorboards, an entire zoo of history deeply carved into the sides. Rough seas, sick nightmares in hammocks for bunks. I wanted it all, and I wanted it so badly that I was severely heartbroken to hear that the pirates killed Barry's entire crew right in front of his eyes; passing Barry the finger of his captain to send back to the British Navy as a warning.

I instinctively comforted Barry, despite feeling uncertain how accurate his tale was and gave him the space he needed; lying in my makeshift hammock conspiring about the sea. There was a certain romance about the brutality. A particular strength in the act. Something about the way the pirates felt so passionately, as though their nature, to declare the sea their own; was utterly alluring to me. The music industry was my sea, and I was ready to be a pirate and send back the finger of a leading man to the record label as a warning to British music. *I owned the sea.*

I left the barge a week later after a long six weeks with the guy. I ended up in south Manchester way, some small town that found my accent incomprehensible. I was in no rush to make my way back to London, and I figured that a change of city would do me good.

I settled into the same routine of clubbing and touring the Manchester night scene in the same search as in London. Only this time, I wore my cowboy boots with short, black ripped, loose pants; most often just a bra and suit jacket with an eye patch always over my right eye. It was the *symbolism* that I liked.

I got the call at midday exactly. I was staring at the clock in my kitchen eating spinach soup when the phone rang at 12 on the dot. I rushed to pick it up.

"Is this a; Pen Jones?"

"It sure is."

"Good. I heard about you crashing a gig in Manchester. I know a record label that wants to meet you. How does 6 o'clock tomorrow sound?"

"Like a dream."

The gig in Manchester was a two-hour impromptu karaoke session at the 'Free Trade Hall,' during their lunch time clean up. I'd arrived (very) early to a 'Three Pencils,' gig and told the staff I was the bands' sound engineer and I needed to test the mic. By the end of my two hours, all twelve staff members, three tourists and a homeless man sat to listen; making it my biggest crowd yet.

I sat at my kitchen table for three hours thinking: *what am I going to wear?* I already knew what I'd sing. I had a substantial number of songs of my own I sung in Manchester that I could do and a couple of covers from my wedding days. The music was sorted, arranged, banked. It was my clothes. I rang Molly.

"I need your help. What shall I wear?"

"Wear that suit."

"No."

"The dress?"

"No."

"Dungaree's?"

"Absolutely not."

"I don't fucking know then. Wear your mum's kitchen table cover for all I care!"

I arrived an hour early with my mother's floral, laced embossed table cover wrapped around me; tied with my father's leather belt he used for a beating when I was a kid. I felt more than dazzling. I felt the best I'd felt in ages. I was confident and assured as I sat waiting. They called *me*; they wanted to hear *me*. For the first time, I hadn't lied, shagged or conned my way into something, and it felt *incredible*.

I was called into the office on Denmark Street and introduced to, let's call him; *Bob*, a music manager. The room smelt of stale cakes and ale. There was an array of gold and silver discs, framed on the wall and a collection of trophies and keepsakes that surrounded me as communally as a pawn shop. The man was thin and pretentious, never looking me in the eye as he spoke.

"You're a woman," were the first words he said to me.

"Well observed."

"Jones? Pen Jones?"

"*Penny* Jones. My name, yes."

"You're supposed to be a man."

I shrugged and said; "I can if you want."

He paused to look me up and down and asked me to stand still as he circled me. I figured he was checking to see if I had a cock hidden in my hair or under one of my belt loops. It was mildly entertaining to see his face when he discovered I was 100% a woman with the potential to be a man.

"You look like a man." He told me, to which I thanked him out of pure British politeness.

I suddenly felt thirteen years old again, getting my period for the first time. I felt naked, stripped of my innocence and youth. I could feel blood dripping from me. Blood that never belonged in me to start. I felt upside down; dangling by my toenails.

Bob was the personification of hope through my naïve eyes. He looked like a chance. On the phone; the man talked of world tours; of shows so big it hurt my head; of albums so groundbreaking; I walked into the office dodging the cracks in the ground beneath me.

I was so full of hope and desire; I was deaf and blind. I saw and heard nothing for what it was. I saw the good people, and I listened to the good bits. The rest was nothing. I agreed to the *'nothing,'* I did everything for the *'nothing,'* because the great things were still playing in my eyes and ringing in my ears.

Hope does crazy things to a girl like me.

"Stand like a man." I stood still.
"Speak like a man", I told him to fuck off in a low voice.
"Walk like a man." I pretended I'd shat myself.
"Sing like a man." I sang normally.
He paused again.
"Not good enough."
I asked him to repeat what he'd just said, as I was sure I hadn't heard him right.

"Not good enough, sweetheart. Not a good enough man and I don't want a girl like you on my books."

"What do you mean; '*a girl like me?*'"

"A prostitute. A bloody, unreliable girl that won't do as she's told."

"I just did everything you asked."

"You gonna fuck me?"

I paused for what felt like a whole lifetime.

"No."

He laughed.

"Then you can leave now, princess."

I didn't leave. There was no chance in hell I was going to do as I was told after that.

"You'll regret not signing me."

"Doubt it. Girl singers just aren't hot right now. And the cold doesn't sell."

"Do you even know what the people want?"

"I want you to leave."

"I want a record contract."

"I want a *fuck*."

"You've already fucked me."

"First time's free, is it?"

I grabbed a gold, glass framed disc from the wall and smashed it on his desk a good ten times before I had nothing left in my hands. Bob cowered like a baby under his desk as I stood on it to kick the pieces around the room.

"Remember the girl who made you shit yourself as it won't be the last time I make you feel stupid for saying no to me." And then I left.

I've met many musicians who are managed by the aforementioned man—excellent musicians and people; who speak highly of him. My experience could've been a mixture of bad moods, on a bad day with a lousy moon cycle. Or he could've just been a horrible, sexist man who underestimated my talent and persistence. I could've lived with not being signed because he didn't think I was a good enough singer or my voice didn't suit his label. But I refuse to be rejected because I was a woman. I left that room feeling hurt and bruised. My womanhood felt punched and scorned for beating so loudly inside of my chest. I felt stupid for acting like a woman. *Why couldn't I have just been a man?*

I needed a drink to numb the weight of oppression and get me through the night; which was a rather constant feeling at that time. I went to the café next door; La Gioconda. I'd never been before that day but was welcomed with wide arms the moment I stepped through the door. It was a hotspot for creativity: the very heart, the very epicentre of England's music family.

Things were leading me to places. A mild interest in pirates led me to Manchester, which led me to Denmark Street and right into the arms of probably the most important and influential place of my career.

I walked straight to the bar and asked for something stronger than coffee, but weaker than acid. I received a pint of vodka and a line of Charly.

The barman sat down with me, letting the rest of the café help themselves to the bar. Everyone was friendly in the sense they'd known each other a long time; the kind of relationship that outstretches all of blood family. I was perfectly happy watching them all natter and giggle amongst themselves; fascinated to discover who was who and what stories they had to tell. There were some truly fascinating people that I'd never come across before: Skinheads, Germans, African black women, transvestites. It was the first of the London hot pot I'd experienced. It was an incredible space and time to be alive—a strange period in time where the radicals were starting to take over. Every single person in the room had their own story marked on their skin, in their hair, their clothes, their sexuality that they oozed onto you like a bad dream. I was temporarily lost. I'd forgotten what had just happened, just on the other side of the wall in the office. I'd forgotten how it felt to be a woman or a man. I was just me, Penny Jones, with a whole lot of other people, being just them. I'd found a place to make a home.

"You're new here?" The barman asked, to which I nodded.
"Welcome. You a singer?"
"How did you know?"
"*You've got stardust all over you.*" He told me, words I've never forgotten.

Fez, the barman, is one of my favourite people I met at the La Gioconda. He saw every soul that walked through and out the door. He served them, served them well, I might add and condoled them. He was the priest of our church. He saw what we didn't. He had eyes, none of us had. He would talk to you about your talent in a way it made you feel as though you were speaking of a stranger's talent. The ability to dissect you from the equation to help you be more rational and unbiased about your talent; was something no one else in the business could do. Everybody who walked through and out the door needed him. Some people thought they'd go in search for someone like him, but would always return. Fez had the answer to everything, and he made an incredible array of cocktails, so there was absolutely no valid reason to leave.

People would run in and shout; *'I need such a such,'* and if that was you, you'd up and run to whatever stint you needed to do. It wasn't unusual for a stranger to run in and ask for a singer, or pianist, or whatever they needed for a last-minute gig or recording. It was an entirely different world: a safe, musical, loving world where I could be needed.

I told Fez what had just happened in the office, and he stood on the table, banging his steel heel as he addressed the entire room. 'I need every single one of ya's to grab something from the kitchen and lob it at next doors windows, okay?'

Without question, they all stood up, wandered into the kitchen, continuing their conversations, and grabbed whatever they could find. Condiments, eggs, meat, bread, tomatoes, fruit, chocolate sauce; they seized the lot. Fez piloted them outside in a line in front of the office building and on the count of three, they all started lobbing the food at the office, absolutely hammering it. It lasted a good while, a solid five minutes of hurling abuse at a bricked building in verbal and physical form. It was *bliss*. Fez kicked open the door and threw a bucket of sauce in the hallway while someone ran in and stole a tennis racket and side table that was sitting at the bottom of the stairs. Those two items were painted gold and hung from the ceiling with rope under a plaque that read; *'the great kitchen raid of the 70s, in retribution for our Penny Jones.'* All the girls, including myself, threw our knickers on the doorstep and promptly left with a gentle breeze.

The building was left a mess, and Bob promptly called the police who gave Fez a stern warning and a £10 fine for the damage. I offered to pay it, but he said; '*it was his honour and retribution to restore justice to the wounded.*' I was touched and healed. Being a woman didn't feel so bad if I could be a woman with great people.

CHAPTER ELEVEN
THE LEMONADE
GIRL!

I believe in magic.

I believe in magic to sustain; to live and to breathe. To be able to put one foot in front of the other, I think there is magic cursing through the streets beneath me. Consuming the air like a wet dream. Dressing the clouds and watering the Earth.

Small splatters of magic; such as your coffee not burning your lips. Mundane moments of magic; like narrowly missing that downpour of rain. Monumental minutes of magic; like writing 'Space Oddity,' on my front step. Breath taking moments that can't be defined within the constructs of normalcy. Moments where the tender hands of God break through the drab clouds and pass down a perfectly shaped manuscript to all my poetic questions.

Sometimes that's all writing is. Sitting patiently, waiting for those hands to come and drop down something invaluable, something prodigious. Sometimes there is every thought and every feeling in every single word. Other times, it's just magic.

Pure, coincidental, beautiful *magic.*

The magic of *'Space Oddity'* was its voids. It's many, dismal voids. The void of a mother, the void of an Earth, the void of belonging; all there amongst the magic. Recording 'Space Oddity,' was all about recreating that void.

Tommy's treehouse was not Tommy's treehouse. It was a treehouse, and he lived in it, but it wasn't Tommy's. It belonged to the child of a wealthy man that lived in a rather big house somewhere around west Brixton. This child confided in Tommy in wanting to be an investigative journalist, and so was more than happy that a tramp with an exciting life was living in her back garden. The child would save her leftover food for Tommy, like feeding a stray cat.

Tommy and the child were more than happy to let me record 'Space Oddity' up in the trees. Tommy boarded up the windows, and the child brought in her mother's best silk blankets from inside and shoved them between all the cracks we could see to *'soundproof'* the shed.

She dangled extension cords out of every bedroom window, leaving a trail of wires hidden amongst the overgrown shoots of grass.

It was a luxurious space with wide sides and a low roof. The ladder was broken, which made hauling the equipment a challenge that lasted way into the night. You could get up there using a slightly weak rung rope ladder. If you jumped enough, you could reach a small part of the infrastructure that you could lean your weight onto to save the rope.

Hauling up amps and a drum kit, however, was an entirely different story; especially when you're also trying to hide from the owners of said garden and treehouse; which is why we hired Julian.

Julian Hows' was a bus driver that worked on the same routes me and Tommy were thieving on. He caught us one day and held us hostage on the bus until he got us to confess. We were both stoned, giggling and teasing, telling him; 'no, *you've* been a naughty boy,' on repeat until we all got bored.

He kept demanding we show him what we'd been stealing.

So, we kept kissing each other and immaturely giggling '*kisses*, we've been stealing *kisses*.'

I like to think Julian found us estranged and alluring, but in truth, I believe we aggravated him like a cheese grater.

"You're eating into my lunch break, I'd like to go get a coffee, if you two don't mind!"

"Get me one!"

"And me!"

Julian ended up leaving us locked on the bus; coming back a few minutes later with three cups of shit coffee and a selection of vending machine sandwiches.

We got crumbs on the backseat and ripped a hole in the back of one of the seats as a rubbish bin. We attempted to hotbox the entire bus, eventually getting caught when it was time for the bus to leave the station. We rode the bus to wherever it was going and did it all over again when Julian finished for the day.

He confided that he hated his job because the management was sexist. At the time I met him; he was a 23-year-old gay man living in Brixton.

In the summer, he wanted to wear skirts, female workers, for London Transport had the right and ability to wear; instead of the heavy-duty trousers in the gummy heat. He was told the only way he could wear a skirt, was if he had a sex change and was employed as a female. Julian said: '*it seems a bit drastic to undergo a sex change to wear the clothes I want to.*'

He quit and wore a skirt with no fear on his last day. He looked insanely handsome.

I paid Julian £5 to distract the front of the house on a routine basis while we scurried past their side door to run into the garden. Julian took the opportunity to raise awareness for gay rights and used the money to hire a whole scholar of his friends to knock on the door and pass on hand-drawn leaflets enlightening facts on a variety of gay right messages.

I think we managed to successfully run past the house three times before the rich man got aggravated at the gay men knocking on his door and he stopped answering.

Then we had to rely on the child to stay awake all night and slip him a sleeping pill Tommy had handy on him, to make sure the racket we were making throughout the night wouldn't wake him up.

We weren't worried about the wife; the child said she was having an affair and would leave through the night anyway.

Terry Cox recorded the drums first; once we got the drums up, we weren't prepared to haul them down again any time soon.

While Terry was playing, I went to La Gioconda and found the first guitarist I could see; Mick Wayne, an incredible guitarist who looked like Jesus and spoke like him too. I found him chatting up a girl who I said was more than welcome to come along, but Mick had lied and told her he was always the front guy.

Mick had a good work ethic, probably the best of us all. He turned up prepared. Despite waking up that morning not knowing he would go on to record a number one; he seemingly walked around with an entire novel worth of music scores banked for a rainy day. Getting the guitar up the treehouse was a doddle until he started playing, and the prodigy child's bedroom light came on. She was at the window Morse coding to Tommy to '*turn it fucking down.*'

I'd had the feeling of Space Oddity for months. '2001: A Space Odyssey' came out in early 1968 and blew my mind in many ways. It left me vibrating, I was numbed for a while. I couldn't sleep if I wanted to. I was stuck in that God awful place as a creator where you have too much in your head you can't start for trying but are neglect of the final piece for it all to make sense. Essentially you have a whole lot of words in your head, with no translation or clue as to what language they're in. It's easier said than done, to just take on the mother tongue and make no sense until you crack it.

I sat in that space for a while. Missing Tommy, who'd done four months in jail for robbing a cops' wallet and filling my own void with myself. I became an egotistical nightmare. I stared at myself a lot, I thought about myself even more. I didn't care for my health, but I wondered what I would look like with green skin or orange feet. I wondered what my wings would look like if I grew a pair. I considered growing a beard. I thought about wearing less clothes, then I thought about wearing more.

The rest of the recording was done within 24 hours, through the day and night. There was a brief moment where we had to hide ourselves and all the equipment when the child's dad came home and was insistent on having a fag outside on his obtuse and expensive looking deckchair.

I'd had no sleep for shy of 36 hours by the time it came to recording my vocals. I'd smoked a lot of weed and drank a lot of spirits to keep myself awake; mixed in with too much coffee and not a lot of food. I should've been a mess, but I don't remember ever feeling better.

As gracious and talented as Mick, Terry, Gus and bassist Herbie Flowers who came along with the strings master; Paul Buckmaster were: they were still *men*. Men who demanded cigarette breaks when cigarette breaks were not yet due since the last one three minutes previous. Men who demanded retakes because they needed a piss halfway through recording. Men who watched wives from the treehouse. Men who wanked behind the bins.

During all of which these men simply acted like *men*, I had to pioneer the entire process in an encouraging (yet not dominant, remember I'm still a *woman*) manner to get the job done. They were all very intrigued and invested in the track, but none of them could be bothered with the mither of hauling and hiding; all the things I had to do to get the job done.

I felt an urgency, and I felt a responsibility they didn't feel. A lot was riding on the track. I had failed and flopped countless times before Space Oddity. I had bragged about my talent to a lot of people who then saw me hanging out my arsehole drunk, or heard demo's of: 'The Laughing Gnome,' which most certainly was not the best decision as a woman in music who wanted to be taken *seriously.*

A lot of men had laughed at my attempt to make music, and I was *bored.* The men I was making music with, were not laughing; they were good men who saw the glimmer of hope in me I occasionally saw too.

But fuck me, they were annoying.

I went outside for some fresh air, an hour into my recording in the very early hours of the morning to see Herbie and Paul laying on the expensive deckchairs stark bollock naked. Mick and Terry had raided the garden shed and were playing a game of tennis over the washing line while drinking the beers in the man's cool box. I caught Herbie trying to break in the house to go for a shit, while Terry already had to get in the fridge. My duties were split between being a singer and *mother* to five pestering kids.

The track was finished with the addition of Tony Visconti on flute and woodwind, recorded in his own home and put on the track by Gus in his mate's studio which we would later record in.

Things just took a little longer than expected. I had anticipated that it would be like blast off and everything would rocket into a star-spangled existence before I could ask where the nearest exit was. It didn't. It didn't even float leisurely like dust in the wind. It merely remained *stagnant.*

I felt invincible the day I recorded Space Oddity, which was essential to me. The moment I heard it through my own speakers in my childhood bedroom was the first time everything felt balanced. It all felt okay. I found sense and reason, and I reveled in it.

I asked the band to give the track to people and make everyone they knew listen; in the hopes, *somebody* would pick it up. It didn't work. I spent a month nagging them all for feedback, asking if anyone had signed us yet or if anyone even liked it. The response was always a shrug and a polite; *'these things take time Pen, have some patience.'* It didn't take time for men; records couldn't be produced quick enough for men. Records by men were being produced at an average of about the same speed they lasted in bed. Similarly, it took women the same amount of time to release a record, as it did for a man to make them come. Male records were as common as a dirty penny and well handled like them too.

I bought all the cassettes I could buy with about £12, which was all I had. I think I managed to buy about 28, which wasn't anywhere near the amount I knew it was going to take. Regardless, I recorded Space Oddity onto the cassette tapes and tried to sell them from my front garden. *I was the lemonade girl!* I sold one to my deaf neighbour across the way for about £2 before moving onto the end of my street and selling a further two to two school kids who were looking to join a band themselves.

I gave them to people on buses, record stores, greengrocers, libraries, pubs, clubs, swimming baths and hospitals. I spent weeks walking around and forcing the cassettes on people who most often tossed it aside or shoved it so far in their handbag it was lost into oblivion. While at the time, it felt like the most tedious and degrading thing I could be doing, it also felt like the *only* thing. There was a sense that we were waiting for the right person to come along, hear it and give us a contract. While I respected the Earth's law of attraction, I was also far too impatient to sit waiting while it happened.

It happened on the day my dad died.

One man came knocking to tell me my father had passed away; while the other, ten minutes later, came to tell me he would release Space Oddity with *honour.*

CHAPTER
TWELVE
BAGUETTE LEGS

So, my dad was dead. Sudden seemed an understatement. I'd never considered he could or would die. It had not been a part of my agenda. I had not once scheduled a bereavement into my game plan. It seemed somewhat inconsiderate of my father to just shit all over my plans in such a morbid fashion. A divorce would've been much more inspiring. Everybody knows a divorce can feed the creative soul much more suitably than a big, bastard death.

Yet, here I was, standing in a morgue, shaking my head sharply in response to the coroner's question: 'Is this your father?'
"Hate to break it to you, Sir, that's not my dad. That's Tina, the Transvestite. I've seen her down the pub. Cracking set of lungs."

Tina was wheeled out, and my dad was wheeled in like a car showroom. I didn't stay for long. Something about the decaying face of your dad doesn't grip you like you think it would.
The funeral was a few days before the release of 'Space Oddity.' I wore a black tailored suit of my dad's, with a pair of red boots. My mother spat on my shoes when she saw me. She wore next to nothing; the grief had consumed her like a heatwave.
I wasn't greatly depressed like my mother. She couldn't shower without it taking her three days to get out of bed first. She never spoke, she failed to eat or drink; and when she did drink, it was neat spirits or wine from a box. I, on the other hand, was mildly intoxicated with the process of death, so was somewhat happy to experience the full grief cycle.

I'd read books on grief in the Victorian era and how they wore armbands for months after a death to alert every one of their grief. It's a sentiment that's always stuck with me. I made my mother a grieving armband out of old socks, and she wore it for four years.

Molly and Tommy arrived at the funeral on the back of a motorbike; head to toe in borrowed red leather. The pair of them carried bottles of whiskey and wore cigarettes in their mouths as they crawled off the stolen bike. They stumbled over gravestones, and faltered over fresh flowers; finally collapsing on top of my father's open grave. My entire family were mortified, but I found humour in my two best friends, stoned to fuck on top of my dad's dead body. My father would've been outraged, so naturally, it made me grin from ear to ear, with tears in my eyes. I was so touched by the sentiment of them being there, I didn't care what state they were in.

The three of us weren't welcomed into the after service or pub, which was fine by me. Tommy, Molly and I had our own ceremony in a service station diner off the M25. We rode the bike down the motorway, stopping for an all-day breakfast at 3am. We asked the waitress if she'd let us have the diner to ourselves, to which she refused, but quickly came to understand we weren't really asking. We caused that much of a raucous, no one stayed for much longer than a coffee, and the waitress joined us not long after 4am.

Molly robbed the petrol station, bringing back to the diner: a football, two tyre pumps, two baguettes, three blocks of cheese and a pack of pens. Tommy made my dad out of the stolen goods and sat him with us at the table. To start, it was a laugh, and we'd ask him stupid shit during our normal conversations about pirate radio and the audacity of morning television. Then, once the drugs and alcohol kicked in, next to the (most likely undercooked) sausage and black pudding, I started to use the football head model of my dad as therapy.

I got angry.

I was mad that he'd died so suddenly, in such a fashion. Upset he hadn't said goodbye or taught me anything worthwhile. Angry he'd left me with nothing but a crazed mother.

I punched my dad in the face, and the football went flying; hitting a poor man in a wheelchair in the face. We grabbed the baguette legs and ran.

I didn't return home for two weeks after that. I probably drove my mother to the edge of insanity, but I was selfishly too bereft to care. I had a reoccurring dream for the entirety of those two weeks that I killed my father and was rightfully incarcerated for my wrongdoing. I killed him by clinging onto him for so long, he died of boredom. I sang until my throat went hoarse, I kissed his cheeks until my lips were dry and I hugged him so tightly I squeezed his organs inside out. I would wake up sweating and shaking.

There was nothing in my life at that time that I missed more than outraging my father.

I missed coming home in bare, bleeding feet with a stranger strapped to my arm. I missed flinging my bra on the kitchen table before breakfast, chewing on last night's leftovers. Smoking in the bath, breaking glasses with my music, shouting about French liberation to our neighbours.

It took me a while to miss my father, who wasn't present in the first place. He wasn't at the dinner tables I was flying my bra on. He wasn't in the kitchen as I shouted at the neighbours; he was long gone. I missed him then, I miss him now. I imagined him in places he never would be or was. I saw him cutting the grass on our village green. I felt him hugging me after breaking. I smelt him after a morning run. I heard him singing along to the radio. I tasted his cooking and boy was it *delicious*. I saw him being a father and felt what it felt to be a daughter. Then I felt the feeling of mourning and felt it like lightning.

Death was real. It wasn't something that happened to your neighbour's cat. Death was something that happened to your mother and father, to your friends and lovers. Death was something that happened to you and to me. Death was in touching distance, it was real, we were all going to die. It was aloof, yet it was imminent.
I smelt death in the washing. I walked through London with death by my side, I know for a fact I reeked of it. I considered leaving death in the middle of the road, praying for a double-decker bus to come and run him *splat*.

He lingers, he chokes; he gets a hold, and he doesn't let go until there's nothing left to hold onto. Until you're a pile of rags and bones, and even then; your clothes will still distinctively have that wash of *death*.

Then just as abruptly as my dad died, 'Space Oddity' came out. It had to come out whether my dead dad liked it or not.

We celebrated the release of Space Oddity and coincidently the moon landing, by having a street party; the road blocked off with a line of speakers playing the record on repeat. It was magnificent, and it felt as though it was going to break the Earth; when all it did was shatter one china mug and make an old woman from two streets down, very mad and irate. It was a great distraction for the grief.

Tommy disappeared for a bit when I had a brief fling with a man who turned out to be a cheat and a homosexual; resurfacing with the desperate plea for me to write more music.

"Will you please fucking write another song. There's nothing to listen to."

"I have nothing to write about."

"You've just had your heartbroken and lost your dad; you're living every writers dream. Write about that, you daft cow."

"It still hurts."

"That's the point. You can't be an artist without tragedy."

So, I sat myself down and wrote. Nothing was good enough. My words were whining and pining while I was tearful and bruised. The songs were too.

Heartbreak songs are just that. Heartbreak songs are just *heartbreak*. They resonate with people, hence why they are commercial and sell well; much better than any other kind of song. Everyone's had their heart broken; *life's a bloody heartbreak.*

Not long after Tommy encouraged me back into writing, did my new manager call me into his office. I was sat like a lemon, wondering what needed to be so formal. I didn't even know my manager had an office, the few times we'd talked were always at La Gioconda, or someone's house or pub.

He looked sheepish when he came in the room, I don't remember him looking at me once.

"I'm not gonna go ahead with the album."

"What do you mean; *you're not gonna go ahead with the album*?"

"I'm not gonna get it produced, book a studio or anything, I'm just not gonna make it happen, *okay*?"

"*Not okay*! You're not gonna do your job, is what you're telling me?"

"You better watch your mouth, girl!"

"Or *what*?"

I left with a black eye and a broken arm. Amongst the madness, he told me 'Space Oddity' was a one-hit-wonder that he thought I didn't write and so he wouldn't stick his neck out on an album that wouldn't work. It seemed the idea of a successful woman was far too ludicrous for his mind to conceive; *I must've been a liar.* He got scared, or his boss got scared, or he never believed in me from the beginning, or maybe he was as delusional as he looked. I didn't care for his reasons for letting me go or thinking the album would flop. He hadn't heard a single lyric or song I had planned for the album; he was just a chicken. A bastard chicken.

The album still had to happen, and it had to happen even more after being told it wouldn't. My stubbornness got the better of me and I devised a plan.

I spent the two weeks after my dad's funeral at Julian's mums house, eating his mother out of house and home. Julian, Tommy and me, were spending pretty much all our time together. Molly had left town for an affair with a German biker, and Tommy felt the need to be on Penny watch while the grief subsided. We were the smallest bunch of misfits London had seen.

Julian was leaving his job around this time too, so the idea of stealing a London bus for a night wasn't as ludicrous as it could've been. He hid on board after his shift finished until everyone left and simply drove it out the bay it should've been sleeping in.

He came to pick Tommy and me up first and then the rest of the band.

We must've spent a good couple of hours driving around London trying to find everyone's houses to pick them up, or trying to get in between residential areas that the double-decker bus wasn't designed for.

John Eager was a friend of a friend of a friend; that I'd never met and hadn't heard play, but I was assured he was a good enough drummer. It was a shame that he lived in the tightest cul-de-sac in London and had to individually haul every single piece of his kit onto and up the bus. We all helped after a long while of watching his little legs scurry heavy equipment while his forehead lined with sweat. We had a production line of musicians from his front garden to the bus; all passing along bits of the drum kit while trying not to wake the neighbours as they carried on their conversations about corduroy flares and Led Zeppelin. Once we were all aboard the bus, it was quite the struggle moving. So much so, everyone got comfy in their spot with their neighbours and remained seated as Julian drove around London and we made a single.

We started recording 'Love You Till Tuesday,' since I had plans of releasing the song as a single and wanted to get it done before the album.
Tommy kept giggling and taking the piss out of the line:
'When you walk out through your door,
I'll wave my flag and shout
Ohh, beautiful baby.'

He thought it was far too romantic for me. The rest of the bus, even the bottom deck, kept shouting '*freak flag*,' every time I went to record, and so it was postponed until they could all get a grip.

There was a lot of laughter. We'd have to keep ducking and hiding if we thought we were gonna get caught as Julian kept driving.

I'd got used to stealing equipment or dragging musicians along to record my album, that I never wanted to record in a studio again at that time. I liked the freedom.

Hauling the equipment, buying extension leads and powers packs didn't even become a hassle as the music started to seep over.

We dropped everyone off at Big Jim's and told them all to crash at his; suggesting we'd help move everything later or walk home. Julian had to get the bus back in the depo on time, which looked ambitious as we were all throwing stuff out of the top deck windows and onto the windy, chewing gum pavements below as the sun was rising.

I walked home with Tommy, bathing in pure euphoria, back to my mother's home. I'd managed to almost kick my mother out of her own home. Me and my mother had a mutual understanding. I don't think we ever liked each other much. She was my mother, I grew up with the understanding that children aren't supposed to particularly like their mother's, even if they're great.

She would soak the washing in vinegar twice daily around this time and leave it hung in the kitchen to ward away unwanted behavior. I think she thought it would stop me from being who I was. I can confirm it didn't.

My dad dying hurt mum pretty severely. Much worse than any of the hurt I caused being myself on stage. She was lost and quiet. She suddenly didn't have anyone to cook for or clean after, she didn't know what to do with herself. When my mum died 25 odd years later, I felt the grief of both of them together; which was tough. I struggled with the guilt I had about my lack of grief towards two distant parent figures in the body of two mediocrely loving people. As people, they were warm and friendly, the kind of strangers you'd spend the night chatting with at the pub. But I didn't want to have conversations about the monarchy over a pint; I wanted to be tucked in at night and told that it was alright if I didn't win, as long as I did my best. As parents, they were weak, and they struggled. I didn't hold any hate or judgement against their lack of parenting skills, I only held resentment towards their lack of love when it was the only thing I needed.

It felt the chance to be loved was buried, and it physically pained me to watch that chance of love be lowered into the ground to be never seen again.

CHAPTER
THIRTEEN
DISTRACTOR
BOX

My luck with managers and record labels was poor to say the least. I felt like the Oliver Twist of the music industry. I asked for more, to get less than before. To be honest, I asked for basic rights and got none. *I stopped wearing a bra when men stopped paying me enough.* My debut album was finally released after I compromised with a record label (recommended through a friend) who gave me one condition: I must change my name. I didn't want to change my name at that point, I had no interest in being anything other than *me* for my debut album. To make me and my music more digestible and sellable; my manager insisted I change my name to something that could be considered *unisex*. He told me it would be like how 'Mary Shelley' wrote 'Frankenstein' anonymously. To which I educated him on the reasons *why* she had to use a pen name, and he asked me; '*do you want to make music or not?*'

I felt like I couldn't argue with that fact because I did want to make music: I *desperately* wanted to make music. It was just my name, I'd already been willing to go under the name of '*Tommy,*' I couldn't feel too protective of Penny when I was being offered a contract with '*Time records.*' Penny was temporarily buried and the singular name; '*Bowie,*' was adopted after the knife I would keep in my pirate boot. The very same knife said manager from '*Time*' pulled on me to tell me he was done with me, two months after the album was released. I was Bowie for a fleeting time before I was: '*The woman who couldn't sell the world, even if she tried really, really hard.*'

I finally met manager Tony Simms in a pub; he wanted to work with me after hearing 'Space Oddity,' so invited me to his office in an industrial estate outside of Brixton.

The conversation for a record deal went something like this:

"Paint me my wall, and I'll get you a record contract."

"And paint your pants too while I'm at it, I guess?"

"What? No, these are tailored. The deal will be off if you so much as get a splash on my trousers. Paint my walls, and I'll sort you something out. Contracts are handed out like P45's nowadays."

"There's got to be more to it than that."

"No. I just really fucking want that wall doing. How many times must I reiterate? It's been staring at me for months. *White-eyed fucking bore.* Paint it blue or orange or something bright; there's cash in the top drawer. Get it done this weekend and I'll throw in a single."

I took the £10 from the drawer, pocketed the cash and stole three tubs of bright orange paint from the hardware store down the road. Molly helped paint the walls all weekend with me. Tony gave us the keys and left us to it; we brought in speakers, and I spent the £10 on a substantial stash of drugs to last us just about the weekend with a couple of bottles of vodka and gin. We slept on the office's sofa and ate all the food in the fridge; which mostly consisted of readymade sandwiches with Tony's name on and strawberry yoghurts.

We drew the words; '*FUCK MANAGEMENT, FREE THE OPPRESSED*,' in large orange letters across the wall, that we then intended on covering up once we'd got stoned enough for the day. By chance, Tony swung by the office to see if we wanted any food.

We both thought we'd be done for when he saw the writing, and I assumed my record contract was long out the window. But Tony took one look at the wall, blurted out one laugh; took a drag of his cigarette and took the paint pot out of my hand. He drew an exclamation mark, put the tin down and joined Molly and me getting high. His office remained like that for years and years. He eventually outgrew the office and called Molly and me in to redecorate with the same wording. It was the last thing me and Molly did together before she died.

I didn't believe Tony would get me a record contract, or stick around for very long. I thought he'd be just like the rest of them. During the entire recording process, I kept saying things like; '*he'll run when he hears this one*,' or '*I'll get a slap for this no doubt.*'

But he never left, or slapped me or did anything but encourage me as I poured myself into the album. He let me in the studio for as long as I wanted; he let me call the album whatever the hell I wanted, and he even let me keep my name if I wanted to.

He was the best thing that happened to me in terms of my career.

Tony's first booking was a slot on Top Of The Pops; an absolutely huge contract that seemed so dazing I didn't believe him. He reiterated the words; 'I've got you a slot on TOTP's,' every day for a whole week until it finally sank in and I rebelled.

I'd been living with Molly for a few months after my dad died. Just weeks before the news of the booking, we'd been to 'Radio Rentals' to buy a TV with Molly's fresh wage packet that was burning a hole in her pocket. We'd both agreed that a telly would be the best thing to keep Tommy occupied and Molly awake during her mid-day naps, due to the sleeping pills prescribed to our neighbour's dog she kept nicking.

Molly waltzed into the store with a sock full of cash, walloped it on the counter and said; 'I'm here to buy a distractor box, give us the best one you've got.'

The stocky man in a tweed hunting cap, and ill-fitting blazer, put on a show and patrolled us both around the store, pointing at every telly, and telling us it was better than the last one.

"Dude, I gotta be on stage in two hours, do you know how long it takes to shave a vagina before a show, c'mon, just sell me a fucking telly!"

Molly got increasingly impatient and started flirting with another customer between begging the shop assistant to bag up a TV sharpish. The man took us both to the counter and asked us for our husband's signatures.

"Does it look like we cook dinner for four each fucking night. We're rock n roll stars, not wives, you cunt. Give me my bastard telly!"

"I'm afraid I can't give you the telly on credit without the signature of a man. Your husband or your father will do."

"How about every single one of my previous lovers, they'll give me a glowing review. Is that enough of a signature?"

"I'm afraid not."

I dragged Molly by her hair, out the store and straight to the nearest bar where she slept with two barmaids and a man who called himself the Devil, and wore pink knee-high socks.

The following morning, I cooked Molly eggs, and boiled two pots of coffee, giving her a packet of fags and a bag of weed to numb the blow. I knew by know the exact recipe to healing Molly.

Molly doesn't forgive or forget easily. She doesn't roll over or let it be. She was once called '*a pimple princess*,' as a kid and has remained *furious* ever since. Angry is her permanent state of mind, coffee and cigarettes make her human.

She rambled like a mad woman all morning about the audacity of the man and the store for not allowing her a TV on credit or giving her any other option. She offered to pay for the telly all upfront in *cash*, but the man still refused. Although that wasn't entirely store policy, that was likely because Molly had started frothing at the mouth screaming obscenities, and pulling down her knickers to show the man exactly where he should shove his policies.

"I know exactly what we need to do. *Call up the girls.*"

Not long after Molly's second pot of coffee did she jump out of her
armchair and spring into action. She gathered every girl she'd ever met
in our living room by the time I'd been to the corner shop for more
cigarettes and tequila.

Apparently, tequila was an essential part of the plan.

There were women in suspenders, dinner ladies, post office
receptionists, barmaids, prostitutes, musicians, artists, and mothers; all
gathered drinking Molly's concoction of tequila, coffee and beer she
served all day every day. It stung your mouth like a wasp but made
you fucking buzz like a bee.

"Right ladies! *Listen up!* We're all missing out on a bastard telly
because we don't wanna fuck the same man every night of the week!"
There was a loud uproar, a melody of women outraged at the
injustice, pumping their fists in the air and stomping their heels against
the carpet.

"So, we're gonna show 'em what happens when women don't get TV!
We're gonna show 'em what channel the fucking riot is on! We're
gonna show 'em we don't need a man for *squat*!"

A second uproar, much louder, tearing my eardrums.

"TV ain't gonna know what's hit it!"

The entire living room shook with the surf of a dozen angry women;
the strongest wave in the ocean.

"Women need TV to drown out their fucking husbands," Molly continued.

Not long after, we all gathered outside 'Radio Rentals,' with bags of photographs. Each woman took photographs of themselves having fun without the presence of a man.

There wasn't a dick in fucking sight.

Women pissed in bars they weren't welcomed into without a man. Women licking bus windows for the hell of it. Women pleasuring themselves, cooking a meal for *one*, close-ups of their hairy legs. All things (*minute and otherwise*) that an independent, shackle-less woman without her husband's signature can do; stuck on the very television screen they can't buy without that same signature.

We plastered all the images on every single TV screen we could see, much to the store managers disarray. All of us were there for hours, putting the photographs back on the TV's as the shop assistants were tearing them down.

Tommy brought us sandwiches, and Tony swung by with a bottle, pulling me to one side quite calming admiring the chaos.

"You need to confirm what song you're doing for TOTP's, sunshine."

"Sorry, Tony. I ain't gonna be a woman on TV until a woman can buy one without a man's signature."

"That's ridiculous. This will be the biggest opportunity of your career."

"*I'm sure I'll be just fine.*"

And off we went to riot.

CHAPTER FOURTEEN
FREE LOVE MILK AND MUSIC

Molly and I jumped in the back of a cattle truck for a dare and ended up on a farm in Hull. It was Julian who dared us to make the jump upon arriving pissed at a set of traffic lights on our way to the next joint one particular rowdy weekday. We clambered in, the pair of us smack blind and tequila tipsy, practically riding a cow all the way up the M1. The cows weren't too happy to be joined by two young girls in dresses short enough they could see what we had for breakfast, but once we got used to their constant stream of shit, and they got used to our giggling; we got along just fine. Molly fell asleep not long after she mounted a cow that promptly bucked her off, tossing her rather unfortunately into the biggest cow pat on the truck. The leftover smack just tickling her nostrils, must've been enough to get her through the night and suppress the stench of shit as she slept with her head on a pillow of cow poo as I made friends with the herd.

The farmer was a northern scruffen who appeared at the back of the truck hours later, wearing fishermen wellies and a distressed beanie. He opened his truck to see Molly Jagger pissing on top of a cowpat while I took a polaroid. The farmer had a gun. I'd never seen a gun that big before, it reached my forehead from where he stood in the northern mud. I panicked and laughed, while Molly pulled down her dress and started mumbling.

"You don't wanna do that, Sir, we can get you smack. You like smack? Of course, you like smack, everybody loves a line of Charly, we can get you some, can't we Pen. Penny?"

I was gone.

The great thing about being friends with Molly Jagger is that she's the most beautiful distraction. Men and women can't take their eyes off her. As soon as Molly started talking, I noticed the gun slowly slipping from my forehead, and I made a run for it before it got ugly.

I took cover in a bush down the track of the farm, waiting for Molly.
I knew she'd be fine.
A girl like her can shag her way out of anything.
Molly arrived panting, her hair matted with shit and her dress torn from bristles and thorns from falling over her own feet. She never told me what happened with the farmer, only saying the words; "even the Devil wouldn't be proud of me," upon her arrival.
We'd done worse.

It was morning by the time we emerged from the farm and onto the windy country lane that seemed to never end as we searched for human life. The first house we came across was a lovely primrose cottage, blooming bushes, birdhouse and all the trimmings of a well-kept English home. We eagerly knocked on the door to be greeted by a lovely, small, pruned lady with a massive fucking shotgun in her hands.
"What do you want!"
"Fucking 'ell, everyone 'round here got guns or did we cross the channel and arrive in fucking America."
"Get off my lawn, you stink of shit." The door slammed shut, and a packet of wet wipes were chucked out the window.

Molly wiped herself clean of cow shit, dipping her hair in the birdbath which outraged the old lady, and sent seventeen bullets in our direction. I know it was seventeen because it was one bullet for every second she gave us to get off her lawn.

The second house we tried, happened to be a taxi driver who said he'd take us further south on his shift if we showered first. Grateful and smug to be getting out of the mess we'd regretfully caused; Molly and I showered together in his upstairs bathroom until we caught the pervert looking through the bathroom window. We forced open the window, knocking him off his wooden ladder and giving him a broken collar bone, which meant our lift was temporarily postponed.

No longer smelling of shit, we assumed people would be more understanding of our situation and willing to help us. I think we forgot what we looked like, how we spoke and the audacity of our demands.
"*I don't care that you've got to drop your kids off at school, Bromley's only like- what, five hours away? You'll be back by tea time!*"
"Fuck off!"
For every door that was slammed in our face, we found another to accoster.

The universe works in strange ways. I left Molly in a telephone box after picking up some loose change from unsuspecting pockets and wondered sluggishly through the street, a headache starting to drown me. The sun was exceptional the first time I met M Ronson. I'll never forget how high it hung, and loud it sang.

M's nicknamed "Sunshine" by the crew because of that day.

I had a wicked hangover, I hadn't slept in three days, and was reciting exactly how to punish Julian when we eventually made it back home. I was like a kettle on the hob that day.

M was mowing someone's lawn, rather decently I might add, not that I cared; for in front of the patch of grass M was mowing, there was a small table with a box of cassette's on.

There was a small paper sign that read; '*I can play guitar, piano, cello and violin. I have a pretty tidy voice too. I don't really want to trim bushes forever; if you know anyone in need of the above, please take a cassette.*'

M didn't notice me staring at the sign for a good long while; I've since discovered M was accustomed to nosy, old women taking cassettes for their grandchildren's Christmas presents, or kids stealing the box for the hell of it and assumed I was one of the latter.

I eventually introduced myself over the sound of the lawnmower. M was brash and confident, knowing exactly what she wanted.

"You play?" I asked.

"I dabble."

"Want to dabble together?"

"I ain't into girls."

"You into music, though?"

"Oh, totally."

We went back to hers and jammed together. I played on the keys a bit while she played on the guitar and violin; singing a few lullabies mixed with chart hits to get her voice in gear. Molly slept in front of her log fire the entire time. I hadn't so much as given M my name yet and we were already talking about compositions and song ideas. I don't think M liked me much when we first met. I don't think having a sleeping beauty who still had a faint whiff of cow shit by my side was particularly appealing. I was incredibly highly strung and impatient due to the hangover too, but she must've seen enough to make her want to stick around. Or maybe she was as desperate as me. She was mowing lawns and begging walkers by for help. There was a commonness with M. I liked her instantly and *deeply*.

When she found out I was the one who wrote: '*Space Oddity*,' all she had to say was; '*I prefer Bowie, Penny does nothing for you.*'

As much as it pained me to say; I knew she was right.

People preferred '*Bowie*,' they recognised and remembered the name. Penny was getting easily confused with 'Penny Lane' or any other American groupie. I didn't want to be a groupie; I'd spent most of my career trying to stay clear of being considered a '*groupie*.'

I figured that if '*Bowie*' was what it was going to take to be remembered, then Bowie will be on my grave.

M got us sorted with a lift back home. She drove us down there under the impression we'd make some music over the weekend, and she'd leave Monday morning.

M drove us home and never went back.

While I was slowly starting to get a name for myself, (*despite it changing constantly*) I still wasn't doing any big shows or TV appearances. I thought that my stand against TOTP's would've gained me some sort of respect, when all it did was further segregate me and my chances. I could sell out a small pub in the middle of nowhere effortlessly; with people who went to their local for a quiet pint, ending up with my gormless face singing about space until a fight broke out with my band. But any gig bigger than an accidental stag do crowd, were slim in chance.

I was typically happier in the pub gigs.

Until *Glastonbury.*

You'd be happy with any size gig until fucking *Glastonbury.* Then you just want the biggest, hippest, most notorious stages on Earth; not an audience member or red curtain *less.*

Glastonbury came to my attention when Marc Bolan was bragging at La Gioconda about his and T-REX's performance at the first ever Glastonbury a year earlier. He described free love, milk and music. Three things I couldn't say no to.

I'd heard rumours of a few familiar bands being booked or asked to join the bill if someone else dropped out. I'd met a few ominous strangers who said they might turn up, see how they felt. It all seemed exorbitantly alluring. I loved the idea that it was a bunch of people in a field they shouldn't be in; singing songs society said they shouldn't singing; loving people, they shouldn't be lovin'.

I had never been a part of something like *Glastonbury* before.

You create a new family in the few hours you're there. You meet your camping neighbours, introduce them to parts of yourself your own mother hasn't met before. You talk about politics in what feels like an environment that could actually change something. Like a circle of electricity, ideas bouncing off one another; the focus of love and hope a lit fire in the middle. Drugs are the costume of choice; the shade is for the weak.

You adapt another tongue, there's words I've only ever heard and spoken at festivals; nostalgic when they reach your bricked doorstep. The sun is not invited, yet it is the best party crasher you've met and stays relentless, despite the desperate cries for a tiny bit of cool. Similarly, the rain is an uninvited guest, although he's not as welcomed or well-received. You lose focus on your human rights, shitting in the grass is what you do back in Brixton after all!

Glastonbury, although *now* a highly regarded and respectful festival, in '71, was rampaged with free-loving people looking for a free time.

I was one of them. I snuck myself on-site and proceeded to sneak myself around the site and backstage for the entire weekend. I used the lads to help hide me backstage. The officials and bands on the bill were much more willing to let respected and well-known people like Marc Bolan and Ray Davies backstage.

I hypocritically acted like a groupie to join them.

We held little campfires and sang some unreleased *'Hunky Dory'* songs to a small handful of people who listened as they kissed or watched the sunset. Marc invited Michael Eavis to come and listen to one of our campfire sets and see how well received and good we were. He came and told us we could go on stage at 4 in the morning if we really wanted. He couldn't promise us a crowd and couldn't fit us on the bill before then because they were worried about waking the neighbours. Therefore, we set out to do the loudest, most outrageous set yet; just to say hello to said neighbours in case they felt left out.

It felt loud at the time, but it absolutely wasn't.

I wore nothing but a sleeping bag covering me from the waist down. The sleeping bag was given to me by a girl with pink dreadlocks who said; '*I should keep that voice of mine warm.*'

To thank her, I wore it on stage with my tits flying free as the sun rose and a crowd of around a dozen people woke up from their tents and saw me performing 'Life On Mars' acoustically.

They came out, sleep in their eyes, mud in their hair, bare feet and mostly chested; looking up at me a little dazed and most definitely confused.

I loved every second of it; pure and utter freedom. I went back home to sleep and shower, revived and awoken. It was that moment that made me want to push for bigger crowds.

I was not stupid or blind. I saw how the handful of people enjoyed the set; I simply wanted to bring that joy to more people.

Music had gone through me like an exorcism at this point. It was so deeply rooted within me; it was happening without me knowing. I was writing number ones without the immense feeling of triumph; not that writing music wasn't satisfying, it has been and always will be for me. I was emancipated with the idea of including an audience into my performance and enhancing my energy with their love and reaction.

It was nearly Christmas when 'Hunky Dory' was released. There was a lot of noise in London, a lot of lights in my eyes. Our Christmas tree was festooned with decorations Tommy made in his spare time. He wasn't working, or thieving; he was wallowing at home if he wasn't with me writing or in the studio. He made Christmas decorations, apple pies, tour t-shirts, really shit tour flyers and setlists. While he enjoyed the lethargies of arts and crafts; he was awful at it. Tommy can be very easily characterised by having no character. You must humour him.

Hunky Dory was recorded in a studio I had been allowed to use, thanks to my manager, Tony. Space Oddity, at the time, was the key to most studio doors, it was well respected, which coincidently made *me* well respected.

I spent the release in bed. I was exhausted by the time the album was done; while it was incredibly rewarding, it was arguably more draining than it was satisfying.

Tommy and M came around, and we played the album on repeat until it was Christmas; when we gave each other kisses under the tree and sang Christmas songs until it was new year's and we got high and spoke our intentions. I don't remember the night, but I remember the morning. I think we had a threesome.

Tommy wanted to figure out what the fuck he was doing, M wanted to keep on doing what she was doing and I wanted to change it all up.

I was ready. *Reinvention was calling.*

CHAPTER FIFTEEN
HEAVEN ON SMACK
AND FRENCH
FRIES

'It was six o'clock in the morning when I arrived on Earth. Seven o'clock when I cried, and eight o'clock when I died. The next day. Morning. Sometime between 4 and 5am. The small hours. The lonely seconds. I was reborn.'

That's what I'd tell the newspapers.

Ziggy Stardust was Tommy's idea. Ziggy was a recycling of Tommy's only other idea he's ever had. Except for his idea for a car that runs on water, which didn't develop past a fucking boat with wheels.

The concept of me being 'Tommy' and looking like a man, heightened my chance of a career. 'Tommy' was the closest I'd come to success. People took me seriously and respected me as a musician. I wanted that back.

So, in the small hours, Ziggy Stardust was born, and by lunchtime, he was a *star.* Success had arrived in a miniature hot wheel's car, and a bitesize Lego figurine had clip-clopped her way to my door to hand me my invitation to stardom.

A slot on *'Top Of The Pops.'*

And this time, *I took it.* Tony didn't let me hesitate for one fucking second. He said: "No more of this revolution bollocks, you can cause a revolution *on* the screen. If you want to reach people, TOTP's is your chance. You'll have millions of people to brainwash as supposed to three deaf cunts down the pub."

Ziggy was the aesthetic of a man being my feminine self. I'd never been more feminine than when I was a man called Ziggy. As a woman, I felt showing my femininity would be a weakness, as a man, it felt like a superpower. I displayed my femininity with such ease, it oozed off my leather crotch. I spoke of space and time as though I owned it. I sang with such vigour, I put the fuck in sex. I gave everything I had ever been to Ziggy as it felt I would disintegrate if I didn't. Ziggy was not a last chance resort; however, I couldn't see past the blackness if Ziggy did not succeed.

I'd planned to go on 'Top Of The Pops' barefoot in what was fundamentally my childhood bedsheet. An adverse statement piece for female sexuality. It had fairies all over it. Tommy wrapped it twice around me at an angle, so my breasts were just about covered and positively plumped.

We tied it around my waist with the dressing rooms' curtain tie, and once I'd painted my eyes with green paint, I felt about ready to go on stage before the producer said: '*absolutely not.*'

He was quite positive viewers would not approve and call in to complain. Despite me telling him it wasn't my problem, he told me it would be my *manager's* problem, and that's essentially the same thing. I had three arguments with my manager, all of them ending in something being thrown. The first argument was relatively civilised; it took place in my dressing room, just the two of us, with no other witnesses to prove how much of a little bitch Tony was being.

He was usually always supportive, even of the things he didn't understand. He'd always shrug, say something like; '*I don't care what you look like as long as you sing good Pen,*' and I'd go on stage with a smile. The second argument happened approximately 10 minutes later after I'd whined like a kid to Tommy and he went protesting to Tony about how unfair and constricting he was being.

The three of us fought like babies until Tommy planted Tony and he went down like a pack of cards on my chaise longue.

After four rounds of whiskey slammers, two ice packs and a whole army of personnel shouting the odds; we had our third argument right backstage; which ended up in me dropping the bedsheet and waltzing onto the stage stark bollock naked one minute before air time. The crowd had a good laugh and so did the crew, as they chased me around the cameras and equipment until I was eventually rugby tackled and dragged backstage where my manager was groveling for our slot to still go ahead.

That's when I held up my hands and told Tony that I had absolutely no other clothes, so I would have to borrow the ones off his back. To say he was unhappy was definitely an understatement; since he saw me arrive in clothes that were hung quite comfortably in the dressing room, but I'm too stubborn for that, and I wanted to win.

Purely to save his job (and my career) did he strip to his boxers and hand me his dull, awful green corduroys and a beige shirt. I still went barefoot, and I put my bra over the shirt for pure femininity.

As for the performance; it was incredible and even though I ran straight off stage to be sick the moment I mimed my last note; my hangover subsided, and I got to enjoy the after-party with a few tense-looking crew members.

The papers the next day wrote about my confused appearance and performance. How I sang feminine but looked like an ogre of a man. They were confused with who I was flirting with. I hugged Eddie Wyatt (the new drummer in the band), pecked M on the lips, all while simultaneously giving a gorgeous young girl the eye in the audience. I was not what television screens were accustomed to at that time.

I was having the time of my life, with all the 15 million people watching through a box in their front room. My sexuality became a national talking point. I'd gone from people outright refusing to talk about me and the outrageous scandal that was me sleeping with a man; to telling 'Melody Maker' that I was *probably* a lesbian.
I met a girl once not long after, who came up to me after a show and said; '*You're that girl that kissed that other girl on the pops. My mother was sick on her roast potatoes when she saw it. It was awesome, thanks, man. Here, meet my girl.*'

That was the power of Ziggy. It seemed I'd unintentionally made homosexuality fashionable. I think it helped liberate a lot of lost men and women. We were still stoned in the street for holding hands; a culture having a figure like Ziggy made people think twice.

Which really is all you can ask of bigots. Tommy was the least bit impressed I'd outed myself as a lesbian while still sleeping about with men, including himself. He said to me; '*you could've at least said you were bisexual you idiot.*'

I didn't care. I was free either way.

Despite the common belief that I woke up with green skin and the encyclopedia of space; Ziggy Stardust was not made overnight. It was a long time coming. It makes no sense to me to think that a rock star (or *anyone* for that matter) is shackled by the confines of *one* voice, *one* person, *one* expression, *one* persona. A rock star can be whoever they want to be, and they can be whoever they want to be in *any* performance.

I would've died of boredom a very long time ago if I weren't able to change my character every now and then. The changing of character was the one thing that kept me occupied as a child, I was positively shocked when I discovered people expected adults to be one person and one person *only*. Ziggy was just a personification of change.

London felt ill. Tremendously and horrifically, a tumor on the brain, kind of sick. It was lying limp in an underfunded and overcrowded NHS hospital bed; oozing puss from its sores and dripping sweat from every orifice. Hooked to a poisoned supply of morphine with the batteries of its life support machine needing a change.

For its children, born and to be born. To its dead, buried and quaking.

To its living, crying and in fear; there was no hope for the death of our city. The children only had bomb sites and shrapnel to play with; it was no wonder London wanted to peacefully slip off the face of the map.

While conservatism was all the range in family households across the nation. Self-expression was undoubtedly the new game *behind* the television screens. I think we all felt it upon ourselves to shock them out their lazyboys and into a bath of captivating self-discovery.
The early 70s was not an era where women flirted with masculine imagery at all. It was a time where we lived in a single, absolute, created society with no pluralism. People found comfort in known truths and known lies and that indefinitely outstretched to the likes of gender and sexuality. No one had time for confusion or question: only known truths, and if you didn't fit that mould, you were a *freak*.
I left Ziggy as a messiah of rock n roll and performed him as such. The audience truly made him come to life: it was exciting to have that relationship with the audience for the first time.

The tour was immense and sudden. Although I had dreamed of exactly what was happening for my entire life; it all felt too unreal and unexpected to possibly be true. There were suddenly lights and a crew with people to manage, and it felt very peculiar.
I was used to shitting in buckets or having to pay a guy behind the bar to be the lighting tech for the night.

Random blokes setting fire to equipment or pissing in the drum barrels was what I was accustomed to; not this sudden star-spangled existence.

The backstage of the tour ran like the backstage of a theatre performance. It was utterly irregular to that of a rock concert. Makeup people and costume designers were running about the place. Security guards on doors with people chatting away about politics behind them. There was the familiar addition of drugs and sex platooned about the place; while that was irregular for the backstage of a theatre performance, it was not unusual for the *70s*.

We went from a tight-knit of people I knew very well and who knew *me* very well; to a whole scholar of people, I didn't know and had no particular interest in getting to know. I felt remote backstage, a little out of proportion to the rest of them.

They all helped me get ready and assisted the smooth running of the show, but I failed to have time for their idle chatter about where Ziggy came from or how my mother was doing.

I very muchly wanted my band and Tommy and a few others to remain strapped by my side at all times.

Of course, this was just an initial reaction to change; I knew I had a lot to learn from the others.

The tour became about what clothes I would wear in three weeks and exactly how much stuffing I'd shove to my groin each day; which depended on the ratio of ticket sales.

My manager insisted I push more socks down there if there were a higher woman to man ratio. I wore things and did things that unintentionally made me a man. Ziggy was fashioned as a man, but I didn't intend on *performing* him as such. I never cared what people saw me as, as long as *I* knew who I was at that time. I added stuffing to my groin for the hell of it one time, and it caught like wildfire that there was a hot new man on the scene.

Even *I* wanted to fuck Ziggy.

I admired the process. It was invigorating to be a part of such a huge show and watch it all assemble around me each night. I was meeting people who genuinely loved my music; performing to audiences of hundreds of men and women having a good time; selling an incredible amount of records; working and meeting some unbelievable musicians and artists.

I was living my dream.

Yet I couldn't focus. A month into the 170 show tour; I started to write and dream up my next album. All the while Ziggy was at large and growing more cosmic, I couldn't help but want to move on.

The first time leaving the country with no idea upon when you will return home is peculiar. That flight is consumed with the thoughts of mothballs in your wardrobe, and will the streets remember my feet when they land again?

I had never had the money nor the means to travel abroad for much longer than a week before. My first time on a proper jumbo plane, and what I had hoped to be my last. I don't enjoy flying much. I tell people it's because I don't like the feeling. But on that first flight, Tommy was violently sick on our plane over to Boston and M refused to stop snorting cocaine off the cockpits door handle, despite the threat of being terminated off the flight immediately. Every time I fly, I can smell the animosity and Charly.

The taxi rolled through the streets of New York, and my eyes widen an inch. I hadn't seen streets I didn't know, which is a bizarre concept, because everything you know, you didn't know at some point. London was etched into my mind so profoundly, it was hard to discipline my eyes in a manner that digested the avenues and blocks of terraced flats.

America was filled to the brim with *stuff*. I was overwhelmed by the amount of *stuff*. America was a stark contrast to London. While London was dying, and wilting away in the ugliest and most pathetic of ways; America seemed to be *thriving*. And not just thriving, but bathing in ineffable ecstasy.

I mean they had Lou Reed and the Velvet bloody Underground for God's sake; it was heaven on smack and French fries. The moment I got a whiff of the Velvet Underground, I was straight at the Chelsea and straight to Warhol like a bloodhound.

I believe I introduced myself to Andy, under the disillusion that I had the right to. I was a '*little wrought of diamonds*,' as Andy would say. I made no sense at that time. I was jet-lagged *permanently*. I was doused in copious amounts of alcohol and narcotics. I was *perfect* for Andy. Andy was stooped upon the Chelsea Hotel front steps. I think he'd been to see Candy Darling, as he had lipstick between his teeth. Nothing other than the feather boa wrapped around his ankles and the bottle of whiskey next to him, intrigued me to sit down by his side.
"I like your feather boa," I told him.
"You can wear it if you like?" He replied, his accent *thick*.
"It suits you more. Matches your eyes."
"My eyes are blue. The boa is blood red."
"*Precisely*."

We spoke about art, which is hardly surprising. Andy had a habit of making every tiny detail into a story. He spoke of the government being an art gallery. Calling the president, the ugly fire extinguisher that did not suit the aesthetic requirements of the art gallery building, but was, unfortunately, a necessary part of the gallery's function in case of art mutiny.

He called street lamps fictional conspiracies for enlightening behaviour and embarked on the history of playful sex and how outdated it was becoming.

There was nothing other than his brilliant mind, and the way he spoke of his mind, that allured me into staying with him and staying with him for the entire time I was in America on the Ziggy tour. He was not just another guy; he was another *world*. While America was a place I had never been, Andy Warhol's mind was a place *nobody* had been. I had discovered another land with Andy.

Andy became an immense influence in the way Ziggy expressed himself in America. While I understood Ziggy, I didn't understand the states. The audience seemed to tick differently than back home; Andy showed me how I could grab them by the eyeballs and make them listen.

Andy spent a lot of time backstage, apparently silent during my entire set each night. Tommy and Andy never got along, to the point where we had to hire another security guard who's only job it was, was to keep the two apart.

Tommy thought he was, and I quote; '*the reason the world is skewered through a kebab of conspiracy.*'

I've never understood his hate towards Andy, who was nothing but a gracious and helpful being; on the contrary to Tommy who smoked all my drugs, ate all my food, spent all my money and contributed absolutely nothing to the music.

It's a good job he was good in the sack.

Andy and I were together for the brief time I was in America. I'm still not sure to this day, what; '*being together with Andy Warhol*' means. At the time, it meant a lot of sex, fun and drugs. It was long evenings of painting, followed by long mornings of expressive sex. Coffee with drag queens and punk rockers. Drugs supplied by street artists as part of his factory outlet. Writing on walls because we're both too high to find any paper. By the time I'd left New York, I'd vandalised 6 hotel rooms of the Chelsea, covered in the scribbles of my next album. Slept with three male hookers, danced in drag at Max's Kansas City, robbed a liquor store by accident and was briefly arrested as a suspect in a rather compelling armed robbery case.

I'd brought my addiction to a dangerous level, overdosing in a tea shop one miserable afternoon. Every show was of course, outstanding and better than the other. Yet I'd also failed to see Tommy the entire time and didn't know how my band were doing. I wouldn't see them until I was walking on stage with them all looking proudly pissed off and rightly so. I was learning how much I loved conflict and needed it to sustain me with the right environment for creative insight. I've since learnt that I can be just as creative *observing* conflict rather than being stuck in the middle of it. I guess America makes you go crazy, or that was my experience anyway.

The only time I saw Tommy was when he overdosed. M has since told me he overdosed for my attention; screaming my name every time he injected. I like to think he would never be that stupid, but with that amount of heroin in your veins, it's anybody's guess.

He just about survived thanks to my persistent haggling with a taxi to take us to the hospital for free, since we'd both spent all our cash that day on drugs. We argued in his sleep.

I was so hurt and so pissed that he'd done something so selfish. He'd been so ignorant to his own addiction, he nearly damn ended it all. It hurt bad. I'm still unsure as to why his overdose hurt me more than my near own, or anyone else's near overdose, but it hurt and kept on hurting for years.

I used to see his froth in my morning coffee. I used to have to scorn Tommy, call him down out of bed, point at the cup and say; 'lo*ok, look what you've done.*'

Tommy would routinely apologise with sleep in his eyes and go back to bed.

It hurt because I knew it was a cry for help, as I'd cried for him a week earlier and overdosed the same. The needle is such a stable comfort in what can seem a paralysing and intimidating world. The familiar bloodstain, the knowing smile on a line of Charly, the routine of rolling a spliff; all home comforts. Addiction is not always about being hooked or obsessed or unable to stop. In fact, addiction is never really about those things. It's about the *void.* The void we all have, the void we all want to fill. The thoughts of death that crawl up your spine as you desperately try and sleep in your childhood bed. The pending doom of debt; the weight of family; the arrogance of a lover. *Voids.* Voids you want so badly to satisfy.

I can tell you now, drugs fill that void impeccably; it's almost as though the drug manufacturers have insight into the shape of every void imaginable and they make them the perfect missing piece. It feels that vicious. Along with the euphoria and the freedom from injecting or snorting or smoking; you feel *anger.* Who manufactured something so incredible and simultaneously incredibly *dangerous?* Who brought this shit into my life?

When you realise it's yourself, that becomes the hardest pill to swallow.

I was one of the good addicts. I'm a much better addict than a person; I was somehow more caring and compassionate when I was on drugs than when I wasn't. They say cocaine stops you feeling, and that's true. While it unquestionably had that effect on me; the sheer feeling of *lack of* feeling made me realise that emotions and feelings aren't the bad thing. Feelings are not the culprit for your own insanity. That's just *you.*

I was kinder on drugs because I wouldn't feel the repercussions of doing a good deed; which I found overwhelming without the cocaine numbing it. I could love freely without worry or without the weight of what I was doing weighing me down into a pit of regret.

I was a responsible addict too. I always made sure my washing was done before I got high.

I just didn't want to feel *all the time*, and I don't think that's a bad thing. We're forced by society to feel *constantly.* Feel *bad* for the poor; feel *happy* for the successful; feel *pain* for war; feel *pride* for your country; feel *hunger* for the advertisements; feel *aroused* at the beauty of the Earth.

Whether it was my instinct to rebel against societal conformity; or a pure desire to lull the voices of emotions inside my head and heart: I just didn't want to feel all the time, and I think that's okay.

What wasn't okay, was my choice of emotional corking.

I should've taken up jogging, but I simply didn't have the knees.

I embrace feeling now. I feel healthier for it. Stronger for feeling, and stronger for allowing myself to explore all the good and all the bad and not feel overwhelmed by it. Stronger for embracing my humanity, no matter how much it petrifies me and my instincts.

I do miss the cocaine though. I just don't have a good enough excuse for public streaking anymore!

Overdosing seemed glamorous at the time. It felt like a *performance*. How brilliant one can bring themselves closer to the final curtain. And everybody was doing it. You couldn't walk around backstage or on a New York street without some limp body overdosing at your feet. You see so many and hear of their near-death experience, it does become glamorous after a while. They described shimmering abysses, filled with pools of your own memories. The lifting of the weight of regret as you slip so close to the edge of life, nothing but how you land matters.

It sounds so abysmally dull and naive now, but as I said:

America really does make you crazy.

It didn't like me either. The record company didn't do a great job at promoting my music before I flew out, meaning no one knew me. I was prepared to do it all over again.

I was new to being signed to a label, I didn't know how things worked or how desires could be pulled in your favour. I was calling back home, telling people that I reckon I'll be out here a while since I'm gonna have to do the whole clubbing and pubs circuit again to get my name out there; which I was more than willing to do.

Having seen more of America now, my optimism at doing every pub and club in America is rather bold. America is a whole lot bigger than London, which became pretty clear the moment I *flew* to the next state.

My management agreed the best thing to do, would be to *lie*. I had lied my entire way here; I wasn't going to start being a saint now. The lie was to sell me as bigger than I was. My management hired all sorts of loons and lackeys, limo's and luxuries, to make me seem the biggest star America had ever seen.

I took one look at my two security guards, very persistent on being my new handbags, and told them I would get them fired if they didn't look the part. I couldn't have two annoying old bald blokes penetrating the Ziggy astrosphere by looking as dull as grey linen is. I made them wear karate suits and yellow eye shadow.

They looked that good I made my entire crew adopt a similar look. I wasn't used to the entourage, I didn't know how to react to having someone stood outside the toilet or someone to collect my dirty clothes and wash them within ten minutes of me blinking; all things somewhat irrelevant to my music.

I felt a little out of control that there were so many people surrounding me, contributing to the lie, boosting my ego 24/7. Choosing what they'd wear and look like, was my contribution.

We'd storm into the record labels office all in suspenders; condoms stuck to the bottom of our knee-high boots; glitter in our hair and on our eyes. They couldn't tell the women from the men. They were that keen to get us out of the office, they'd say *yes* to anything. Including agreeing to us buying 150 bras to hang on washing lines, we hung over the audience. That was M's idea. She initially said; 'a mixture of used knickers, bras, condoms, boxers, dildo's, whips and chains;' but apparently, management only heard the word: '*bra.*'

M replaced a womanly shaped hole Molly Jagger left behind when she fled London, just in time for it dying. I loved spending company with the guys, but I needed female company and M was perfect for it. M was the best guitarist I'd seen, and the world got to see it too. I would be on stage, staring at M explode right in front of my eyes and wonder how I got so lucky. How did I stumble upon the greatest guitarist to exist in someone's front garden?

I've always found something irresistible about M, which she is rather passive about. You tell her she's good and she'll say something like; '*A banana is good for breakfast, go get a banana to play.*'

During Ziggy Stardust, M was a confidant when America was cruel to me. She'd be in my room with Eddie's stash of weed, and we'd sit up all night watching shit TV. On stage, she was my confidant too. M shares the same reactivity with the crowd as I do. I can taste the ambiguity if the audience isn't on the same wavelength, in the same way, I can smell the adrenaline as they heave out every verse with passion.

M is just as explosive and reactive as me.

I don't know whether it was because we both knew, more than the rest of the male band members, how privileged and lucky we were to even be on that stage and singing our songs.

We'd fought our way onto that stage, performing was the long sigh at the top of the mountain. I was no stranger to the girl who couldn't name two states in America, and here I was *fucking* in them.

I was the luckiest girl in the world, and I knew it. I had made it; I had finally done it. The climb was worth the view. I was finally on stage, singing to an audience that wanted to be there and wanted to hear my songs. The songs that I wrote in my childhood bedroom about a childhood dream. My songs that didn't make sense, yet people *found* sense in them.

I was exactly where I wanted to be and doing exactly what I had wanted since I first picked up a recorder all those years ago. It had happened so quickly, although at no speed at all. People tend to forget the ten years of ground work I put in prior to Ziggy exploding on TV screens.

I had intentions of Ziggy existing for a year, and then I would be Penny again, or Bowie, or someone else; I didn't know in America, other than I knew I would reinvent *very soon.*

Being a woman, I learnt, is all about *sacrifices.* I don't want to sacrifice my womanhood to be successful. I don't want to be a *man* to be successful as a *woman.* I don't want to *accept* that I should be a man to be successful- and I *don't.* But at that moment in time, I learnt that I had to sacrifice a year of my womanhood so that I could have *decades'* worth of being a woman and being a woman in *success* and *wealth.*

Sexism was a commodity, sexism supported the economy. Being a woman was practically a rebellious act in itself. Every time a woman dared be a woman, and fractured the stagnated image society had painted of the female gender; *the pound collapsed.*

While I was more than happy to rip up a few pound notes; I was more interested in *supporting* women who wanted to make a living for themselves.

By being Ziggy, who I had created as a creature of intent to provide comfort, empowerment and a little bit of sex and fun; (*'cos it is rock n roll after all*) I'd created a small gateway for women. At the end of the day, no matter who or what people thought Ziggy and I was; the fact is, I was a woman being Ziggy, who was quite plainly androgynous. You're right in thinking it was a political statement, of course it fucking was, it had to be.

I had to be a political statement to be seen and heard because god forbid I just be a woman. I wasn't a man, so I had to be creative in how I earned a living and made people listen and respect me. I was a woman being *exactly* who I wanted to be, whether people saw that or not.

Being Ziggy gained me access to television, something no other female rockstar had achieved so quickly or predominantly. It gained me a million-person audience to use my voice as a woman. It allowed me to earn a living without the support of a man. It gained me access to a recording studio to produce the music I loved; *safely*, with talented and *honest* people. It meant I could create a pathway for the future of female artists. Being Ziggy was the best thing I ever did.

CHAPTER SIXTEEN 51 PIGS

Back in around 1969, myself, Tommy and Molly occupied a house in Bromley. I didn't know how it came to be at the time, I don't remember now either, and I assume a copious number of drugs were to blame. Tommy tells people he fought in a gruesome fight for ownership of it but survived unscathed without a scratch. Molly used to say: '*we just walked on in and claimed it as ours as we did the music industry.*' I've always liked that version, so I'll stick with that, but rest assured it wasn't ours by any stretch. It was abysmally derelict but beautiful. Swallowed in green shoots of grass and weeds we used as rabbit food for Tommy's new-found pet obsession. Ivory roots covered the ground for miles. It felt like quicksand in between the vine roots, but really it was just deep and quenching mud. There was one route into the house and one route out; you daren't try another course, not *alone.*

The door was about the only stable thing. A large iron frame with colourful stain glass that embellished no coherent shape or pattern. And then the hallway, a grand space with no doors, just holes in the walls that lead to room after room. There were two kitchens, two Larder's, three living rooms and a study on the bottom floor. Five bedrooms, a study and three bathrooms on the second floor and an attic space which was just one big open room.
I was never too sure whether the floor was going to fall through, which was part of the excitement.

I assume we discovered the house after a night out, getting lost coming back home as that's my first memory there. We spent that night jumping off the furniture. We pretended the floor was quicksand and threw ourselves off bannisters, onto chandeliers and up bookcases to avoid being slain by the sand. I awoke in the attic with half a dressing table on top of me. Molly broke her hand, I believe by falling out of the wardrobe, and Tommy woke up in the garden shed.

We revisited a couple of weeks later to find it in the exact same state we'd left it in. We all left a sock hidden in a specific place in a room. We didn't know who owned the house or if it was occupied, which seemed unlikely given the general state of the house. Yet there was still furniture in every room and clothes in the wardrobe. Pots and pans in the cupboards, books on the shelves, drawers full of letters and bric-a-brac. When we came back, the socks were still there, untouched and so we claimed the house our own.

Molly and I brought our roller skates to the house once and spent an entire weekend skating around. We tried and ultimately failed, to race down the stairs, resulting in us smashing the bottom panel of the front door, creating a permanent draft to the already freezing house. The attic was the best place to skate since it was a completely open and long space with no carpets or snags to trip us up. We'd create synchronised routines and perform them to the second bedrooms collection of creepy dolls.

The house made us act like kids. We made a rule to not allow drugs into the home and to only go to the house to escape from all the mess that essentially our drug use endued. That rule lasted about two years. We did have a party there once, and *only* the once. We knew it was risky and required a lot of logistics since the place wasn't exactly *safe,* which definitely appealed to us more. We wrote down a list of house rules and stuck a copy in every room which went totally a miss. We also lined the one path into the house with lanterns, so everyone knew which way to go. Which of course was ignored and about an hour in, we all had to haul a bald man out of the mud, and into an ambulance with two broken ankles. One of the floors on the second floor went through and a young girl, who really was too young and should've been in bed; fell through, and her poor little white legs were dangling through the kitchen ceiling. Tommy saved her and walked the girl home to two very concerned parents shouting and bawling about how she'd escaped down the drain pipe.

The party bizarrely attracted a lot of young people who similarly escaped out of their conformity catholic homes, down the drainpipe and found themselves in the middle of an intense game of bowling in our attic. We used bottles of beer for skittles and a ball of elastic bands as the bowling ball and collected a lovely pile of smashed glass that didn't get moved for years.

We did eventually buy the house after a few years of abusing it. The owners were an elderly couple that had lived in the house their entire lives and then moved to Italy a few years before their deaths. They kept the house in the family, and it was owned by one of their grandchildren, but no one lived there since they'd all moved to Italy. I bought the house by myself with the money I earnt from the Ziggy Stardust tour and asked Tommy to move in on the condition he spent his days doing it up and fixing all the holes and mess we'd made. I did regret asking him since he was by no means good with his hands and within the first week of owning the house, he made the hole in the floor bigger; broke a bath; toppled over my favourite wardrobe and somehow managed to put a hole through one of the steps in the main staircase just by walking down them.

We took all the studio equipment I'd gathered, from my mum's house and made a studio in one of the bedrooms. Tommy decorated the room in a mixture of old bedsheets and loose scraps of fabric he took from a haberdashery's skip. He nailed them into the ceiling and left them to hang so you'd have to bat away bits of cotton just to get into the room. It wasn't his best idea, but neither was pinning the drum kit to the floor which wasn't stable enough to hold up a baby chick. We had to abandon that room; left hopeless, soulless and floorless; swiftly redecorating a second room much more practical in the traditional sense of a studio.

I played the project manager on that one.

It was home, but more importantly, it was a place of sanity amidst the utter chaos. During my gigs, I'd stare out at the crowd; the masses of people all living their own lives in their own heads. I was always marveled at how the crowd itself was chaos; just a dumping of lots of people screaming in a square. Secondary to the chaos in their own heads, adding more bedlam to the anarchy. How within each crowd, there's hundreds of singular messes all living in single heads. There are thousands of people wondering when they're going to die; hundreds asking what this all means; fifty or so asking how it is they feel so alive and a handful wondering if they've got time to go take a piss before the next song. I stand on the stage, quite alone, amongst this mess, this chaos and utter bedlam in beautiful disarray; wondering myself: how it is I feel this alive.

The house is a lighthouse upon that mess, the common, regular, sudden, awful mess that is created nightly, daily, frequently.
Often, I would collapse through the iron doors and sit on the bottom step of the staircase with a cigarette and slice of cake (chocolate, of course), listening to Tommy talk about his day or asking him to read poetry to me. We'd often fall asleep on that step and be awoken by Tony who'd demand we pack within minutes for a tour. I'd kiss the bottom step, say a quiet goodbye to the house and arrive back to the house months later with a huge smile and sigh of relief.
Home. Where sanity sleeps so your insanity can breathe.

Without doubt, that house was the best thing me and Tommy ever stole.

When we left our sanctuary for the 'Aladdin Sane' tour around America; I was more than disheartened to arrive at the feet of southern roughen: '*Bill,*' outside the supposed '*house*', we were to spend the tour living in. I never learnt Bills surname or middle name, or if Bill was even his real name (which I didn't suspect). But Bill lived next door, and by next door, I mean to say; he lived in the farmhouse about 2 miles down a beaten track that needed a good weeding. Bill owned, what he claimed to be, *half of America*, but was actually about ten acres of land and a farmhouse. He owned two horses; one horse named Shelia, he would ride to mine to annoy me, and a grey boy called Tommy, which was confusing when I'd go to call Tommy in for tea and get a horse at my window chomping on the fresh carrots.
Bill was a crazy bastard. He won't mind me calling him a mad bastard, because when I left after the tour; he set fire to the house and sent me a delicate looking envelope with some of the ashes inside. *First-class stamp.*

Our house was a western-style shack that had mould in the bathtub, no matter what you did. Every floorboard and door creaked; the fire spat out thick and scorching hot black soot when it wasn't lit, and none of the locks on the doors worked. The windows were shuttered with woodlice infested planks of wood and our front yard was a breeding ground for migrating birds.

We'd never had much luck with homes; our only respite was that we never stayed in them very long. One was haunted by children you could hear screaming for their mothers in the night. Another set on fire out of the blue and the apartment we had in New York, got broken into and most of Tommy's clothes and his entire comic book collection was nicked.

We wanted a break from the city and hotels, asking for somewhere with no neighbours. We thought we could settle with one neighbour, but Bill was a nightmare.

It was mostly Tommy to blame for our poor relationship with Bill, who called him a '*red-necked bastard*,' after hearing someone say it at the airport. It was the first thing he said to him. The second being: '*put the gun down Billy, let's settle this like real men.*'

Bill encouraged Tommy to keep up his old (and they were *old* at the time) thieving habits and recruited him with the odd job. The strangest job was stealing a Shetland pony.

Tommy did this by also stealing our tour bus from outside the gig in Texas and driving it to the neighbouring farm where he took Bill's neighbours pony by clumping it over the head with one of the amps left in the bus. Tommy's tactic was impeccable in *transporting* the pony, but awful when it came to keeping the pony *alive*. Tommy delivered the, *what he assumed to be*, alive and well Shetland pony named Virginia to Bills front door; only to discover the following day that Virginia was well and truly deceased and attracting flies on our living room rug.

After that debacle, Tommy avoided Bill at all costs for about a week until Bill delivered his homemade cherry pie with a note saying; 'I want a pig and no bacon.'

In Tommy's head; 51 pigs are 50 times better than one pig. In Bill's: (I can't believe I'm putting this in writing) *sane* mind; 51 pigs are 50 times more *trouble*, cost and effort.

So, when Tommy *accidentally* released 51 pigs from an abattoir and put them in our tour bus *again*, he had one unhappy Bill, 20 odd furious crew members clearing up pig shit and 51 pigs to look after. Tommy was sent back to England a week early while we all cleared up the mess he left behind like a tornado.

While Tommy was grounded, the tour continued. One particular night had poorly ended due to a lad kicking off in the crowd. He beat up a girl for stepping on his toe, *bloody short-fused patriarchy*. We had to cut the set short while a medical team could get through the crowd and to her aid.

I'd had enough of the fighting. I proposed an idea to Tony, who rolled his eyes in silence but put the plan in motion straight away. I think the band only agreed because they were all knackered and just wanted to get on with the after-party. I told security that they were strictly *only* allowed to let in women and to turn down every single identifying man that tried to get into the following concert. It was just a statement, nothing else. I just wanted one gig where women felt safe in the crowd, away from bastards with wandering hands. A concert where women could dance and mosh safely if they wished to. I also wanted a gig for women as a symbol of how much women love rock n roll too. It was the best and happiest crowd I've ever seen smiling back up to me, and the band had a bloody good time backstage afterwards.

I don't want to give the bad press the satisfaction; but not many other people, other than myself, the band and the audience enjoyed the gig. After that night, a group of men staged a protest outside, which was one of the funniest things I've ever seen. A group of about 25 white men stood in a circle shouting: '*ROCK N ROLL IS FOR ALL.*' To me, the idea of a man protesting for equal rights after one '*all women*' gig, only emphasises the absurdity of gender inequality. Can't women have just *one* night; just *one* fucking night! Men get safe access to rock n roll *every* fucking night of the week, it just wasn't the same for women.

I didn't think men would be so highly strung over the empowerment, safety and happiness of a few hundred women for *one fucking night*! But here I am still receiving death threats from the titled 'male empowerment' group: 'MALE JUSTICE.'

They've written me many letters over the years from polite notices of their protests outside my gigs; to the newly released t-shirts for sale on their website; to a descriptive list on why I should quit my job. I must admit, '*Justin*' who '*manages all-female disruption*' sounds like a right laugh.

Most of the letters cited the following:

'As men, we feel as though your shows are not welcoming for all. We at, 'MALE JUSTICE,' are fighting for the involvement of men. We feel left out, and more to the point disregarded in the participation of your shows and music. We urge you to appeal to men in all aspects of your show and career. It would, in fact, boost your figures, so we hope you take kindly to this letter, as we really are trying to help you.'

They all went in the fire (sorry Justin), except the odd few I found too funny to burn. 'MALE JUSTICE,' attended pretty much every single one of my gigs between the years of 1973-1980. When the new decade came in, I think they turned on another genre of music for their woes. They were the most *in denial* groupies I've ever met, and every single one of them were *men*. M slept with at least half of them and went on to marry one of them, so I don't know just how secure their values ever were.

I'm all for making men feel comfortable and accepted, but not at the *expense* of women.

It was, in fact, the 'MALE JUSTICE' team that inspired and encouraged me to include choreographed dancing in my performances to piss them off. I wanted a choreographed dance to compliment all the elements of the show we'd forked out for. We had lights and stage designs and costumes; to me, all that was missing was a bit of ostentatious dancing.

But, I asked myself, what kind of dancing is gonna match the strikingly vivid bolt of lightning on the cover of my 'Aladdin Sane' album?

You're right, *pole dancing.*

I'd seen Candy Darling do it back in America on the last two tours and was always aroused at the idea.

My fascination started pre-tour, before 'MALE JUSTICE,' with a drunken night at '*Mary's,*' the local underground swing bar back in Bromley.

Mary's was called 'The Circle' in the day. It was a place where you could go get high communally. I think it actually sold records, but everyone just brought their own and played them on the record player in the middle. I don't really know how any business made any money in the 70s; everyone was free lovin' and giving or too high for money to mean shit.

It'd take us shy of two hours to walk to Mary's, which we had to do because no taxi or bus would take us. We'd have to get drunk enough to *want* to wrap our legs around a pole and get chaffing for weeks. I say *we*; I do mean Tommy and me.

We've been inseparable since we met; even in a strip joint.

When my name was getting more well known, I could get a lift from someone which wasn't as much fun. One time, a man in his sixties, gave Tommy and me a lift and we ended up going to his Aunts birthday party to surprise her and sing for the night. He paid me more money than a booker and fed me cheese sandwiches and vol-au-vents between songs.

We'd get to Mary's, order a bottle of anything and jump straight on the stage. It was a place for freaks, for sinners and for *Catholics*. It happened to be directly underneath a cathedral; you had to enter through the confession booth; it was all very muchly Devil approved and God on probation.

Mary hired a few good dancers; male and female, for the stages. It wasn't a place for punters, it was a place for expression and to get pissed doing it.

The dancers were paid in booze and cigarettes- not exploited for their talents, everyone was an addict of some degree; so that payment was more desirable.

As soon as me and Tommy would enter the room; the dancers would jump down, and an audience would form.

Tommy and I would spend the two hours stumbling there, plotting and scheming precisely what we were going to do on stage; so that by the time we got there, all we had to do was throw away our petticoats (with most of our dignity in the pockets) and start the show.

Tommy, as talented as he is; is not a great dancer, never mind *pole dancer*. His physique is most desirable, and he has a lot of *other* great qualities; like crowd teasing and '*boxer line taunting*,' as he named it. '*Boxer line taunting*,' is the closest thing to stripping an unwed Catholic is allowed to see. But, the testimony that he wrapped his lusciously long and envious legs around the pole, dusted in my red high heels and fell on his arse within two minutes of every show; proves that Tommy should be kept *behind* the stage. He's just always been up for a laugh and something new. It's a shame his stamina is *atrocious*.

I, on the other hand, was like a poster around that pole; seamlessly gliding around its smoothed edges. After a while at least; no one is a duck to water when it comes to pole dancing. I met Cindy mid-tour, and she choreographed a routine for the rest of the tour. Cindy wanted me to give in to the stereotypical pole dancing and feminine image by wearing lots of skimpy clothes and stockings. I told her she could have her fun in rehearsal; then I was back to wearing whatever I wanted when the tour came around.

I wasn't very lenient or sympathetic at that time. I didn't want to just wear my knickers on stage, and I was bored of doing things other people wanted me to do. There was nothing but pure amusement as a reason for me freezing my tits off on stage. That and for the sex appeal, of course.

But I felt sexiest in a suit, so that's what I wore; amongst ripped dresses and shorts with band tees and men's shirts. Basically, anything I could find last minute backstage or something meticulously planned months in advance: there was nothing in between when it came to my fashion. The Ziggy Stardust tour might've ran like the backstage of a theatre and pioneered such habits for future tours, but the wardrobe department remained a little out of control. We were all undoubtedly a little out of control at this point; it made sense our fashion was too. Plus, my team knew it was pointless and counterproductive to tell me what to wear.

No one told me what to wear.

CHAPTER SEVENTEEN
TERRIBLE
LOVE LETTERS
TO SLEEP

'WHAT PART OF BOWIE IS BIG?'

Are you suffering from confusion? That'll be *Bowie*. People are saying she's, or *it's* the next big thing, but that's a symptom of confusion. As someone who isn't currently suffering with the illness, I can confirm the only thing *big* about 'Bowie,' is her *breasts*. Double D to be precise.

We caught up with Bowie's bra backstage and here is what it had to say:

'Yeah, it's pretty great. Bowie gives me freedom, so I work in the day hauling her gigantic breasts and then she gives me the evenings off while she gets her back to carry them. It's been a hard adjustment from working for Tiny Titty Tina to being Bowie's breast' best friend, but I just love what I do!'

We'll be going backstage with Bowie's knickers next week to see just *how* wet she's making the charts!'

I'd never read anything about myself before, other than my own diaries, but they weren't inflammatory or about my breasts except that one time a kid at school spat chewing gum down my shirt and my nipple got stuck to my bra for three days. I wasn't accustomed to being written about or thought about. The idea that people would take an interest in anything other than my music seemed utterly irrelevant and outright stupid. Which, with the power of hindsight, makes me kind of crazy. I was naïve for thinking that a successful woman wouldn't be talked about and *not just talked about* but talked about the way she looked or who she fucked.

My music was irrelevant. The only place my music sold was in the record stores. My music didn't sell on magazine paper, and the newspapers knew that all too well. They'd known that for a very long time. Sex sells. Pretty sells. Fake sells. *My music written about objectively* does not and *will not* sell.

Still, I was horrified at the prospect that young girls would read such trash and form an image of myself based upon my talking bra and next week's knicker installation. Mortified that my voice or music was deemed irrelevant when I had a pair of tits they could talk about. It, therefore, made sense that men in music were written fairly based upon their music because they didn't have a pair of tits to be written about, and we all know the only thing worth writing about is tits.

I called up Molly after reading the article; she answered after 5 rings with a; 'I'm really busy fucking unless you're *really* upset or dying,' to which I responded: 'you're now really *not* busy.'
We talked for hours and hours devising our plan. The initial plan was to protest outside the magazine building, but then we both got high, and that shed light on how stupid that idea was, so we arranged the photoshoot instead. Molly had been with Frank Wood for over a year at this point, the longest Molly had been with any man other than the band, and that doesn't count because she wasn't sleeping with them (*all the time*).

That meant I had to trust the guy because if he had the patience and respect to stay around Molly *willingly*, for over a year, he must be pretty special.

I put all recording and tours on hold and flew out to France, arriving in a flat in Paris with Molly and Frank.

The initial idea was a nude shoot, artistically and creatively controlled by Molly and me to hide what we wanted and reveal what we wanted. The moment Paris and drugs got involved was the moment it went slightly off track. Fruit got included, cigarettes burnt the set, sex was exchanged, laughs were the soundtrack to the whole thing and by the end; the film was tossed out the window and onto the street; mistaken for the ashtray under the influence.

Whenever I got high after that day, I would get paranoid that a stranger in Paris had picked up the film and developed it; to the point where I'd call my manager every single time for a good year and tell him to; '*prepare for the worst and start going on damage control now.*' It never happened, I don't know where that roll of film ended up.

We shot again the next day *sober*, which was tedious, but it got the job done. The images were revealing enough for the seventies, but not revealing enough for the industry; precisely what we wanted. It was our little fight back, us grabbing hold of the reins and telling them we were in control and in control of our *own* bodies.

We printed the images on flyers with the tagline; '*we're more than our pussy's!*'

Then we plastered them all around Paris before catching a flight back to London and doing the same. The news had already broken in London, and the flyers were old news by the time they were up on lamp posts.

Most people were not impressed that the image of two women clutching hold of their vaginas were casually plastered on the same streets their children played conkers on. The moment we put a poster up, a mother tore it down.

I distributed a few hundred to as many addicts, dealers and general reprobates I could find hiding in London's dark spots. I paid most of them a small amount of money to spread the posters like chlamydia wherever they could thrust our femininity. This meant they were seen by the right kind of people: *my kind of people.* The forgotten; the sinners; the abused; the underrepresented.

If anyone's gonna grab their pussy for a cause; it's gonna be the girl that's got no choice but to sell hers to feed her child. You're not gonna catch a middle-class mother with two irons and four children at university, grabbing her crotch in the name of feminism. Those bitches wouldn't know what feminism was if their middle class, cocktail party friend baked it in a casserole and choked her on it. The entirety of London's underground saw the poster, and I'd have random women walk past me on the street; look me dead in the eye and thrust their pussy to me in the act of alliance.

I'd smile and go about my day knowing the revolution was coming.

The magazine in question followed up the next week with my knicker chat and then the week later they had a feast on the photographs, writing:

'UNDERDOG BRA AND KNICKERS FOR BIG BOOBED BOWIE SACKED AS BOWIE GOES INDEPENDENT AND TRIES TO RUN HER OWN COMPANY BY HERSELF!

The statement suggests she's in control of herself, but stripping naked and posting those photographs through people's doors is not a sign of sanity. The poor thing thought she could take on her own 'company' all by herself. How naïve. Everyone knows it takes a whole army of men to raise a woman.

We spoke to the bra who formally worked for Bowie for 6 months, and this is what he had to say: 'I'm pretty heartbroken, it was a good job, and it paid well. She's gone mad and is not gonna do herself any favours working without me. She can't go about her daily life without me! She thinks that being free from her assistants is going to be liberating, but she won't last. She'll be putting those big breasts of hers in the freezer for a break before she knows it!'

I oddly found the third article more amusing than outraging, and I didn't rise to it. I'd made my stand, and I'd said all I had to say. Fighting against the magazine for a second time would've started a feud I didn't have time to fight.

I had to resume the tour and get back on with things whether I liked what was being written or not. I tried not to pay attention or read anything about myself, which was easier said than done when they started to write about who I was leaving hotel rooms or apartments with, rather than my music. I'm not actually sure whether I've *ever* read an article written about my music- good or bad. I've read plenty on my sex life, but none about my *music.*

There's a whole book on Eddie's drumming called; '*how Eddie Wyatt's drumming made the world better and Bowie hotter.'*

Which is a 226-page love letter to my drummer who read it and called it '*art*,' before shagging the author promptly as a Great British thank you!

I knew I couldn't control what people were writing about me, but a fucking sentence on my lyrical writing would've been nice!

The 'Aladdin Sane' tour started how it always started; with excess arguments and drugs.

America seemed to make everything worse, but we just couldn't help ourselves. It's full of a lot of people I despise, and they have a lot of rules and living arrangements that put me on edge. I guess I just don't like performing to a room full of people who believe it's their '*right to bear arms*' 24/7 and bare those arms with guns to my concert. It put me on edge that someone could open fire at any given moment, and when it actually happened, was the exact moment I irrationally decided I was never going back.

I was being escorted out of the venue that particular night in San Francisco when a gristly voice yelled; 'SLUT'S GO TO HELL,' and shot the cigarette out my hand.

I was escorted out of precaution to hospital, where I was treated with a minor burn on my arm where the mixture of cigarette ash and bullet shrapnel had grazed my forearm.

I don't know to this day what happened to the man, but I'm sure I'll meet him when my time comes in *hell*.

It was a crazy time to be alive. I could write music, but with significant consequences. Before, the consequences had been a result of me *not* being able to play or record music. Now, these consequences, *like being shot at*, were a *direct repercussion* from making and recording music.

And when you experience trauma because of what you love, a complex kind of happens. You question whether what you love, is, in fact, worth loving; despite knowing with all you have, that life wouldn't be worth it without that love. But then the realisation that your life is at risk by doing the thing you love comes into your head, and I just got *stoned* to deal with it. And then I got stoned again and *again* until the scar on my arm faded, and I got a tattoo of a rocket back in London to cover it up, to try and forget it *and America.*

It worked for a while before my record label made me go back, which was where the drug addiction got a whole lot worse, and I overdosed again; although this time it wasn't as pretty.

It was a whole coma and two months less pretty than the last time.

Last time I overdosed was during the Aladdin Sane tour in our little American shack.

The time I spent alone on that tour was invaded by nightmares upon nightmares of my past. My rape, my abortion, my hardship, the fights, the overdoses. All the lowest of the lows, and not a sighting of the highest of highs that I'd had over the years. I felt hands I didn't want to feel, voices I didn't want to hear and images I had done my absolute best to bury and burn to never be seen again. When you lose your self-respect, or more specifically, when it is *fucked* out of you: a party seems like a great idea.

Then you host said party and swiftly realise, at somewhere between
five and six in the morning; when you're knee-deep in some stranger's
sick, your thighs mysteriously wet for blood, arm dripping pus from a
needle infection. A party is never a good idea unless it's your birthday
and you're *seven*.

Or when you attend a festival and lose a week of your life.

There's sick on my shoes, two empty baggies on my heel, a sunburnt
neck and two legs I can't feel. I'm playing twister with my tent, staring
at my neighbour of a crackhead, thinking what a fucking joke. He's
pissing on the pasta he's just boiled, and his tent's just caught fire. I tell
myself that's not me. I'm not that kind of addict. I'm a *beautiful* kind
of addict. The type of addict that writes poems and stories and
motorway banners that deter kids from making the same mistakes.
Only I've just shagged a 50-year-old bloke in a portaloo for a gram,
and now I can't find my hands.

I tried to stop abusing drugs for a bit. I told myself that I wouldn't take
any kind of drug on my own, which was a good thing in many ways
and a terrible idea in many others. My head was showing me a reel of
horrific things, and I couldn't even drown myself in enough cocaine to
forgot about it because I *suddenly* had a *conscience*.

I disconnected myself from everything I could quite physically
disconnect myself from, including clothes. Then I locked myself in
my American shack; telling Tommy to only let me out when I came to
the door and told him exactly what was in my head with no
retribution.

To cry and to mean it. I barricaded the doors with furniture to makeshift a lock. Tommy had come back to America at this point, and thank whatever God there is, he did.

I cut myself a gash on my leg so long the scar looks like I'm permanently wearing nude tights with a run on the shin. I cut my hair to the same length as Tommy's: *short.* I ate vegetable soup every single day for two and a half weeks, and I cried into it every single night.

I took heroin five times a day for a week straight and only survived because Tommy slept outside the shack the whole time and would check in on me through the window. He kicked the door down one evening, riding with me on horseback through the streets of New Orleans to the nearest hospital; where I was treated for two days before being kicked out with a pot of ice cream and a new hospital robe.

I'd bled so much onto the bed sheets you would never have known they were white, and I injected so much heroin into my arm I'd collapsed a vein and could no longer tolerate it in my body without being violently *sick.*

I couldn't remember how my body was supposed to feel, yet I was sure it wasn't this. Organs restlessly decaying with the ferocity of a new born inside of my skin that ached and drooled its hollowness. The itchiness as desperate as love for air. The pounding in my head subterranean beneath my thoughts. Every inch of me riddled with nihilistic terror.

I was, to be mild, *fucked.*

The insanity had finally hit me. My family curse had struck.

I was insane.

I had to be insane to shoot up so much to overdose for the third time, and I had to be mad to go straight back into writing and touring as though everything was hunky-dory.

As though I hadn't really nearly died; as though I hadn't thought about ending it all. As though I hadn't been the luckiest woman on Earth to be who I was and fucking *survive.*

Insanity is the people's war, and I was ravished by it.

There's truth in the fact you need insanity for art, I understand that now. No sane person can create art; for they have not surrendered their sanity to the arms of art and welcomed paint, or paper into their lungs to heave up their dredged sentiments onto sacrificial scraps of life.

Alongside insanity is addiction, in all its forms. Drug and alcohol addiction is somewhat most desired and accessible if your art form is within the virtuosity expanse of the artistic spectrum. However, addiction of sleep, of politics, of biscuits, of travel, of desire and of theft; are all noble pursuits of addiction if a crippling amount of unstable dependency is how you must surrender yourself.

I am, of course, partly if not *wholly* to blame for my suffering at that time. I hadn't spent the time to heal or recover; only to create; which is only a small part of the healing process.

I used things I shouldn't have to suppress how I felt, and even when I was capable of healing and moving on; I didn't. I blamed the world, I blamed my family curse and I arrogantly still do. My relationship with life is far too complex to put into words that have any meaning. It's beyond the classic: I love it, I need it, I hate it, it hates me. It's beyond a Hollywood script. I'm even afraid to say my relationship with life is more complicated than a Quentin Tarantino love story epic. He would direct the beginning exceptionally well; maybe even make me cry at the ending. But the whole mess in the middle would be precisely that: a *mess*. Not even a pretty mess, just a fucking *mess*. Lots of me hearing life telling me to stop or slow down and me doing the opposite because I'm too stubborn to even listen to life. *Imagine that!* Too stubborn for life, too lively for death. What a conflict the curse of life is.

So, rehab called, and I gave it a go because I needed some new inspiration and I'd heard from a lot of other musicians, that they wrote some of their best songs while watching their fellow addicts fuck up their lives even more.

'My problem with God is that, if he wanted me to live, then why the fuck did he make cocaine? Or why did he make the man or woman who made cocaine; or why did he make humans want and need cocaine? All I'm saying is; why would God want the opposite of me from what he created?

Why didn't he make apples addictive?'

Those were the first words I wrote in my rehab diary that inevitably got taken from me until further notice when the rehab techniques started working a little more.

I was reluctant (to say the least) to get clean. No one else was, and what fun was to be had sober? At that point in time, I'd never done anything fun sober in my life, other than play with bubbles as a kid and even then, I think I drank the liquid between running in circles.

My biggest problem was *sleeping*. Before the drugs, when I slept at night, I had terrible dreams. I envy anyone who wakes up in the morning and calls me to tell me they; '*slept like a baby thinking of marshmallows on friendly fires with the loves of their life's.*' *Good for you, Caroline, when I fall asleep all I see is death. Death in the shape of everyone I've ever fucking known.*

So, I took drugs to help me sleep because we all know that drugs stop you dreaming. And it was bliss. Let me tell you, I will never *romanticise* drug consumption, but I also won't *lie*. Drugs are *bliss*. I can't deny that. I don't encourage you taking drugs, because the bliss (as good as it is) is incredibly short and the horror that pursues lasts a hell of a lot longer- *trust me*. The belly aches, the sickness, the shits, the lying, the despondency, the comedown, the tears, the fallouts and the fights: they tend to last a *lifetime*. The moment you're an addict is the moment you sign up for a lifetime supply of front row tickets to your own show on '*how you gonna fuck up your life this time, pal?*' It's only fun to see the *once* I assure you.

I spent the entire time in rehab sleep-deprived, crawling up the walls begging for sleep. Apparently, that's a good sign, and it becomes a real low point when you're aware that begging for *anything* other than drugs means you're on the road to recovery.

I begged and begged for sleep. I don't know who I begged, but I bloody begged them for nights on end until I lost my voice and wrote terrible love letters to sleep; addressed to the rehabs secretary.

When I came out, I was greeted with a whole stack of magazines and newspapers that'd written about my intricate relationship with cocaine, and 12 drug binging stories (all lies) from people I trusted, sold for a couple of quid. My band weren't arsed that I'd been in rehab, as I wouldn't have been arsed if they'd fallen off the face of the Earth for 6 months either.

We functioned like a band when there was music. When there wasn't music involved; we were all single entities trying desperately not to be suckered into the void we were using music to fill. *Just your average functioning humans.*

The papers wrote about my endless nights of cocaine-snorting, lesbian loving, town mayor fucking in inner cities across the world. According to one magazine, I fucked a mayor in France while *simultaneously* fucking a dinner lady in Wolverhampton on the same night.

I must say they made it all sound a lot more glamorous than it was.

My nights under the influence were mostly spent trying to find my keys, then realising they were in my hands and then forgetting what the keys were for, while still looking for the keys in my hands. I wish I fucked a French mayor, but like most things they wrote, *it just wasn't true.*

Rehab wasn't a miracle that cured me. I didn't leave the rehab building thinking; '*I never, ever, ever want to even see cocaine again.'* No, I left rehab feeling tired and horny with the mindset of; '*if cocaine is presented to me I will think for longer about the implications of taking it, but I will no doubt and indefinitely snort it up my hooter because it's fucking cocaine and it would be rude not to!'*
It wasn't until a good few years later that I had my '*rehab'* moment. Rehab is great if it works, if not; it's just a complete waste of time and money. Rehab worked wonders on Eddie, but it unquestionably made me and Tommy better humans but *worse* addicts.

I was awful when under the influence. You'd think you'd gone back in time and were under Nazi occupation if you met me when under the influence at that time. I had no moral compass. I ignorantly blamed it on the fact that it felt as though the *world* had no moral compass when it came to its respect for *me*, but that's my well-bred arrogance talking. I was a bitch because of the drugs, and that's the end of it.

But for the '*Aladdin Sane'* tour, I was still a '*raging cocaine whore bitch,*' which was the press' cute new nickname for me.

Trying to stay clean in a rock n roll band, is like trying to dry the dishes with a soaking wet tea towel. It's just ineffective and a waste of time.

CHAPTER SEVENTEEN
BENJI

I'd had a pretty nasty stomach for a couple of days in America during the 'Diamond Dogs' tour; that I put down to the travelling, food and change of water. All the things people say to assure you you're not about to drop down stone-cold dead in a foreign country. A bad stomach is a side effect of lots of drugs. I was comfortably used to shitting myself in uncomfortable places. A bad stomach could also be a side effect of bad anxiety, something I was also used to.

I hated being a woman in my twenties as my body shifted and changed through dynamics I didn't understand. I was gaining weight in places I didn't know I could gain weight because of hormones I didn't think I had, jumping around inside of me. I was paranoid of falling pregnant every time I brushed past a man. I was stuck feeling helpless about gender equality, while simultaneously bathing in a degree of privilege that my 16-year-old self would never have conceived. I was replaying my rape and replaying my abortion on a toxic loop, like an 80's boy band that willingly jammed itself in the CD player. I was fingering myself most nights and then feeling bad about it and fucking some stranger as though it was my *duty,* and then I would have to drink to numb the inadequate thoughts floating about. I was an alcoholic, drug addict, masturbating, egotistic, musician whose music I couldn't even define because I was too busy worrying about my hair loss because of the fucking hormones! It wasn't like I had a mother who could direct me or a friend who could help me. My mother was too delusional to remember her twenties and my friends were all too stoned to sympathise or care that it was happening to them too.

This time felt different. This feeling inside of me was not the low-level hum of anxiety I was used to, or the extreme pit of regret I carried with me. This was much, *much* different; but I had a show to do. The adrenaline had wholly consumed my stomach by the time I was on stage and performing.

Until I miscarried.

Of course, at the time, I didn't entirely know what was going on. I assumed my period had finally come and come *heavily*. If anything, for the first few seconds bleeding, I was relieved. Then the pain in my stomach became unbearable, and I ran off stage and into the bathroom where the blood *also* became unbearable.

I'd never miscarried before, it's not something you're taught. There's no schooling on '*how to be a girl.'* There's no timeline to womanhood you're given alongside your first tampon.

I didn't know the difference between period blood and miscarriage blood and among the pure panic, I don't know anyone that would.

I hobbled off the stage, disorientated and dazed. It felt as though there was no floor beneath me and concrete walls trapping me by each of my wrists; tightening by the second.

While I could run, it felt as though I were getting nowhere. Like Scooby-Doo running down corridors with the same bricks and the same décor just passing by as he runs and runs and runs.

The bathroom felt as far away as the edge of the Earth, and I collapsed through the door, prepared to plunge off the face of the planet in a heartbeat.

Of course, I didn't, and it strangely shocked me more. I was panting, bleeding, spinning and howling about the Earth on the piss-stained floor of a hired portaloo. The stories this portaloo must hold, and now I'm adding to the novel. I was sick on my legs at the thought. It was a messy affair.

M ran into the bathroom, to be greeted with a wide-eyed me, legs apart, knickers around my ankles blood and sick everywhere. In the panic and pain of it all, I'd rolled around the floor meaning I'd pushed the blood around like flour on a rolling pin. It was all over the floor, the walls, the toilet, the sink, my hands, legs, hair- *everywhere,* just *everywhere.* It must've been in my eyes too, for I couldn't rid the image for months.

It wasn't until M came in, that I started to panic as she shouts for help and an ambulance. At this point, I have stopped bleeding, I'm just drenched in blood like I've just casually bathed in a bath of it. Or I'm the star of a poorly prepared horror film that has gone horribly wrong. The adrenaline was still surging through mine and everyone's veins. I don't think rock n roll stars are entirely trained for these kinds of ordeals.

Dump them in the middle of a revolution, or a drugs den and they'll thrive. But dump a rock n roll crew in the middle of a horrific miscarriage, and they all step aside nonchalantly, as I clean myself up the best I can, to tremble back on stage and finish the set, 3 songs early. I really don't like to let folk down.

By the end of the set, the adrenaline had most definitely worn off, and the agony of the whole experience was pretty damn hard to swallow as I rode in the ambulance feeling numb in shock and grief. No one needed to tell me what had just happened, I knew exactly what had happened. I'd just miscarried on stage in front of 10 thousand people. It might sound silly, as those 10 thousand people didn't know I was miscarrying; in fact, a few days later they were told I had a stomach bug, and that was the reason for the shorter set. Yet, in my head, I'd just shared the most intimate experience of my life with 10 thousand odd strangers and the father, somewhere, behind the stage, *unaware*. 10 thousand people had just seen my baby leave me. My baby *die*.

It felt so cruel for it to be so public. To be a woman and have every single part, even your *womb*, publically viewed. Everybody had an opinion on every part of my body, and now it seemed they could have front row access to my miscarriage as well. I understood the timing of my miscarriage was nobody's fault or planning, but the aftermath of being a woman in rock n roll who had lost their child on stage was *mortifying*.

When the news eventually left the safe confines of my personal life; I would get asked when I was going to try for the next one in nearly every interview. People would ask what I would have called the child; they wondered if Tommy really was the father; they asked what kind of miscarriage it was and whether my drug consumption was the cause of it.

When Tommy, the *father*, was interviewed; he was asked what it was like touring with the band, and what to expect from us musically in the upcoming album.

There were no boundaries to the questions I was being asked, or *point*, to be honest.

And when you've miscarried so publically, you start to believe the boundaries are gone yourself. In my eyes, everyone's seen me with the blood of my dead child underneath my fingernails that I spent weeks scrubbing off. Everyone's seen the foetus of my child on the cold, dirty portaloo floor. I have no other secrets, everyone else has seen me naked, what is left of my privacy?

At the time, it felt like I had nothing left.

I lay in that hospital bed as the doctor confirmed that I had miscarried and talked through the next couple of weeks and what I should and shouldn't do. It all went completely over my head as I watched Tommy between the slatted blinds burst into tears, screaming before running off to a dirty, filthy squat to shoot up on his own for two weeks.

I guess if I still wasn't miscarrying, I would've gone on a two-week heroin binge too but, you know; *priorities.*

I was alone and very muchly scared. 28 years old, the feeling of my child just tingling inside of me. The unfairness of existence; the fingertip distance of another life making my hands turn numb; the desperate and desolate ache of missing something you never had. That's the strangest feeling that there is no word for.

Missing something you never had.

What is there to miss? Lost opportunities, what could have been, a different life?

I didn't know I was pregnant, but I missed that kid deeply as soon as it was gone.

I missed something I never had.

How do you miss something that you don't know what it looked like, something so faceless and soundless, as you realise you miss a voice you've never heard? You miss a touch you've never had and a smell you've never smelt. You miss hugging it, despite not knowing what that hug ever felt like. You miss talking to it, despite never even hearing the sound of its voice. You start to miss these things you've never had in your life before, and now you've tasted them you can't get enough. I decided that even if it was just a memory to miss; I was going to miss it and miss it badly, deeply and ragingly to keep the memory alive. I had no idea why I felt the need to keep on missing something I never had and let it drive me crazy to the point of further addiction, but I did it anyway.

Tommy went on his binge, got it all out of his system (his feelings, not the drugs that is) and came home with barely any eyes or functioning veins. He collapsed on the kitchen floor and overdosed right at my feet for the second time.

He was admitted into the hospital and came around a couple of days later when our child had died exactly three weeks to the day.

A coma for an addict is a good night's sleep. He came to, revitalised and sympathetic. Me putting Tommy in an ambulance and allowing him to fuck up two weeks of his life by overdosing was my way of being compassionate. Or as sympathetic as you can be to the father of your miscarried child who's an addict that went on a two-week binge, while you lay on your bathroom floor for three days crying and vomiting.

Him, finally putting his addiction to one side for a couple of hours and nodding while I cried in his hospital bed; was *his* way of being sympathetic and for the love of God we functioned, and still function like that now.

We talked for a bit about what had happened, although neither of us had anything mature or sensible to say. Neither of us were ready or indeed wanted a child at that time, it was more just naturally a shock to both (arguably more *my*) system.

Tommy rattled on about how he lay on the mattress in the squat and thought about a child running around him in circles, and he said it drove him crazy.

We then argued about how the child wouldn't be in the squat, and all children would drive him crazy and then we gave up talking responsibly and lay in silence for a bit more.

Tommy instead wrote me a letter, posted through the bedroom door a couple of weeks later noting how sorry he was. Sorry for not being there, sorry for the loss, sorry for the ache and sorry for everything bad that had ever happened in the whole wide world. He incited how he couldn't make any good from this or couldn't make any good from any bad and honestly told me how that is what makes him feel an inadequate human. When he realises, there's so much bad in the world, and he can't always control it. When bad things happen to the people he loves, and he can't do squat about it; he shoots and snorts until he can't feel a thing to notice the difference.

He named the child Benji and told me it had blue eyes and black hair, which genetically didn't make sense, but he was very handsome, so I let it slide. Tommy wrote about struggling to comprehend my pain and asked me to explain it to him in detail. All I could say was; *put your grief in your stomach and try to swallow that.*

The letter finished with more apologies and an explanation of why he will be a good father, *just not today.*

I have not yet been a child enough to be an adult. I have not yet recovered from life enough to give it, and I have not yet forgiven myself or repaid you the respect and the gratitude you and the child deserves for harmony to be in our lives.

Cohabitation with a child, while the instability is still rocking in my stomach, seems mediocrely crazy.

I will surrender everything when the time comes, I think you know that. I am not making excuses. I'm a fucked up addict, with no job or direction in life as of yet; everything I fucking do is an excuse. Maybe parenthood will be my direction, who knows. I'm really, incredibly sorry for the grief you've experienced and the pain we've experienced together. I hope you know I'll always be here, a little fucked, but still here.

Yours, Tommy.'

And that was that. You lose your child, you talk about it, you cry, you pretend to grieve, you start to grieve, you think you're grieving, then you actually begin grieving and then you *stop*, although never, *not really.*

I'm still grieving now, wondering where the child would be in this book instead of this segment. Would Benji be backstage at Glastonbury, would Benji be with us on our Europe roadtrip? Who knows?

Benji's quite comfortable in this part of the book. Some people must be a part of the tragic moments; otherwise, *Earth would be so very lonely.*

CHAPTER EIGHTEEN
I THINK I'M DYING
LET'S GET
OUTTA HERE!

Me and Molly made a promise when we were kids, that if one of us turned up, suddenly, out of the blue with a campervan and a boot full of booze: we'd drop whatever we were doing, and go on a road trip for the foreseeable future. So, when Molly turned up outside my Bromley home (the one we stole) in a blue VW, honking on the horn shouting: '*I think I'm dying, let's get outta here!* I dropped everything and hopped in the van with my passport, notebook, guitar and a handful of cash and cards.

"Where we are going?"

"Where d'ya wanna go?"

"Anywhere."

"Does anywhere have a café I can piss in?"

"I doubt it. But I bet it has a toilet!"

Molly had packed the essentials. Drugs, alcohol, cowboy hats, our favourite music cassettes and six French novels she begged me to read. She packed some niche French music for me to listen to, every single Little Richard album, some Elvis tracks, a bit of Elton John, all of the Rolling Stone's cassettes for a good sing-along and a handful of singles we liked. They were on rotation with our drug intake. It was Little Richard, snort a line; Elvis, smoke a spliff; Rolling Stones, another line, and then a single of our choice, and inject a vein. Stop at a petrol station for a piss, *repeat.* A blissful order of pandemonium.

Molly painfully drove under the influence down to Dover, where we got the ferry over to Calais. Once we were in France, we just kept driving. Both of us were accustomed to not sleeping, and more importantly, *functioning* outstandingly well without sleep. I think we both took it in turns to drive for three solid days without rest. We stopped off at a lake we both found pretty, somewhere near Chamonix, before driving straight through to Italy.

Molly had a brief affair once with an Italian and would be flown out on his credit card to his summer villa once every two weeks for a good six months. The wife was going to find out about the affair, so Molly blackmailed him and said she'd keep quiet if he gave her the house, which she'd grown rather fond of. It was a typical Italian villa on the very top of a steeping, cobbled street mountain with nothing but greenery and an array of rainbow plants surrounding the house as though it were amidst a kaleidoscopic jungle. The kitchen was a marbled masterpiece and the garden, like something from a Greek fantasy. Every bedroom had its own bathroom, and every bathroom had its own Jacuzzi. The house conveniently came with its personal chef and cleaner, meaning the fortnight we spent there was exhausted in exuberance luxury.

Molly always did have excellent taste in men to have an affair with.

We left Italy when Molly lit a fire in the garden and simultaneously forgot about the fire. Meaning half the beautiful Italian jungle was consumed in flames that destroyed many of wildlife's homes and one out shack shed Molly used to shag the husband's son in.

We drove to Switzerland for a bit, sleeping in the van outside petrol stations because we couldn't find anywhere that lived up to the Italian house expectations until we found a lovely, monstrous unoccupied house in Montreux on Lake Geneva that was calling for us. We could both afford to pay for a rental house or a quirky hotel that sold homemade muffins, and it wasn't like Switzerland lacked beautiful homes or hotels. But me and Molly hadn't stolen anything in a very long time, and the road trip was all about nostalgia. We used to take clothes from dustbins back in London when we first met, and bits of embroidery buttons from outside factory's too.

So, we broke into the home of a very nice-looking family who had a whole wall dedicated to their family photos and decadent hunting life, in the name of nostalgia. We stayed there for four nights; which was the length of time no one was home, escaping rather rapidly out of the master bedroom window, bombing into the pool and dragging ourselves into our campervan and off into the night. Molly developed a pretty bad dose of Bronchitis around this time, sleeping in the back of the camper for four days while I got us over to Austria.

We both liked Austria. I think it was mostly because there wasn't much there and neither of us had been around Austria much on tour or holiday. We found and paid, for a chic little shack in the hills next to a ski slope that was out of season and stayed for a month.

Our neighbours were lovely, we got to know them pretty well, they still write me a Christmas card each year. Mindy and Sam Durrell were an English couple that moved out to Austria with their son Marcus, who was a ski instructor. Mindy was a translator and attempted to teach us both German which failed with Molly. She'd only just learnt French, and the drugs were burning out the rest of her brain. It's a good job Mindy, and Sam had a relaxed '*northern*,' ethos on life because Molly had started to make a habit out of getting stoned at 4am and rolling down the ski slope naked. Mindy would have to bandage her up every morning before I had even awoken, as she'd tumble daily slap bang into the back of their 4by4. Molly was a human cockerel waking up the Durrell's. I'd wake up to find a bruised and dirty, exposed Molly Jagger on my doorstep giggling to herself.

I'd read during the day, lying on the patch of grass in front of the house, while Molly slept for a couple of hours. Sam would cook every night on their BBQ and invite us down for tea, which we'd gladly eat. We'd exchange a bag of weed for supper eat night, which Mindy and Sam didn't seem to have a problem with.

One night we all ate too little and drank too much, and me and Molly ended up performing a very loose rendition of '*Can't you hear me knocking*,' on top of Mindy and Sam's house.

We enthusiastically jumped up and down together, bursting through the roof, landing conveniently on top of Mindy and Sam's king-sized bed. The next day we skinny-dipped in the nearby lake and Molly drowned trying to retrieve her hat from the bottom of the lake. We rushed to hospital where they managed to clear her lungs of water and revive her, diagnosing her with acute kidney failure too. Molly stole a bag full of morphine and demanded I break her out before the doctor came back. I plonked her in the back of the campervan, still hooked up to a steady supply of morphine that she then controlled herself, and by the time we got back to the house she'd passed out again, and I turned straight back around.

I selfishly left her in hospital for a week while I went hiking with Mindy, camping on top of a nearby mountain that did not shelter us from a theatrical storm that flooded our camping area. We trekked back down the following day to find Molly shagging Sam outside, which promptly ended our time in Austria. I don't think the fact Molly is dead is the only reason Mindy doesn't send Molly a Christmas card.

I was starting to miss Tommy, and home and making music by this point, but Molly was just getting into it. She was thriving. Ultimately dying too, but thriving none the less.
A girl can thrive in the conditions of death, like a weed can spurt from un-watered ground.

The mischief of pissing in petrol stations and eating fast food every night. Of lying in double beds until mid-afternoon, reading French novels with frothy coffee. Drinking and smoking with exotic foreign people and fucking them too; all with no repercussions or responsibilities. Back in Italy, we went shopping for ball gowns, that we wore to breakfast the following day and entirely ruined by swimming lengths underwater in the icy pool. In Austria, we bought Lederhosen and crashed a local wedding, singing for the bride and groom in recompense. Molly dove off a ten-foot diving board in Monteux on Lake Geneva, submerging into the tar looking lake and remerging with a gash on her forehead. We drove through a red light on our way to Germany and were stopped by two handsome police officers who invited us to a formal dinner for the German Police. We attended, wearing hot pants and leather jackets, abruptly thrown out for offering the super intendant a gram of smack.

The road trip was Molly's dream. Everything she'd ever dreamed of doing, all the chaos you could possibly imagine- we endued. We got lost in a national park in France and were found a day later by a park ranger who fought off a deer with his bare fists, as we were escorted back to the entrance. I pissed in the sink of a wealthy Frenchman who offered us champagne and oysters.
I rode a horse through the streets of Milan, with the words: 'dance with me,' on the back of my jacket; forming a congregation of people and couples all slow dancing to the national anthem performed by buskers in the main square.

We broke into a French farm and spray painted all the cows pink. Molly broke into a school and played tennis all afternoon on their large tennis courts with very little clothes on. We hosted a house party in a house we didn't own or pay for, emptying the pool to fill it with balls to make an adult-sized ball pit perfect for a dreamy orgy on the French Riviera. We went to sleep in France one night on our way back to England and awoke on a rather large and luxurious boat in the middle of the ocean off a Greek island. Molly crashed a speedboat into a bar and was fined for the damage. It was *pandemonium*.

We had to stay in Greece for longer than we would've liked to because we couldn't find the van. We had no idea whether we'd left it somewhere in Greece and couldn't find it or, left it in France. We had no idea and no memory. So, we'd spend two hours a day trekking around different Greek islands in the hunt for a blue VW. We eventually found one and broke into it, thinking it was ours, quickly discovering it wasn't when a child started crying, and its father punched us both for breaking and entering.

In Rhodes, we both grew fond of a little bar called '*Hop,*' that a lovely short man named Barak owned with his partner Alec. I painted their dance floor, which was a communion of tiles. I painted each one a different colour, so they had a rainbow, which, when under the influence, looked absolutely exceptional if you span around. Molly swear she saw the meaning of life spinning around on that floor under the influence of enough smack to tranquillise 7 horses.

"The colours man, that's what it means. The phantasmagoria, man."
"Do you know what phantasmagoria means?"
"I'm an economics kid, Penny. I know what everything means."

We slept above the bar, sharing a double bed for a few weeks before I got bored of Molly kicking me in her sleep. I'd wake up before the sun and watch it rise on a very particular rock by the sea. The rock looked like Tommy from the side, it felt more than arousing to sit on his face. I missed him and home profoundly. Much more deeply than I thought I would. And much more deeply than I ever had before. A few years earlier, I would've fled the country and travelled Europe with Molly bearing absolute joy, without burden or care for anyone I would leave behind. I didn't have anyone to miss.

Now, I realised, I did. I had people and things to miss. I had built a life to miss. I had created things and met people that I would deeply ache for. I yearned for my home that I had poured so much love into. I hungered for Tommy's arms, and I longed for my saxophone.
I wasn't a kid anymore.
A kid with no accountabilities or obligations. I had a cat. I had six plants in the kitchen to water. I had a frequent enough shag in Tommy, he was (although not officially) my boyfriend. I had a house to dust, and a career to maintain. I had a record label to appease, and a manager to pay.
Molly had all of these things too, but I think she also had enough drugs to forget about it.

I'd ask her every morning what her middle name was, and it was a different name every day, my favourite being: Molly: 'Molly, *Molly Jagger.*'

She was sick. Quite tearfully sick. It became horrifically apparent in Greece when she took too much acid and metamorphosed into this world where everyone were bugs, and she kept trying to stamp on us all to squish us or catch us in a fly net. She wouldn't eat unless you fed her while she was dozing off to sleep. She could only sleep if you slipped a bit of brandy into whatever she was drinking, and that would only cause more fuss as she hated brandy because it always made her sick.

It was purgatory. I couldn't watch Molly suffer or mess up her life anymore. The chaos wasn't fun anymore. We got in a taxi to the airport where I put Molly on a plane to Minnesota and myself on a flight back home. A mutual friend of ours was waiting for her at the airport to take her to the Hazelden Foundation treatment centre, where she had a bed for treatment.

I was anxious about letting her on a plane by herself but had got rather used to creating a good enough cocktail to wipe her out for 20 odd hours when I needed to.

I mustn't have got the cocktail quite right this time, as she awoke mid-flight screaming and kicking. Splitting an air hostess' head open and spitting on a five-year-old child who called her a nut job. She was arrested when she landed and never made it to rehab.

That misshapen flight was quite possibly the death of her.

CHAPTER NINETEEN
FRIENDS WITH LOVER AFFLICTIONS

When I arrived home, I walked through the airport to see my face on the front of the daily mail. An unfavourable photograph of me in my early twenties, stumbling outside a club that I can't remember. Tommy told the Daily Mail I was raped by a booker and aborted the child illegally. Turns out my Tommy was never '*cured*' while I was dealing with the miscarriage.

His addiction had only got worse.

He sold my story to the daily mail for one night of narcotic euphoria. The only words I said to him were; *I hope it was worth it.*

Tommy was the only person who knew of my rape and my trauma, telling him these exact words; 'this is the *one thing* I need control over and don't want anyone knowing. If you do tell anyone, I will shoot you.' He was there that night when I was raped. I didn't really have a choice but to tell him what he already knew.

So, I put a gun to his head. It wasn't hard to get a hold of a gun, even easier for someone so absolutely desperate they'd do anything to get it. I got a gun, I stormed straight into the house, I pinned him up against the wall, and I put the gun to his head.

In the moment, I was the least bit hurt about my story being released, which was the thing that surprised me the most. I thought that my story of rape and abortion, being out in the world; would be like relocating my heavenly house onto the grounds of hell. It wasn't. People were compassionate and understanding, and when I said; 'I don't wanna talk about it,' most of the time, people respected that.

I was the most hurt that I had told him it would be the *one* thing that would hurt me the most, yet he did it anyway. And didn't just do it, he did it for one night of getting high in a squat on his own. His addiction was incomprehensively out of control, and I was the least bit bothered.

We were all out of control. Plummeting, cascading and free-falling into obscurity.

I had my own parachute to worry about.

The gun was to his head, his eyes were wet, his arms still bleeding from interrupting his shooting, the belt dangling limply like his soul out of its cage. There was still compassion in his eyes, yet no remorse. I begged him for an answer, I asked him for a why and all he could say was; the *money.*

They paid him a hundred quid for the story, which was barely enough to keep him sane for a single night.

I shot him in the foot and walked away. I didn't see him for *four months.* He was sent to rehab that next day after his hospital discharge for his toe and told that the rest of the band would not go see him until he could apologise and *mean* it. In the first week, I received 72 apology letters all starting with; '*I'm so sorry,*' and ending with; '*but the addiction is just too much.*'

Then I started getting hate mail from him. Long, ludicrous letters inciting how much he hated me for putting him in there and how I was the most vile human for shooting him in the foot. Then I received drawings of him stabbing me or shooting me, or one time, *rather creatively*; hanging me by my pubic hair in a crane in the sky, over a 60-foot canyon.

Then he wasn't allowed to send me anything and called me once a day leaving the same message; '*I want to sort this out, call me back.*' Eventually, he stopped all contact until one day, out of the blue, I received a neat looking letter with gracefully written handwriting addressed to; *My Penny.*

It read;

'My Penny,

Don't hate me. Think illy of me. Find me vile, fucking pin a picture of me to a dartboard and routinely stab my eyes out. Throw me off a cliff in your dreams, throw me off a cliff in real life. Wish me aids, wish me death, wish me an end so vile and horrific it hurts you too.

But don't hate me. I could stand death, but I couldn't stand you hating me. I would end it all, and I wouldn't rest easy, wouldn't rest at all. I'd be a wallowing, weeping shit failure of a ghost that even the underworld would spit back out.

You are suffering for my wrong doing. You're in pain because of my addiction; it's not fair, or right or acceptable. While I wish there was something I could do to make this all okay, I understand it could never possibly be okay.

I don't want your redemption or forgiveness; I do not deserve it. I don't wish for anything at all from you.

My only hope is that you can heal. I hope the Earth is kinder to you than I was and I hope it helps you recover because nothing I could ever do or say *will* and I understand that, as much as I hate it.

I hate myself. I hate you for not shooting me in the fucking head. I want to feel the pain you felt, but I know I have friends that good they'd never do anything close to the hurt I caused you; which makes me wish you'd fucking shot me more.

I want to be able to sit in the same room as you again. I want to be able to watch you laugh again. I want to make love to you so bad, I'm sore. I want to be able to hear you sing still. Ridding me of those things will not punish me for they are engraved in my head- so much so, they were the images that got me through this. This awful *this*. If you want to punish me: hate me and I'll accept that. I will not protest, I will understand.

If you want to seek revenge; tempt me with drugs enough, and I will no doubt fail and get hooked again. I've always had lousy self-control, I fell in love with you after a shag for Christ sake. If you want to forgive me; do so at your own doing; for I have accepted the fact I do not deserve forgiveness from anyone- *you or God.*

If, by any miracle, you want to still love me, or like me, or tolerate me in very small doses; it will be you I'll be praying to at night. *My God.*

You'll take on that shape, that holy crucifying shape; for if you still have that love inside of you; you must be made of utter stardust. I'm telling you, Penny, I don't know why you would even *tolerate* a boy like myself.

Yet that is what I can see you doing. I have dreams of you smiling at me in a corridor one day, and the world aligning back into order. I have these dreams where you are the one who hands life to children; where you are the one that presses a button to make people smile. I don't know what the Earth did to deserve you, but it must've felt fucking incredible when it put you on this soil.

Sorry isn't enough, but it is truly all I have.

If my life were enough, you know I'd give it to you.

I'm deeply sorry; I've been deeply wrong.

Take from this, the unnerving hidden face of utter cruelty and never trust a man like you so graciously trusted me.

I will take that honour to my grave, as my greatest triumph.

I still love you and forever will.

Sorry.

Tommy.'

I read it and wept. Tommy meant every word. He'd bled onto that page and was now sat in a rehab bed, entirely empty except for his regret and tears. I didn't feel sorry for him, but I did miss him *deeply*. I thought that made me a crazy person until his words made me realise I was only human. Only human to miss my best friend. Only human to miss someone who made me laugh and smile and forget the world existed. Only human not to hate someone who did me wrong, so to save my own dignity and self-worth.

I called up the centre and told them he could be released whenever they felt he was ready, which was the next week. I also called up the rest of the band and told him he'd be coming home. They were madder than me, out of respect and commodore towards myself. They protected me, they loved me, they didn't want to see me hurt again and were pained at the hurt that had been caused. I was proud of them, teary towards their small acts of compassion.

M put my gun to Tommy's head the moment he came through the door while Eddie whipped his back repeatedly with a bike chain. Tommy was the least bit surprised and had not a single care in his eyes.

Shooting him would be too kind, he still had *some suffering* to do.

I welcomed him into my arms where he wept for half an hour, routinely sobbing the words; '*I'm sorry,*' until the night came and I made him sleep. By morning there was music coming from every room in the house, and all seemed to function as it once did.

And we kept on beating and beating and beating, and the noise of the hurt seamlessly faded into the background. I haven't *forgiven* him exactly; I don't think I ever could. But I don't *hate* him, I could never *hate* him.

I love him. I love him like I love the night.

I simply *need* it.

The thing is with Tommy; I still don't know at what point our relationship changed. I don't know when we went from friends to lovers, I don't know how that happens. I don't know what part of the universe prescribes friends with lover afflictions. I guess I must thank it, whatever, or *whoever* it is that made me look at Tommy one day and think: '*fuck, I think I'm in love.*'

And not just *in love,* but like really, seriously, mind-numbingly *in love.* The kind of love that doesn't need any other words after it. I love him. *That's all.*

There's a lot of different forms of love. You don't love chocolate the same way you love your mum. You don't love your best mate, the same way you love your bed: but you love them all the same. That's why it's so tricky. Differentiating, the fakes from the reals. Tommy was my real diamond, but I think he must've been a fake to start; which is what makes our relationship so complicated.

He caused all the chaos in my life, meaning naturally, I wanted to banish that part of my life far, far away. But every time I did, I either got bored or went insane, and the two are fuel for addiction and dismay, and I would just miss him more than I wouldn't want him. There comes a time where you must think: what hurts the most? The havoc? Or not having him around? It's always not having him around. It's always going to be that. Chaos can be fun if you make it. Missing someone is *never* fun. You can't have a party out of losing someone, the same way you can have a party out of a scandal in the Daily Mail.

It wasn't long, however, before the shock settled in and things fizzled out. The band were not as gracious towards Tommy as I was. They'd spit on everything he owned and most often still buckle his knees with a bike chain if they could get him alone. I'd relentlessly told them to forget about it and stop avenging them on my behalf, but they made it perfectly clear that I had nothing to do with it. They were individually disgusted with what their friend had done to their other friend, and I think I'd kept them in the studio too long for them to see sense. I couldn't forget that beneath all the hurt, he was an addict. Just like the rest of us. We all knew what he was going through, and he was the only one who'd successfully completed a substantial amount of time in rehab with mostly beneficial effects. If anything, he was better than the rest of us. By societal standards anyhow.
We took a small break, and Tommy left.

For the first time in Tommy's life, he made a decision by himself. I gave him the idea, but he made the decision to board a plane and leave for Berlin himself. We were civil, and things were fine, but they were *just fine* and being '*just fine*' hurts after a while. There wasn't as much laughter in the house, things could get awkward if we wanted them too and we only really spoke if we had to. I didn't hate him, I never could, and I know he didn't hate me. We just didn't *love* each other. I couldn't find the strength to conjure up enough lies to make it all seem more than '*fine.*' Neither of us had the strength for that at that particular time.

He chose Berlin because it was the one place he hadn't had the chance to properly explore yet when we'd been over to Europe touring. I packed his socks (he always forgets socks), made him a sandwich and said a small goodbye as he left for the airport. I wasn't particularly sad. I knew things would be different and I'd have to adapt to not having, what at times, felt like a child around my ankles 24/7. That kind of adaptation happens quietly and swiftly, almost overnight. That form of adaptation is not what books are written about, or people become professors for. It's the loneliest form of adjustment, and yet the most liberating.

I woke in the following weeks, to find myself more productive and focused than I'd felt in years. I was capable of cleaning and organising without distraction or effort.

I could write in quiet and comfort knowing that no one would walk through the door and throw pennies at my feet to annoy me and get my attention to play catch outside with the neighbour's cat.

I continued my natural process of writing and creating, singing and performing; with a haze of *lull.* I was quite centred and calmed. It was a welcomed change from the calamity of drug-infused, suicidal euphoria Tommy endorsed upon my daily life as natural as he breathed.

I knew he was a good man, with good intentions; but it was hard to remember that when my life was so much cleaner and arguably happier without him in it. I had the feeling that I'd wasted years of my life with him, yet I knew that were a lie because I didn't know *how exactly* I'd wasted them. I couldn't give you *one* reason; not even the drug use or constant childish arguing, as to how he spent my years. So, I knew it not to be true, and I knew I would eventually miss him, and that sucked.

He didn't write or call, and I didn't either. I didn't think we would, I simply assumed he'd turn up at my doorstep one day and be back in my life as though he were never gone. When a year went by, I feared that he would never come to my doorstep again, and that's when I started to miss him. I missed the childish arguments. I missed him leaving his socks in my shoes. I missed him chewing straws and putting them in my mouth when I yawned.

I missed him reading newspaper clippings backwards and asking me to figure out the story. I missed the way he walked, it always made me laugh. I missed his forms of encouragement, and I missed him sitting in the corner of my room watching. Just *watching*. He watched everything *a lot*. He was good at that: *watching*.

He'd watch how I'd write and how I'd read. He'd watch how I got dressed and how I tied my shoes. He was always very boy-like when he did it. He wore the enthusiasm of a young schoolboy wanting to learn from his professor rather well.

He's always looked like a child to me.

Maybe it was my maternal instincts that made me fear for his wellbeing in the big city of Berlin in such a turbulent time. Perhaps it was my own naivety lathered in denial for how I truly felt towards him. I just woke up one morning and suddenly couldn't stand the thought of my Tommy all alone in Berlin. It was the same morning I got the very first postcard from him, the first contact we'd had in *18 months*.

'*My Penny,*

I woke up yesterday head to toe dripping with sweat. I'd dreamt you were ill, really sick again and it woke me. It felt so real, I feel so tormented. Are you well? You know I see omens in my dreams, please keep yourself safe Pen. I couldn't forgive myself if you were sick and I hadn't reached out.

*Berlin is keeping me warm, but it's not without conflict. I've shared
your music plenty. You've become a beacon of hope amongst some
of us. Take pride in that.*

*Hope you're well,
I've missed you.*

Your Tommy.'

Me and Tommy both share the sight of omens in our dreams. We're
riddled with the unfortunate ability to see premonitions amongst our
slumber thoughts. It can be a hindrance or a help; mostly the first
kind. I'd been suffering from a blocked ear and wretched cough for
shy of a week before Tommy's letter. I'd thought nothing of it and
continued to not worry about it as I boarded a plane and flew to
Tommy.
I couldn't reply in writing, I had to see him.

I didn't care for pettiness or why we went our separate ways in the first
place. I wanted him, at that moment in time, I missed him deeply,
and I wanted him. For comfort, for laughter and for fun. I went with
no intentions or plans other than to sit with Tommy and talk for what
I'd hoped would be weeks' worth of unifying.

Tommy was the same as Tommy had always been. A thieving, child with a warm and welcoming heart. His apartment was above a bakery on a quiet and unsuspecting street on the East side of the Berlin wall. He had a whole collection of English books scattered on the floor, an array of coats strewn on chairs and dirty dishes piled neatly in the bathroom. When I asked him why the pots weren't in the kitchen, he simply said: '*Camouflage*,' and I somehow knew *exactly* what he meant.

We drank German wine and ate English food. He read me stories from German newspapers and introduced me to all his neighbours with pride. I slept next to him on his pull-out bed in the living room space and showered after him, so I could graciously use the warmer water. We'd have two cigarettes and a pot of coffee each after sex. I danced for him every Sunday morning as our religion. He made pancakes every single morning and sang the same melody every night. I'd never heard it before, but I liked it. Tommy read to me little bits he'd written, which was a welcomed surprise since I had never read any of his writing before. I don't think he wrote before Berlin, it was a kind place to him.

We went out to the odd bar to drink and dance. It was unusual for us to keep so low key and close together in quietness, but we did. It was a deep connection that we suddenly shared in Berlin. I didn't want to dance in a room full of sweaty Germans, I wanted to sit on his lap in his small apartment as he told me about the bakery's recipe for pretzels.

I didn't care for drugs or even for the intensity of music at that time. Not to say I'd forgotten about music and stopped wanting to create and write. That's never been the case. I was just able to put that part of me that always needed noise and lyrics and performance; to one side for a few weeks to breathe. That's what it felt like more than anything: *breathing*. I realised how choked I was in London and it was nice to be able to breathe again.

Tommy was just able to be him, without the band, without me, without anyone or anything telling him otherwise or whipping him with a bike chain for *one mistake*.

Berlin was the best thing for Tommy. And *us*.

Then, I rather suddenly fell ill. The cold I had developed quite drastically seized my lungs, and it became apparent that I needed a doctor and needed one *quick*. Tommy was as frantic as he's always been and scuppered me into his arms, patrolling his street crying out for a doctor. I was too weak to walk or scream with him; I merely lay limp in his arms and fell in and out of consciousness.

He went from door to door, begging and offering all the money and clothes he had for a doctor or someone who could offer me refuge or anything to help. I disintegrated into the night, barely able to keep my eyes open as my lungs grew weaker, and my breathing slowed.

I had no intention of dying, yet I knew I was close to an end. I had assumed the end was death at that moment. I never knew it would be life: *life as I knew it*.

Tommy's search for help waned into the morning when he was punched several times for waking up angry men who had work in the morning. We travelled through homes and gardens so not to be caught by the guards patrolling the wall. In the end, Tommy approached a guard. He lay me on the ground, my back became sodden with the fresh morning dew, and my head almost caved into the concrete as he stepped away from my body which silently begged for his return. I watched him lift his arms above his head as three men pointed their guns at his chest and he screamed; 'HELP HER PLEASE, SHE NEEDS A DOCTOR NOW!'

The guards remained silent, vigilant and cold as Tommy wailed for help and begged for mercy. He threw all the money he had at the guards' feet and begged them to take me to the other side and to a doctor.

I couldn't open my eyes anymore; they were swollen with agony.

The last words I heard from Tommy were: 'Please, if only you knew who she is to me and the world; you don't have to bring her back, I just have to save her. *She can't die.*'

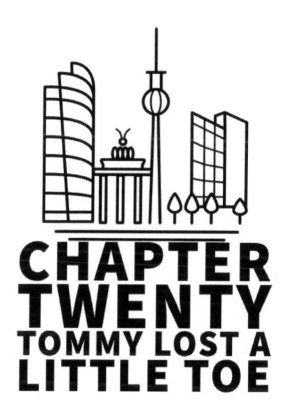

CHAPTER TWENTY
TOMMY LOST A LITTLE TOE

I awoke in a western German hospital with unfamiliar wires and tubes
sticking in and out of me. I was riddled with a fever and wrought with
paranoid feelings of disorientation. I was immediately sick on my
chest, and then I choked on a wire. I spent two weeks in the hospital
on enough morphine to make it feel like an hour. I met many nurses
and many patients, all of whom had been bitten by the cold and
insufferable conditions of *life*. Next to me was a black man named
Iggy Rock who'd purposefully cut the words: '*rock*' on his chest with a
shard of glass from a beer bottle. He moaned relentlessly through the
night, leading me to dream of smothering him with my pillow. He had
an American accent and told me he was part of the army, which I
knew to be a lie; since I'd met many soldiers in my time and Iggy
harboured an entirely different crazy than the crazy soldiers' harbour.

It wasn't long at all before I was kicked out of the hospital and told to
return home. It felt like seconds, I was unbelievably disorientated and
sick. I could still taste my own stomach in my mouth. I didn't have a
home. I didn't have *anything*. My passport, money, clothes; everything
I owned and brought with me was on the other side of the wall. Those
paranoid feelings of disorientation were the least bit paranoid. I really
was lost and all alone.
This side of the wall seemed crueller. It seemed colder and denser.
The air seemed thicker, it took a significant amount of difficulty for
me to breath and swallow regularly. I was most often sick every 20
steps or so when I left the hospital.

All of me wanted to crawl backwards and beg for a bed for a night, a week, a month; I had no idea or concept of time. I had no idea where I was or who anyone was. I wasn't compos enough to speak the language.

I could barely remember to breathe.

Yet still, me and Iggy were discharged at the same time and found ourselves sat upon the same front steps of the hospital *waiting*. Waiting for what, I don't know. We were just *waiting*. I might have had him sat beside me, but I'd never felt more alone in my life. I remembered being five years old and running through a field with a neighbour. We found a stream and a dam the village had made after minor flooding. We broke the dam and fled the scene up into a tree. I'd never been out that late before, it was as though I'd never seen the night before. I'd only ever seen that darkness from my bedroom window, tainted by glass and reflections. I'd never seen the stars in their crystal-clear ceremony. I'd never felt that warped chill wrap around your shoulders and nestle between your toes. I'd never heard the music of the night: owls, bats, foxes.

Being all alone and lost in Western Berlin was like I'd never seen daylight before. Never felt a car whizzing past you enough to knock you off your feet. Never had a headache at the droning sound of constant conversation.

Never squinted at the sun, or added a layer in the chill. Never so much as opened my eyes to the sun or watched an entire city suddenly shelter from the rain.

I was unsure I knew how to live, let alone *survive*. It felt as though I'd never had to do that before: *live*. And live so vicariously and cautiously so to not surrender to defeat.

I was trodden on by paranoia and fear. I could barely move for the first couple of hours, stuck on the hospital steps hoping and waiting for a miracle. I wanted to sleep to dream, so I could see what omens I would face. But the cold and the morphine still running through my veins meant I would be awake for a further 48 hours without a single visit from a single omen.

I found the nearest shelter I could in a woman whom I found reading poetry on a park bench. She was called Elspeth, and she welcomed me into her home without question. She fed me, bathed me, kept me warm and loved. She refused to take in Iggy, stating she didn't have the room. We sombrely went our separate ways.

I couldn't remember any of the German Mindy had taught me in those first few weeks. We communicated through songs at her home. I riffled through her extensive vinyl collection and pointed at English lyrics to congregate sentences together.

Our own Frankenstein of languages.

She had a copy of 'Space Oddity,' which made me cry. I couldn't find the strength to tell her it was me, I told her my name was '*Olivia*,' and that I'd boarded the wrong flight and was separated from my family.

Elspeth worked as a dressmaker in her family's shop and told me I could earn a living there to get enough money to fly back home. It seemed such ill fate that it must be *sewing* that haunts my every turmoil. I explained I couldn't sew which she told me was incredibly '*progressive of a woman to not know the hands of textiles;*' via a collection of lyrics including Dire Straits and Elvis.

I explained I belonged to an English religion of women called: '*kooks,*' who believe in the liberation of household enslaved women, and she tutted. She told me she enjoyed sewing; *It brought her peace.*

Instead, I cleaned the floor and swept up loose threads. On occasion, I delivered garments to homes across West Berlin and took orders for repairs. I'd made it clear I simply wanted the money to be out of her hair. The moment I earnt my first paycheck, I used a telephone to call home.

"Hello?" I spoke to the dead telephone line.

"Tony, hello? Hello?"

I called six times that day, to six different people, blowing about a quarter of my money. No one picked up. I left the number of a local telephone box and spent my evenings sat outside of it, waiting for a call. No one did. My manager had a stroke that untimely evening and the rest of the band were keeping him company. With him in hospital and the band being incompetent, they didn't think to check the phone as they graciously cared for Tony for weeks.

They knew I'd gone to Berlin to visit Tommy, and had no reason to worry or call, especially since I'd begged them to leave me alone for a couple of months while I spent time with Tommy.

I slept on Elspeth's chair in her living room and wrote on pieces of newspaper she'd kindly lend me to occupy myself. Elspeth wasn't very well off, nor were her family. Despite being on the West, all their money was tied up in the East with her father's car company.

I was incredibly lucky that she let me stay as long as she did, as I was hardly the perfect guest. I snuck out at night, desperately trying to find a gap in the wall or find someone I knew. If I wasn't needed at work, I'd be at a bar forcing some guy to buy me a drink so I could stay hydrated enough to try and desperately find someone I knew, or that maybe knew me. The severe pneumonia had shrunk my body inside out. I was beyond recognisable from my glam album covers and TV appearances.

What was an innocent trip to visit Tommy, had turned into a dystopian reality. I was as much a part of Western Berlin culture as the furniture. I was as agonised and pained as the natives, at the separation and turmoil the wall brought.

Our love was an inhumane feature of the Berlin wall. It was that dreary, grim block that supplied me with the appreciation and devotion I needed to survive.

I watched the suffering of mothers ripped from their sons; I heard widowers wail at the misfortune and torment of not being able to see their husbands' graves. I tasted the vulgarity of separation for economic gain, and I felt the agony of two entities, *one people;* ripped apart by an attempt on peace and democracy.

The baker whose daughter was alone on '*the other side,*' just feet away. They waved at each other every morning, but the baker was never to touch his daughter again for she died of pneumonia. Doctors fled; whole villages had nothing but bandages for their sores. Ordinary people who carried bibles ripped from their congregation and their place of worship as their sacred roof, their *church,* remains behind what was just brick and mortar.

How powerful brick and mortar were and *powerless* the government for enforcing such materials in their place.

The animosity and inner fight the people suffered. The knowledge that the wall prevented a likely war, but it did not bring peace in recompense.

Where, they asked, was their reconciliation? Their safe place, their *home?* If their home was bound by brick, mortar and barbed wire, are they but prisoners in their own land? Do they have freedom, or was freedom the material used to make the wall stick?

It was Molly who saved me, a small and humbling notion. I saw a Rolling Stones poster flapping in the wind around a lamppost and waited the weeks until the gig.

I went backstage to find her against all the odds, underneath a bar table, shaking, rocking back and forth screaming about the criminality of *berets*. She'd taken ecstasy and couldn't feel her legs.

I found the rest of the band and carried Molly back to their hotel when I begged them to help me get back to the Eastside. While I felt the most comforted I had in weeks since being discharged from the hospital, I just wanted Tommy back. He'd saved my life.

It was Keith that went over to the Eastside first, taking him three days to find Tommy who'd moved out of the apartment he was living in since he could no longer afford the rent after giving away all his money to help me. He was living in a shared flat, that was no doubt a squat. I never got to see it. Keith's first words to me when he came back were: '*he's riding again.*' Which meant Tommy was back on the heroin.

I didn't care. I just needed to be back with him.

I could feel him breathing. I would go out in the morning, place my hand on the same brick in the same part of the wall and feel him breathing. *Hear* him breathing. East Berlin kept him alive and gave me his breathes as a soundtrack to Eastern culture I couldn't experience.

I had all the clubs and bars in West Berlin to occupy my head, but nothing occupied my state of mind quite like he did. Demanding to be heard and touched and loved. Demanding to be thought of and about and for.

Seeing him again was a moment sworn to be sensationalised and romanticised. His face was worn in hurt, embellished with lazy stubble and heavy bags under his eyes.

He personified the wall. He was grey and dim. He had mortar between his limbs and barbed wire around his heart, but like the wall; he was penetrable and weak in notion.

I embraced him and welcomed him back into my life, knowing I would never, *ever* let him go again. I sacrificed my peace for love. I'd finally given in to my stubbornness. I was undoubtedly in love with him.

Tommy mumbled about how sorry he was, something I was all too familiar with hearing. But this time, I digested his every word and felt it- *believed it.* He cried at how glad he was to see me alive, and I joined him in communal lachrymose. We'd been suckered into the depths of political turmoil and all other things seemed so weak in meaning against surviving separation. That's all we did. *Fight to be reunited.* Fight against adversity and unify in the arms of hate for estrangement.

We were bubbling in this revelation when he dropped to one knee and begged me to marry him. Four guards shot bullets at our feet. Tommy lost a little toe and I, a shoe that belonged to Elspeth.

We ran smiling in the face of oppression, knowing we'd defeated the wall despite it still standing and segregating love. We fled Germany and went back home to the band house where we slept in refuge for weeks.

I wrote through the night and slept through the day, like the beginning of my journey. I slept next to Tommy in the same bed, comforting him when he awoke with nightmares of the bullets and the psychological bruises stamped in his head. He was dope sick for a bit again too, which was merely but a slight cough in the wreckage of the aftermath of Berlin.

I know myself to be better for it; but it was tough to swallow the brutalities of such a city, living in what seemed to be the same modern times as us.

Living seemed such a luxury after *surviving* Berlin.

We weren't the greatest love story to be near the wall- *no*, that was the demolition of the wall itself. But we were a good by-product of government insanity.

I never would've been a wife if the wall didn't teach me *love*.

CHAPTER TWENTY ONE
THE DEVIL TOOK A PISS ON MY ARM

The wall was just an eyesore to the view, not the heart, before I fell ill in Berlin. Berlin knew how to be fun, in ways London couldn't even fathom. Berlin had bars and clubs that seemed futuristic beyond means. There were bars that served cocaine and tequila by the bucket 24/7, like a petrol station for the damned. Clubs that played music deeply infused with the culture of a drowning city. Cinema's showing dirty films with kids on the front row. Shops brimming with spandex next to granny knickers. Nothing could surprise the eye in Berlin, except the *wall*.

I could only write about my relationship with Berlin back at home. My entire time there, I never wrote a single word on the agony of living there. I couldn't bring myself to. As a writer, I believe you must live through something to write of it. It was contextualised in my dreams as something of an unfortunate estrangement. We were an unfortunate case of the wall. Yet, I knew the *entirety of Berlin* was an unfortunate case of the wall. Mine and Tommy's story is like every other person who lived and experienced Berlin at that time: *harrowing.* I wish I was sensationalising the facts, but you didn't *live* in Berlin at that time, you really did *survive* it.

Yet, the action of survival creates a never-ending stream of inspiration, and I made three albums from that act of survival.

'Low,' 'Heroes,' and 'Lodger.'

All of which, I couldn't have made without Iggy Rock.

It was M that said; '*I know this guy you're going to love and he's performing at such a place tonight.*' So, I said *alright,* put on my cowboy boots and went to the concert alone with a small chip on my shoulder. M had told me that this guy was pretty cool and making waves no one else had made. I knew I was jealous, and I had every right to be.

I watched this guitarist pour vodka and coke on this guy's alight arm to try and dampen the fire, and that was when I saw Iggy.

I couldn't believe it was him.

Iggy Rock ran on stage screaming with his left arm completely ablaze, yelling to an empty concert hall an hour before his gig: '*The devil took a piss on my arm!*'

He was eventually tackled by whom I presumed was his manager and bathed in water before being carried back off stage where he was bandaged in a collection of his own band t-shirts.

I went backstage to see him, finding Iggy lay on top of a snooker table with his arm in a bowl of ice and his fingers in a girl. I didn't cower away because it was a somewhat familiar scene in the profession we shared.

"American solider Iggy Rock, how's the scar?"

"Mucus lung, morphine addict, *whatever your name was.* I didn't think you'd make it."

"*Of all the people to survive,*" I said with no end.

Iggy gave me a warm hug, and we shared a small spliff for half an hour before he went on stage to a garishly rowdy round of applause.

He was electric on stage from the moment I saw his bare feet. He was a bare-chested, bare-legged beast of a man protruding around on that stage as though he'd fought in a jousting match for ownership of the very wooden planks he was gyrating upon. He crawled on shards of glass, he cut his own skin, he verbally attacked himself and if that wasn't enough; he literally kicked a group of white men out the venue for styling their blonde hair into makeshift afro's, hailing it as a '*sin a black man physically could not witness.*'

Iggy Rock had that inspirational quality that people have told me I have too. I take that kind of thing very seriously and a heavenly compliment if I'm being likened to the characteristics of Iggy. He'd make you want to create, which is an incredibly valuable and insightful thing. Not a lot of people have that aura about them, but Iggy reeks of it. I'd spend an hour with him and feel more energised and revitalised than if I slept for a year and only ate the recommended 5 vegetables a day. Iggy Rock was good for mind, body and soul. That's what makes him so compelling and irresistible.

We've remained friends, arguably more than friends. If you produce and create music together, you're more than friends. You might adopt a sibling relationship, a parental one or maybe a caretaking role like an Uncle or an Aunt; but you enter the studio as friends and leave as something *more*. I'd say Iggy Rock is like a brother to me. Much better than my actual half brother, *God rest his soul.*

Iggy had spoken to me on multiple occasions about connecting deeper and more fundamentally with his audience. He'd always say: *'but if I can jump in the middle of all that energy, it'll fucking keep me up, it'll fucking lift me to the arms of God in the fucking sky. I'm gonna do it. I'm gonna jump, and I know they'll fucking catch me. I'll retire right there and then if not.'*

Thankfully the crowd did catch him, and fortunately, he didn't have to retire that night. They were awfully confused. Of course, now *stage diving* is such a fundamental part of any rock n roll concert, it almost seems ludicrous to question whether Iggy would've been caught or not.

You have to remember as the pioneer of stage diving, his faith in an audience reciprocating his energy and resisting their natural human instinct to move out the way of anything heavy falling on their fucking heads; was *unknown* at that time.

I watched with pure and utter fear in my stomach as he pummelled into the crowd to be caught by a sea of welcoming arms and ear-splitting throats, biting his ankles and ripping his pants clean off him. He arose a little dishevelled, and I think astounded, but continued through the night as though he hadn't just pioneered a necessary crusade and element in rock n roll. That was who he was. He could've invented the Earth, and he still would've walked away from his creation as though he were walking away from a mediocre cake at a bake sale.

Rock stars are well educated; being a crackerjack is part of our vernacular. Supposedly, there's a few shy off the mark, but most of us are relatively well educated for a bunch of crooked drug addicts with daddy issues, who use a procession of beats to sustain and breathe. I've often wondered what dictionary rockstars were read as kids because it sure ain't your average Oxford Collins.

I once came into Iggy Rocks dressing room to find him hanging upside down; a clothes hanger clipped to the bottom of his jeans. He had sick drooling out of his mouth, and there was still beer bottle glass in tufts of his hair where he smashed the bottle on his own head, leaving a protruding bruise and lump in the shape of a 50p coin. He pointed at me and quite calmly stated:

"You know what the problem is Pen? The industry is run by dilettante's, and I'm singing peppy fucking records to a bunch of nihilists. I ain't got a problem with the nihilism, bring on the revolution. I've got a problem with the dilettantes making me feel contempt. I ain't contempt. I'm Iggy fucking Rock, where's the assimilation?"

The most unusual part was the fact a literary outburst like that, was not unusual. It was as though Iggy swallowed a few pages of a dictionary every couple of grams he snorted to keep a balance. The rock n roll diet.

He wasn't on his own, either. Every other rock star I knew would slip in a Latin phrase every now and then.

I romanticised the idea that there was a specialised dictionary in a particular library just for rock stars who gained access to the holy book by slipping the librarian a gram of smack and a 70-date tour schedule around America.

It's always astounded me how literate rock stars are even, and perhaps more so, when under the influence. I could never form sentences in interviews that sounded close to being temperate, never mind beautiful confessions of literary romance.

I mean, that's why I'm a writer.

I'd stumble and stutter. On seven known occasions, I used words I didn't understand and got caught out. Including the word: 'bourgeois,' which I innocently confused for an exquisite French dish. I wasn't the typical rock star at that time. I was a little too rough around the edges for that. A little too naïve in a sense I clutched hold of childish innocence and refused to let go as though it were a buoy and I were drowning in a sickly sea of realism.

There was something about myself and Iggy being two oppressed outcasts facing adversity together that unified our music and established the halfway point for our behaviour and society. A warm hut with tiki-straws and pina colada cocktails served every half hour. A clairvoyant with a northern accent as our bouncer. A back catalogue of Little Richard tracks as the password to get in.

Together, the halfway house we'd made unintentionally established a place where people could accept our behaviour via our music; simultaneously popularising our personal adversities into mainstream enlightenments. Our mission was not acceptance but expressionism. Yet we'd gained a small amount of approval along the way as influential figures.

Iggy has been my confidant for years now, and at that time, I would often speak about the things I did to get where I was, and he would sit in silence listening to me intently.

He never really had much to say as for advice, except these final words one day after I told him how a respected television show didn't want me because of what I wore and how I danced: 'Don't worry Pen, you could have it harder. At least you're not *black.*'

CHAPTER
TWENTY TWO
A MILLION
SYNONYMS

'The Berlin Trilogy,' happened as something of a reflex of life. Everything had changed, and I sensed more change was to come.

I was right.

I was pregnant.

All I could manage when I found out, was to sit there numbly like a dog with its tongue out, hypnotised by the thought of what was to be. Playing with questions such as: do I actually want a child? What happens if I die when it's young? Will I be a good enough mother? How do you get a child to sleep? How much bribing is bad for its health? What happens if I can't do it? *What the fuck do I do now?*

I collapsed in shock on the bathroom floor, breaking my nose as I smashed my head against the bath.

I awoke with the pregnancy stick clutched in my hand and blood dripping down my face, and it was at that point that I thought: rock n roll with a bump is only like opera with a smashed glass. You expect it *eventually* if you're doing it right.

I told Tommy I was pregnant straight away as I learnt from taking him to the abortion clinic all those years ago; waiting until it's too late, is not the humane thing to do.

I simply said: "I'm pregnant."

He took a long pause and looked disappointed. The kind of disappointed when you don't win on the arcade machine. *Childlike disappointment.*

"You got *rid* of my child." He told me. I was shocked. Not that I had forgotten, but it seemed so distant I was unsure as to whether it had really happened or not in that moment. I'd buried that fact so deeply within me, it simply didn't exist in the open.

I had been through every step of the grieving process, over and over again, morning and night like a washing routine. He wasn't a part of it. It wasn't his kid I aborted, it had to be the booker's. It was his kid that I *miscarried*, I would never abort Tommy's child. Not *Tommy's*.

I was so sure I was the world's worst mother. I had the world's *worst* womb; that would be the badge I'd get on Mother's Day. I'd killed a child and miscarried another. How could I even hold a life in that womb when it had been a battlefield for so long? It just felt wrong. All the good and tranquil feeling of pregnancy were suddenly gone. I was now *petrified*.

"That was a long time ago."

"It's still dead in a bin in some London backstreet."

"Woah, Tommy. I *lost* that child."

"No. You got *rid* of it."

"I was 19, Tommy."

"It was *my* kid too."

"We don't know that."

"You hope to know that. Why can I trust you want that kid now, if it is even my kid?"

"Of course, it's your child Tommy!"

"You got rid of it already?"

"I think we should have this conversation another day."

We didn't speak for four weeks. Tommy went on his biggest binge and disappeared for the entire time. He didn't know I knew exactly where he was at all times. I would never have let him walk away into oblivion after finding out something like that. What would any addict do when their past resurfaces? I had a few people keep eyes on him, in every squat, on every street he went and near damn killed himself each morning and night.

While he was acting like a fool, I went to Paris and hid for a month while our child nested and grew. My bump was visible by the time he emerged with red raw eyes and saggy skin. He looked nothing like Tommy and nothing like a father.

I booked him back into rehab and told him he could come out when the baby was born.

I was lucky enough to be working on an album to distract myself at the time, else me and the baby would've gone insane.

I was actually in the recording studio, perched on a stool when my waters broke. The entire studio was full of men, not a single woman in the house; which of course meant I had to calm the blokes down between delivering my own child. The only way the guys knew something was up, was because the water went on the wires at my feet and sparked the equipment.

They immediately went to the equipment, tutting, shouting about who spilt beer on the cables. Meanwhile, I'm panting like I've just run a marathon without two lungs, and it takes them until my first contraction where I scream into the mic to get their attention. Six out of eight of them ran. Two of them had grandma's who had suddenly fallen ill, one had a dead dog, two more had to be somewhere else, and the other genuinely fainted.

The two men left standing, in utter disarray and panic, grabbed the spinning chair from the studio and placed me on it; wheeling me through the hallway and carrying me down the stairs like I was on a throne. Although I didn't really feel like royalty, as the guys argued about whether they recorded my last tape or not as I'm plummeting out of everything I've ever known and into motherhood.

With the baby imminently due; I begged everyone I could get my hands on, to call Tommy and get him here whether he was still a junkie or not. I didn't care at that moment. I didn't care whether he'd arrive with heroin dripping from his arms and cocaine still on his lips; I just wanted him there. I didn't feel alone, I had my baby with me; it was him and me against the world, and I knew it would be fine. But I also knew how much Tommy needed this. He needed to see his baby, he needed to go through this with me.

Someone rang Tommy, and I've been told he cried in shock. His treatment wasn't quite finished by about a month.

The centre didn't want to let him go in case anything triggered another spiral so close to his recovery. While I couldn't have cared less at the time what a snotty-nosed bitch at a rehabilitation centre thought about my fiancé, I can see her theory now.

Tommy escaped. He got every single inmate to cause havoc by doing whatever they wanted. Some shat in the canteen, some just screamed and shouted, and I believe a few got quite aggressive, which was not Tommy's intention, but it meant that everyone was distracted long enough to not notice him slip away.

In true Tommy style, he didn't quite anticipate his next step and started running in a direction, hoping for a sign for the hospital. He eventually resorted to screaming at strangers, asking where the hospital was. It's worth noting, he was wearing a hospital gown, tag and all, I don't blame anyone who ran away in fear for their lives.

After jumping out of three taxis', mid-journey to avoid paying and walking another 2 and a half hours because he got lost; he finally arrived with bleeding feet and a very sweaty forehead.

Just the *four* hours after our son Albie Jones was born weighing 8 pounds 2, with blue eyes and a large birthmark on his right leg. I still don't know what the better feeling was. Seeing my newborn son, or my fiancé after 6 months. I say that, because my fiancé hadn't just ripped me a new vagina, so I strongly felt a lot more kin to him, than the crying child in my arms.

Tommy got in the hospital bed next to me, his sweat equaling mine and held me for what must've been a good 6 hours before we all fell asleep as one peaceful family.

We didn't speak, mostly due to the persistently crying child, for a good five weeks after Albie was born. When we did talk, Tommy mainly sobbed so much I couldn't make sense out of what he was trying to say. I wrote him a letter while he was in rehab, noting how it was just easier to think it wasn't his child. Especially now Albie was in our arms, it was near impossible to imagine aborting a child with the same eyes. Everything was just different back then. Being a pregnant woman was different back then; *I* was different back then. I'd only known Tommy for hours at that time. Tommy's emotions got the better of him when reasoning about the abortion.
Albie became the focus, and we haven't spoken of it since.

Being a mother is more painful than being an addict. There's much more trauma being a mum than an addict. All trauma is your own as an addict; you self-inflict your own personal trauma.

Not as a mother. You'd never self-inflict trauma because you don't want to hurt your baby. You must feel your baby's trauma as well as your own, and that's heartbreaking.

What's more heartbreaking is; I was a better addict than a person *and* a mother.

I struggled instantly with motherhood. It was the *guilt.*

I felt an indescribable amount of grief towards the fact I didn't love my son the moment he arrived *like I should've.* You're told that: it's all worth it when you see his little face; it'll all make sense when you hold him in your arms; you'll fall in love with him, the moment he arrives. *I didn't.*

I know now that it's not that uncommon and there's plenty of women who struggle to feel that unbridled companion with their child the moment it arrives, due to shock and the overwhelming and sudden change or perhaps even postnatal depression. But the guilt and shame I felt for not loving him the way I thought I was supposed to, instantly made me feel tremendously uncomfortable around my child.

I didn't want to touch him for months. I was overwhelmed with confusion. All I could think when I looked at this strange little bundle of flesh and bones was: how the fuck did that evolve in my stomach and how did I get it out? Why is it in my house? How is it mine? What do I do with it? What does it want? Why can't it communicate with me?

I'm going out of my godforsaken mind!

Tommy was incredible and took to fatherhood *instantly*. He finally found his calling in life, and it was phenomenal to see. But I was a shit mother at first. I let him cry and whine because I didn't know what to do and I assumed I'd only make it worse. I didn't cuddle him because he looked too fragile and I was far too paranoid of breaking him in two. I refused to 'goo-goo ga ga' in his face because I didn't want to belittle him; meaning that he grew up far too fast and the next time I blinked he was two years old and in my arms in A&E.

That's when I fell in love with him because I was so terrified he was going to die, and I knew I would never forgive myself for not loving him when I had him. So, I loved him. It came naturally, and that was the strangest part to me. All of these instincts and things I never knew I knew; I suddenly put into practice to care and love for my child. I didn't think I had that kind of compassion inside of me until he broke his leg chasing Tommy and the neighbour's cat.

Motherhood is the craziest of trips.

While music is the black tar heroin going right into the vein, motherhood is the bad batch of pills you didn't know you needed.

Albie was a kid who wanted to do it all. He wanted to do every sport, read every book, climb every tree, eat every food, watch everybody and everything. Of course, all children are naturally born with instincts towards what they *can't* have. But mix those instincts in with such a heavy tour schedule, and you get an insecure mother thinking that she's not good enough, or doing enough or taking her son to enough outdoor play adventures during the week.

While I love my child with all my heart, I never signed up to surrender my career for his life. I don't care if that makes me selfish. I learnt how to balance motherhood with my job, and it was a balance that took a little while longer than I wanted to perfect, but I got there in the end.

Tommy became a full-time stay at home dad, sacrificing any chance of him discovering a career for *my* career.

I owe him everything for that chance.

I could go to the studio and create; I could sit upstairs for an hour or two to write, and I could go on tour and take Albie with me knowing he was safe with my Tommy.

My career has always meant the absolute most to me, *always*. I've never wanted to be a mother more than I've wanted to be a musician and that's quite tough to swallow now I have a child of my own. There are days where it makes me feel like the foulest mother ever, but I take it with a pinch of salt, knowing I've always done my best for my child.

Mothers are always under such scrutiny for the way they behave. Whether they are loving enough or giving enough. Whether they've sacrificed enough of themselves or whether they're rich enough.

It's always a matter of: '*have you prioritised your child over absolutely everything in your life, including yourself?*' If you haven't, you simply aren't considered *good enough*.

It's absurd to expect a woman to give up everything just because they have become a mother. Being a mother doesn't change the fact that you're still a woman. A woman with needs and dreams and her own set of lungs to worry about.

There's so much pressure on being the perfect mother. When we think about our own mothers, we can all think about a mistake they've made or how they weren't quite perfect in raising you. Maybe she missed your sports day once, or perhaps she became an alcoholic. Maybe she refused to say; '*I love you,*' or perhaps she fought with your dad relentlessly. As well as being a woman and a mother, she's also *human*.

All mothers are human.

I gave Albie too much sugar for years; I let him go to bed without brushing his teeth if he wanted; I left him on his own around addicts who were still using once while I went for a piss. He probably saw me drink too much and definitely saw me do cocaine a couple of times; I called him a little shit when he was 6, and he cried; I swore in front of him his entire upbringing. I gave him a porn mag for his 15th birthday; I didn't go to every one of his parent's evenings because I was always on tour; I told him '*it was just a bruise,*' when he came home with a bruised foot that actually turned out to be broken. I've lied to him countless times and once, I stole a chocolate bar from a shop just for the thrill of it and I blamed it on him.

I know. I'm *evil.* I'm an evil mother for my mistakes.

Fact of the matter is: there is no exact right or wrong path to raising your child. There's no manual or script on how your child's life is supposed to go. There's no step by step guide on how to get him to bed on time and make sure he eats enough vegetables. There's just *you*, figuring out this completely new and unknown territory all by yourself.

Because while you may be, what is generally considered as *lucky*, to have your partner who's figuring out the landscape of fatherhood; motherhood is an entirely different level of terrain. Motherhood comes with a lot more bears around the corners and a lot more middle-aged women calling you a *'fucking bitch'* for calling their child a *'stuck up snob with greasy hair and a snotty t-shirt.'*

I don't have to justify how much Albie means to me or how much my career does. I also don't have to explain why I chose to maintain my career, perhaps at the expense of a few less nights with my child. I'm a mother who loves my kid, and I don't know when that stopped being enough.

Now a mother who loves their kid must *also* be the CEO of a major conglomerate business; skinny and flawless-looking with no scars. Present at all times of the day for everything; supportive of everything the child does, even if what the child has done is wrong. A great cook and an even better personal trainer for the other mums who are *so* *desperate* to be good enough.

Some women are born with maternal instincts developed and flourishing within their daily life from the early ages of existence, and other women, like how I consider myself; with instincts buried *deep* within them. That's what makes every mother different. The instinct of maternal compassion is not one I bestowed initially, meaning I was regarded as a cold and unloving mother to start.

But it's alright if those instincts are a little harder to reach.

Mother's and the way they raise their children create the people of the world we pass by on the street and buy coffee from. If every mother loved their child the same, in the same way: we'd all be the same person, the same by-product of the same maternal love.

The world wouldn't go around. Some mothers must raise their son's to be soldiers, while other's raise their daughters to be butchers. Some mothers must teach their child to survive, while other mothers must teach their child to skip. Some mothers must raise their child to be political leaders who enforce war, and some mothers love their child enough; they stop it.

That's the power of a mother.

People are often intimidated by a mother with a career because they don't know how to box her. She's not just a mother or just a career woman- she's both. The idea that a woman has to singularly be one thing is poorly outdated and illogical; for a woman to be a mother in the first place; she must be at least a dozen things first. A *lover* is one of them.

I chose to make sure I still had a career while being a mother because I was in a fortunate position to have both. I'd also worked bloody hard to get where I was and couldn't stomach giving it up so easily. I could go to work and be a mum in equal balance. I hate people thinking that I'd rather be at work than with my child, that's simply not the case. I've always found work and creating such an integral part of my being, that I deem it wrong and irresponsible if I were to deny my soul, to spend time with my child as a person devoid of themselves. My career makes me who I am. I am music. I am a writer. I am a creator. I have to be those things to sustain and be myself: the self that my child knows and loves.

It's reckless thinking anyway. Most mothers work alongside being a mother to fund their child's needs. Mothers *need* to work to remain financially stable.

Having 'a career,' is no different to having 'a job;' and people should be less hard on mothers who make decisions against the natural current for their children. It's a mother's job to love her child and a woman's responsibility to love herself enough that making mistakes as a mother is *ok*.

Because no child is perfect, so no *mother* should be either.

I always thought that being a rock star, on a stage every night, would be the most powerful thing I would do as a woman, but I was wrong. Being a *mother* is the most powerful thing I've ever done and continue to do.

No matter how shit I am at it, or how much of a rocky start I had. I love Albie, undoubtedly and beautifully.

It's a striking kind of love. It's unforgiving and relentless.

It's a bond unbreakable by death or any other sentiment that presents itself as more powerful than the relationship between mother and child.

Of all the things, I can put into words; how much I love him, is never one of them.

I can incite how beautiful I think the trees are and how disgusted I am at the government. I can write a hundred-page love letter to the birds and their chirps and songs, but never a single page for Albie. Not because I don't love him, I just don't have the words.

It seems unreasonable to use the same word to describe my devotion to my son as I use to describe my like for chocolate. *Love*.

Of all the words in the English language; I am disappointed that there are nearly two thousand synonyms for the word sad and not one word good enough to describe the love I have for my little Albie.

It would take a million synonyms for the word love to describe our bond and even then, I think I'd still be missing *one*.

CHAPTER
TWENTY THREE
WHEN DID IT
HURT TO BE ALIVE?

Molly Jagger finally took too many drugs and shot herself in the head on my wedding day.

Of all the people, I anticipated might overdose at my wedding, it was not Molly. I'd talked to Tommy for months on end about him not touching a single drug offered on our wedding day; but by the time I found Molly in a pool of blood in her room, I said: *fuck it,* and ordered everyone get high to fix the whole damn thing. The wedding was imminently cancelled, and we got married a couple of months later; a small service in a Parisian church. We kept it small to minimise the number of potential deaths, since everyone who was initially clean, was now using again to deal with Molly's death.

It was a shit time. She left a hole in London, and it yearned for her miserably; like a seventeen-year-old boy wallowing in his bed, riddled to his core with heartbreak in the adolescent degree. London was poor at mourning. It rained for years, and the wind cried out for her every time I walked down its street: *whiny bastard.*

We all had to pick ourselves up and move along, of course.

We'd become something of a beacon of rock n roll. We had to show strength and love in the face of fear and death. If we broke, what would they have to hold on to? That's how it felt, anyhow. We were *music.* If there's ever a time when people need to hear music, it's when the grim reaper comes a knocking and steals the wind from your throat.

We had to keep going for the music's sake. For the *people*'s sake.

Who am I to confirm that surviving and sustaining on this planet for 70 odd years is better than not existing at all, anyway? She could be having a constant party for all we know. I like to think she is. I hate the thought of her amongst the wet soil, it sends my teeth chattering. Molly Jagger is too good for a grave, too good for death.

I don't know what the alternative to life or death is: but she deserves it.

I miss her every day. *I think we all do.*

Molly had written me a letter a few years before she died telling me that she felt sick. She said: *"I don't feel nauseous, my stomach isn't churning, but I still feel sick. Sick of it all. I feel like a kid that can't keep life down. I don't know how to swallow this one Pen. It hurts. When did it hurt to be alive? I don't remember being diagnosed a lifetime, I feel so sick, I'm so tired."*

I took it to her funeral and dropped it in her grave. I wanted her to have something to remind her of how much she hated being alive. I thought it might make death a little easier.

I don't remember much about her funeral or how we all mourned. I just remember there was a lot of musicians with guitars strapped to their backs; black leather jackets and lots of grown men with smudged black eyeliner. There was a lot of press which was, of course, sickening but I don't think any of us expected any different.

Front page news in life *and death.*

The funeral procession was solemn and drab because the streets were littered with mourning teenagers wearing '*Molly Jagger*'t-shirts or stylish black dresses. Myself, Tommy and M were in one car, with one empty seat reserved for Iggy, who didn't make it on time. About halfway through the procession, I'm startled upright by a frenzied looking Iggy Rock banging on the blacked-out windows shouting my name in search for the right car. He'd knocked on every single car until I flung our car door open and in Iggy hops wearing a kilt and nothing else. I asked him what the hell he was wearing and he looked me up and down and said: '*the right and respectable clothing.*' He got too stoned and therefore confused about kilts and funeral attire.

After the funeral, we had a large gathering which was costumed with drugs and alcohol. Molly had apparently told Ronnie Wood that she wanted a disco floor at the reception after her funeral, which I found hard to believe, but it was a good time. Ronnie arranged for 'Queen' to perform at the reception, which they did for a large number of narcotics on a wooden casket in the back room. We ended the service four days later in a bar in Newcastle, with feather boas around our ankles and handcuffs around our wrists. M and I had been caught with enough marijuana on us to look like possession with intent to supply. We both had a good night's kip, and I was released the following day, picked up by Tony who drove us straight to the airport, still in our funeral dresses, ready for the tour.

By this point, I was already keen to stop touring for a while, and the tour hadn't even begun yet. I didn't tell anyone that I was thinking of taking a break and spending more time with Albie, except Tommy, who was ready for me to stop too.

This was 'The Serious Moonlight' tour, I couldn't stop now. 'Let's Dance,' was number one and 'China Girl' was heading for number two. I should've been elated, top of the world, celebrating in style. Instead, I was still severely mourning Molly; up all night with Albie on tour and continuously keeping Tommy off the gear while still weening myself. Despite having nine months off pregnant with Albie, I had a few mistaken nights the following months after he was born, including closer the time of Molly's death. It was a recreational thing, not quite an addiction, but I had a kid this time around, and drugs were just not what I should've been doing.

It was quite comfortable at that time to pretend everything was more than okay, and we all did so exceptionally well. Success for creative types cannot be easily defined. In sport, you are successful if you win a match or score the winning point. You are rewarded with a trophy or a medal or a better playing position. In academia, you're successful if you get the highest grade and you're rewarded with accolades and titles.

In the realms of imagination, success can be; finally making sense out of a thought into words, or completing the last brushstroke of a painting. Success is often the end of something; the finishing of a song, the final product. It's the composition of time, effort and finality that is success for creative people. The satisfaction of creation. The relief you're not insane. The release of your creativity that was stored inside you all that time. The process from idea to product.

For me, success was not chart hits or money. I created because I wanted to desperately share music and art with the world, and in most regards, I *needed* to create and share as a matter of existing. Creating is so deeply rooted within me; I don't know the source of the disease, but I have endured the symptoms my entire life.

Creating is as natural as breathing and just as equally important to me.

My career felt as though it had dwindled, not necessarily for the bad, but it had definitely sidetracked from my initial intentions. Deciding to stop for a while after the 'Serious Moonlight' tour, was simply a shot at refueling and refocusing myself and my team back on to the importance of creating for *art* and not creating for *money.*

I took Tommy and little Albie on a road trip around Europe instead, in an attempt to have some quality family time while I could and in a small ode to Molly. Albie had just turned five, and I wanted to do something together before he had to go off to school. I hired an identical VW transporter camper van in blue, the very same as the one me and Molly took around Europe.

I borrowed it off a very old friend who had a weed farm underneath his mother's art gallery. We went to the gallery to pick it up and got caught in an expo on natural erotica in historical art, and was asked to strip for a painting while our mate was signaling the panic alarm that the weed farm had caught fire. I believe Tommy rushed to help put the fire out while a lovely lady named Linda painted my gash in water colour.

We took the van straight to France where we pitched up in Troyes near a chemical plant; it wasn't the best view but it was quiet, and the pool was cold. A little too chilly for Albie who was relentlessly grumpy on the first week of our travels. Me and Tommy played poker each night and broke the fold-out bed shagging.

When we tried to leave the campsite, the man who owned the joint, pulled out a shotgun and demanded I sing a few songs that night before I could leave. I don't remember feeling threatened by the gun, having just come back from America, but he did say he'd play ABBA through the loudspeakers and God Bless my Albie; but we learnt very early on in his life how much he detests that groovy band. He'd purposefully shit himself every time 'Voulez-Vous' came on the radio out of protest up to the age of about 9; it all was very tense.

We were finally allowed to leave after a quick sing-a-long, much to the owner's dismay, and set off to Spain where we planned to lay naked on the beach for weeks on end drinking sangria and eating Tapas.

Instead, we got caught at border control with a small number of drugs, which was surprisingly not the problem. The problem was the model machete my five-year-old son had stolen from our trip to a medieval museum in which we paid fifteen euros each so Albie could have a shit.

Unbeknownst to us all, he'd stuffed this jagged black knife into his rucksack, simultaneously tearing a hole in the bag and hid it under his bunk. We were fined, and I think they reported us to British Social services, but nothing came of that. During the questioning, we were held for about four hours in a square room with nothing but two cups of shit tea and a packet of French Garibaldis. Given Albie was only five, just had two French men steal his new toy and hadn't eaten properly in over four hours; he charged out of the containment room and fell straight down a flight of stairs, only to hobble out of the emergency exit and sneak into a lovely Irish family's motorhome. It was about this point in my motherhood journey that I realised having children is great if they're well behaved; having children is difficult if they like to settle all their angst and disputes by shitting in unforgettable places.

On this unruly occasion, it was the lap of an Irishman, who was attempting to help my sons broken ankle. We left shamefully for the hospital and then the coast; getting two flat tyres and having half our stuff stolen from our boot while I chased Albie around the petrol pump in the process.

We did manage to have a week of calm, burying Tommy in the sand and paddling in the sea. Albie built a very phallic-looking sandcastle, and Tommy trod on a crab. I got sunburnt and food poisoning, but between the redness and sick it was a lovely time.

We bought kites and ran, as the sun set, down the length of the beach; we hired bikes to ride around the town and trekked up into the mountains where we spent the afternoon by a waterfall. I met a lovely woman who owned an English café down the seafront and sold a clothing collection she sewed in her spare time at the local market. Maria wrote Albie a poem called 'sugar boys like you,' and embroidered it onto a blanket he still has in his room today.

My favourite part is:

'and Albie,
your mother doesn't have the words,
she gave them to the world,
her second greatest gift
after you.
And Albie,
the world has your mother's words,
but you'll always have her heart
and she'll always love you.'

It's beautiful. Maria's words were the closest thing to perfection, I could offer Albie at that time. He obviously gave no thought to it back then and was, in fact, sick on the blanket that night, but has loved it ineffably ever since. In fact, he kept it in his school bag during his entire time at primary and high school and has even driven himself to Italy in a matter of days after he left it on a skiing holiday in his late 30s.

Maria has sent us a Christmas card ever since with a photograph of the view from her apartment, and I never get bored of staring at it.

We then moved further along the Spanish coast, getting lost due to Tommy's terrible map reading skills and the fact Albie had decided he wanted to eat his dinner off the map the previous night. Meaning half of Spain was no longer land and water but one giant meatball stain. Albie wasn't sleeping very well, so we took advantage every time he did doze off, meaning this particular night we drove for hours to keep him asleep. Eventually, panic parking where we believed was just on the side of a road.

We were all awoken shy of two hours later to the sound of what can only be described as the world ending. A woundingly loud alarm, raging between each ear, followed by a gigantic stampede and a solid rocking of the entire campervan. I bolted upright, grabbing Albie instinctively; while a stark bollock naked Tommy flings open the caravan door to reveal a blanket of young Spanish kids gawping at my Tommy's tiny prawn.

We'd apparently parked in the middle of a school playground, and they had an end of year show to rehearse.

We drove off, *promptly*; driving and driving and driving until Tommy's flushed cheeks returned to his normal colour and we could laugh about the whole ordeal.

I was exhausted by this point. Touring and performing night after night, had nothing on the tiresome routine of being a mother night after night. The comedown of a tour mixed in with the constant travelling and wiping of Albie's arse in petrol station toilets had done me in. For the second-time road tripping, I missed home. I might've had Tommy and Albie, the only things that mattered, but I wanted my home. My bed, my slippers, my favourite mug. I wanted to know how hot the shower was going to be. I wanted to know there wasn't going to be a bible in the drawer next to my bed. I wanted clean and non-scratchy sheets.

We drove home in silence for most of the journey. Tommy was enjoying being free and feared I'd get straight back on the road touring as soon as we returned home, despite me assuring him I wouldn't. Albie slept, finally, solidly and happily. I think he was glad to be home too.

I walked through the door, dropped my bag on the bottom step and kissed it softly. Tommy joined me after putting Albie in bed, bringing me a letter from our post box. It was a little dusty, it looked like it'd been there for months.

I knew from the handwriting I was going to cry.

And I did cry. I cried so hard: I sobbed, in fact.

It tore a muscle in my chest, or did it break my heart?

It was one final letter from my Molly, sent just before she died.

CHAPTER
TWENTY FOUR
ANOTHER YOUNG
GIRL SCOUT
HAVING A GO

The letter was short, and her handwriting was a mess. It was clear her body shook writing the entire thing. It was almost incomprehensible and most definitely unrecognisable in terms of her character. She'd always address her letters to 'My Pensive Penny,' this letter urgently started with a simple 'Pen.'

She asked how I was and told me she'd seen a black cat that must've rolled in blossom, for his white forehead was pink. '*It made me smile like the Cheshire cat,*' she wrote.

It was most peculiar of Molly to dwell. She never dwelled or reminisced or even so much as recognised her past existed. Molly Jagger didn't have a past. She had the present. She never spoke about her future, that didn't exist either.

She lived solely for the day and for the day alone.

Which was why it sent a chill down my entire body for her to write the phrase: '*I remembered, the other day, you telling me the story about Hollywood.*'

The particular story was from a good few years back, a couple of months or so after I'd come back from Berlin. Tony had booked me a role in a film amid the glamour that is Hollywood. I'd enquired frequently about acting in small, independent films and Tony had said he'd take care of it. I was greeted on set by a handful of people, and sent straight to hair and makeup where I was dolled up with a blonde wig and an industrial layer of makeup; a contact lens for my eye. I was dressed in a nightgown and robe and nothing else, with no idea what role I was to fill at this point.

The director then came in to brief me, telling me I was a secretary at a nutrition firm called 'Sarah.' I initially thought: *'great, I've never been a secretary at a nutrition firm called Sarah!'* Until, I then learnt Sarah was having an affair with one of the nutritionists named 'Donald,' who appeared in his slim looking underpants and sticker that read: 'Here to nourish and educate: DONALD.'

I stormed out onto set where I finally got to see the readymade bed and naked man rehearsing angles with two of the cameramen.

It was a *porno.*

No way around the fact; it was a hard-core, low-budgeted, poorly scripted: *porno.*

I'd been scripted into my first film, which was a porno. Sarah was in a porno. Tony booked me into a *porno.*

A fucking *porno!*

I told Tony he would be sacked if he did anything like that again; to which he confessed was entirely fair. Tony only stayed in my life out of pure fear. I can admit now, that I was terrified of being left on my own in the industry and so put up with more than I had to, to not be alone.

I must say though; I have nothing against porn; having on occasion spent many of pleasurable nights enjoying its realms. I simply had a problem with Tony tricking me into performing in a porn film for what seemed like his amusement and his amusement alone. I'd always liked the idea of acting, as I'd done it on stage most nights of most of my life. I'd spent most of my career in character, so it didn't feel too unusual to do it in front of a camera.

There's not a lot of different roles for women in film. The roles available for women most often include dumb blonde, the woman in distress, single mother, woman having an affair. They most often have blonde hair, big boobs, small waists and speak in such a voice, it's hard to believe being deaf isn't a kindness. They're ripped from the world of modelling and plonked in the middle of a thin plot for the aesthetic. Because a fat girl shagging the priest just doesn't look as good. I didn't want to play the *obvious* woman. I had no interest in playing every single woman that's ever been on our screens. I was interested in giving the underrepresented a voice.

I didn't want to be the starring role, *just because I could* either. I didn't deserve it for a start. I hadn't slaved my way at drama school being bullied by a bitch who has a horse named '*Pippin*' and a father in the Arts. There were thousands of women in the world who would've done anything for the meetings I had in rooms with men promising me the world; *I* wasn't one of them. I wanted small roles in mediocrely big films. I wanted to experiment. I wanted to play characters who were nothing like me, so I had a chance to feel what it would be like to be someone else for the day. I wanted a stable form of escapism that didn't end in me overdosing or selling my soul to a rehab.

Hollywood was like the friend's house that you hated because his dad was a creep, but his mum made the best brownies. Hollywood was warm and layered and a lot of fun, but not without its flaws, of course. Hollywood funds the flaw commodity. Hollywood wouldn't exist if it wasn't for flaws, they *profit* from flaws.

Every Hollywood script I read; every novel; soap drama and modelling advertisement described and portrayed women by their *hair*. More specifically: whether a woman had *blonde* or *brown* hair. And therefore, had either or characteristics. Men in the same scripts and novels were described with desires and fears; with motives and distastes. 'A 22-year old builder with a passion for cycling and a fear of being alone.'

Compared to: 'A 22-year-old blonde woman with lusciously long legs, an enviable waist and polished nails who works on reception.'

I shaved my head.

That way, people didn't have a choice. They had to write about my interests and my fears or call me bald, which no one liked to do. If they wanted me in the script, I had to be bald. I refused to wear a wig. It shocked people because most of my career was founded upon my appearance, and here I was bald and ultimately without one.

I scrapped Hollywood not long after I went bald and learnt that I'd have to fuck for a role. I was too old for that shit. I did star in a few music videos instead though.

I auditioned and got a small part in Duran Duran's '*Girls on Film,*' music video. You know the one. The one you asked your mum if it's real or in your dreams. My part was cut, but I was a sexy clown, which wasn't all too hot, so that's probably why it got cut. One time I was asked to work on a low budget film as a favour for a friend and ended up being robbed in New York.

This was a long time ago, just after Ziggy Stardust and I didn't have a whole team of personnel with me at all times. Both my handbag and suitcase were taken in a hit n run robbing that landed me with two bruised eyes and a sprained ankle as I tried to run after the bastards.

I was asked to feature in a lot of low budget films for friends back then, which I was very keen to do. At the time, I never had any intentions of acting, it was just something I found fun and found even more invigorating when I started getting more involved within the industry. I knew a lot of creative people and a lot of photographers who had dreams of becoming storytellers through short underground films.

I featured as a dinner lady who sold crack cocaine to the kids, in a film by a pawnshop owner named Chance. I was a mother who hadn't had sex in a year, so cheated on her husband with her local fishmonger; in a film by a woman with four children herself, named Angie Andrews. I've been a swimming instructor; a man who has a fascination for UFO's; Elvis Presley's biggest fan and I've even played a squirrel in a very underground film that I don't think has ever seen the light of day.

Most of the underground New York stuff I did for friends, has never seen the light of day; mostly because it was utter rubbish or partly due to financial or technological issues. There was always a lot of that on those sets. Lots of sound and camera problems.

While I played a young woman who'd just come out of prison for GBH and was adjusting to everyday life; the director 'Samuel Mathews,' lit a cigarette and put it out on the camera wires by accident, setting the entire apartment living room on fire. We never finished the film.

They were all extraordinary chances for me to explore my acting skills and range and meet lots of creative people who had incredible cinematic visions. I think it's a shame that underground, smaller writers and wannabe directors, aren't given the same chances as back in the 70s. Nowadays, all the films coming out of the box office are remakes of old classics, which seems unreasonable when there are so many young and talented storytellers with incredible ideas being overlooked and underfunded. All the youth are being ignored and underfunded.

When I was young, we were hated, which I think is better than simply being disregarded like the youth are today. The youth aren't involved in politics because bigots believe they don't know what they're doing. Tell me that every single old white man in parliament knows precisely what he's doing and maybe I'll change my mind.

The youth will probably agree they don't know what to do to fix our world either; but they still have ideas, feelings and beliefs that should not be discarded. The young matter. Indie films are the epitome of the young mattering, and we don't see enough of them anymore.

I've always believed in the youth. That's my religion. Molly believed in the youth too. She'd go back to her University every single year, find ten kids that intrigued her and pay for their tuition in full. She donated 10% of her earnings every year to a mixture of children's charities, including a foundation that supported kids in the arts. Molly taught kids how to sing through the same programme for six years. Molly had no doubt that a kid was going to change the world. We'd done it. We were kids when we wrote our music and released it to the world. We didn't end world hunger, but the act of making music is a world-changing thing. It made Molly tingle to her core, knowing that kids will be bashing drums, ripping chords and defying melodies for years to come.

And that it would change the world *forever.*

She recited in her letter, how humoured she was at the idea of me in a porno and then went on to recount the time I met a man, whose aftershave was a strong musk of misogyny, in Tony's office.

I went into his office to be greeted by a scruffy haired *boy* in the music industry. He was polite enough to start with pouring me a drink and lighting me a cigarette as we chatted about London and its haunts.

Then he pulled out a spreadsheet, and that's the moment I lost my calm.

This boy had invited himself into my manager's office with a hefty cheque book his father gave him, simply to piss me off. Tony knew it would send a fist threw his wall, which is why he was conveniently *'elsewhere'* living of his cheque for a couple of weeks after.

The *'boy in the industry'* was entirely trying to tell me what to do. It's worth noting this boy was eighteen years old and had performed on stage nine times (he was very adamant on telling me this repeatedly) and had one released song and an album in the making with his father's record label.

He advised me to use flyers as a form of publicity alongside the interviews I was doing. While complimenting me on my vocal range, he simultaneously told me to lower the pitch on my next album to appeal to more females since *'they don't like loud music, but I'm sure they'll appreciate another young girl scout having a go.'*

I was stunned that this was acceptable. I knew damn right that I couldn't walk into an established male performer manager's office to tell him what fucking words to put on his flyers. I knew for a fact, I couldn't do that because I'd be launched by his fists into the next room for insinuating he didn't know what he was doing and that I could tell him how to do it better.

I'd just released *'Heroes.'*

Molly's letter recited that story with immaculate detail and then finished with:

'*We've met so many cunts like him, Penny. So many bookers who want their soul encrusted in diamonds for a cheap quid. I want you to stick it to the man. Stick it to the cunt. You've done it excellently so far, rather impeccably I might add. But do it one more time for me. Stick it to the man one more time. Your Bromley house, the one we so beautifully stole. I know you love it. I know it's home. But how about you make it home for fifty or so girls. Fifty or so girls sticking it to the man. A music school Penny. Make a fucking music school for me. Teach the girls how to change the world. Change the world together. A safe place, where these girls can jam and skiffle and sing and scream and fuck each other. We would've done anything for a place like that. Imagine the chaos we would've caused. We would've shagged the teachers, thrown the beds out the window and written an album all within the first week. I'd love it if you could Pen. It's a dream of mine I think I'm too late to pursue. Call it: 'Stick it to man Academy,' if you like, I'll let you have that one on me. I'm sorry I don't think I'll be able to visit. Teach them how to do the Misfit Flash- that should be a first-week priority.*

Enjoy, Pen. Really, enjoy it. You'll be the best professor of sticking it to the man this world's ever seen.
Keep on livin'.
I love you.
Your Molly.'

CHAPTER
TWENTY FIVE
STICK IT TO
THE MAN ACADEMY

'Stick It To The Man Academy,' open its doors in 1997. I spent five odd years rebuilding the house, after reluctantly moving into our new home in the middle of nowhere in the Lake District. I set about turning the Bromley house into the academy with plans to build outhouses on the land surrounding the house. I had no idea how long building work and planning permissions took to go through. I didn't know anyone in the council I could shag either to get it through quicker. Altogether, from planning to creating, it took around 5 years to get the academy up and running. It might've taken longer, but it was much easier to put together than an album. I was starting from scratch and could be as creative as I wanted.

I couldn't let Molly down. If the academy was her dying wish, it was going to be executed and executed so perfectly, she'd be howling with pride from her grave.

The house was turned into the main building of the academy, with a further three outhouse buildings made for more dormitory's and rehearsing spaces. The whole house was stripped to become structurally sound so no kids would fall through the floor. Tommy and I didn't care much for the weak flooring, even when Albie was a kid, as he was too light to make a hole. But apparently, when you have other people's adolescent children on your property, you have to make the place structurally sound or face being sued every other week. The hallway, staircase and main door are the only things intact with the original arrangement of the building.

The staircase is still my favourite part of the house, and my magical bottom step has been marked as something of a place of historical heritage on the site. The newbies kiss the step as part of an initiation, right on the mark where a student in our first-ever term at the school, graphitised lip marks on the step during the night.

The walls of the two living rooms and study on the bottom floor were knocked down to be one whole open space as the dining hall. While the two kitchens at either end remain kitchens. One is a functioning catering kitchen and the other, equally functions like that too, with added extras for culinary classes for our girls. The two larder spaces remain in use as larders for the food we must store quite tightly to avoid girls with the munchies grabbing a midnight snack. We dug a tunnel underneath the first floor for more storage and easy access for the chefs from one kitchen to another without walking through the dining hall. The girls quite swiftly found the secret tunnels and took the tunnel hostage in many drunken nights during initiation and more. The second floor remains relatively intact and is the main study floor. The five bedrooms were turned into four classrooms. A music room, dance room, general study room and what we call the 'riot room.' The fifth bedroom, which was mine and Tommy's, has remained intact and under lock and key for more sentimental reasons than anything else. I've been called to the school in the middle of the night on three separate occasions now, to lecture three different girls who were caught trying to pick the lock.

The bathrooms have all remained unharmed, with the second-floor study operating as our Head Mistresses office.

The Headmistress of 'Stick It To The Man Academy,' is the only woman I knew who'd be capable of leading 100 odd unruly girls into stardom.

Kitty Burkhart, of the *Magnolia Society.*

Finally, the wide-open space of the attic was transformed into dormitory spaces for 20 girls.

The academy is not explicitly a boarding school. We have fifty girls who remain with us at all times and about 50 others who come for classes and lectures on a weekly, fortnightly or daily basis. Every girl's schedule is different and altered to her, her needs and dreams.

It's almost organised chaos.

We built two outbuildings for the remaining boarding students; about 20 girls in each building. The last outhouse, which also happens to be the furthest from the main building, is a three-story small house with five recording studios on the top two floors, a chapel and empty hall on the bottom floor. The hall is for rehearsing or performing, with a stage about the same size as an average pub or club floor. I replicated it to look like a grubby, 70s English pub scene with a sink in the corner to piss in and all. In the dining room of the main building, hangs the side table and tennis racket from the great kitchen raid of the 70s. I believe one of the recent initiations is to try and climb the walls to grab it down.

The whole school is lavished with the same ethos. Covered in small details that replicate the reality and brutality of life on the road, life on stage, on tour, in the industry. The rooms are small and shared with one bathroom between about 6 girls, which Kitty tells me is a constant nightmare around the same time each month. We make the girls live on a tour bus for seven days every other two months, driving them down the motorway one selected night to familiarise their stomachs with service station food. Every girl that comes through the academy can recite every service station South, East and possibly North of England. We quiz them on it once a year.

We bring in industry professionals to critique their work and even hire actors to be '*meanies*,' as the girls call them, whose only job is to rip the shit out of the girl's work. That technique is often criticised by the parents who have their child crying down the phone every night for a week, but it's more effective than offensive, so we keep it in our curricular.

The girls that attend the academy want to be there more than anything else. They'd do anything to be there, and that's precisely the kind of girl we want. The recruitment process is a long one. Headmistress Kitty Burkhart herself, along with my charming M; scour the country for girls with talent. They attend open mic nights, pubs, clubs and school performances in search for girls with skill and determination.

Kitty and M handpick 15 girls a year for tuition, the rest of the girls are picked from the application process. We don't care about grades or even past experience. We've had hundreds of chicks come through the programme without ever performing on stage before. The idea of the school is to get the girls ready for the stage and career in music, we can do that without any experience, and often it's better if the girls don't know what to expect. We recruit musicians, singers, scientists, writers, translators, designers, artists, producers, wannabe agents and managers and more. If we see talent in a girl, she's ours if she wants it. We've recruited dancers that were just too good to turn down, and last year we recruited our first musical scientist who worked on a study about the gender of sound.

We ask the girls to send in a photograph of themselves 'dressed to riot,' and a two-page letter on a different topic each year. 'Write about female birds in the desert.' 'What do you think about pleated skirts?' 'Which 'The Smiths' album is the worst,' was our most recent one. The letter is just to get to know the girl and her voice because that's all that matters. We want girls with new and unique voices. Girls who aren't afraid to say exactly what they think and feel. Girls with all the nerve to change the world and all the hairspray to do it in a term. We then interview the girls which I attend each year. I wouldn't miss the interview day for the world, it's the highlight of my year. Hundreds of girls fleeing to my home to come play for me, there's nothing much better than that! Tommy comes too, although that's a secret.

There's a locked door at the top of the hall in the far outhouse where you can watch from above without being seen. Tommy's been up there with Albie every year since it's opened.

The girls have five minutes to do and talk about whatever they want. Some intricately describe their love for the trombone, while others chat to me about American politics. One kid once dismantled a tampon on my desk to tell me about the industry, which was rather interesting. She was recruited to the school and is now head of technical design for Tampax.

Not all the girls go onto a musical career, and that's not what we explicitly advertise. We advertise the advocacy for female empowerment. We attempt to give these girls whatever tools they need to achieve whatever the hell it is they want to achieve. We had a young girl of colour come into audition who spoke about her horrific family history for her five minutes. Jacqui showed me her drawings for an aircraft she was adamant would revolutionise space travel. We didn't have a specific astrophysics teacher but admired her determination and her passion. She was from an incredibly deprived and unfortunate family who couldn't afford to put her through university and were losing their family home due to their father's death. We took her in on an honorary scholarship, and I let her family stay in mine and Tommy's bedroom for the few months they needed to get back on their feet.

Jacqui now works for NASA, and I believe her aircraft designs are in the making, and ready to revolutionise space travel. Not all graduates become musicians, but they *all* become feminist icons.

I love visiting the school, which I do about three times a year, alongside the interviews if I can. I'd go more if it weren't for touring or recording. I have visited throughout the night a few times to record and jam in one of the recording studios. I'm rather fond of one particular studio on the top floor with the view of the house in all its glory. It's called the 'Angie' suite, after a twenty-two-year-old girl I once met who wore a school uniform for the comfort of it. She flew out to Japan where she'd heard there were plenty of girls like her, who wore a school uniform for the fun of it. Utterly oblivious to the industry of young girls in school uniform sold on the street; she flew out to chase a dream of musical stardom, and I've never discovered if it came true. I've spent hours staring out that window, thinking of Angie Young and what I could've done to help protect her, singing an Australian lullaby she taught me.

I visit for the end of year performance too, which most of the girls loathe due to its likeness to a 'real school' assembly. We don't really do assemblies at 'Stick it to the man.' We have a weekly jam instead. All the tables of the dining hall get pushed to the side, and everyone attends with whatever instrument they play, or just them and their voice. You don't have to play or sing; a lot of the girls will just watch, enjoy or dance, but the opportunity to skiffle is there.

We try to make every opportunity we can, an opportunity to skiffle.

There's many 'extra-curricular' activities available at the school too, a collection which has grown and developed throughout the years. We have a shooting range at the bottom of our land, behind the chapel house. We teach code on a Thursday, French on a Tuesday, German on a Friday and a short course in Russian for two months every October and November. There are weekly martial arts and self-defence training on a Monday morning, which the girls absolutely adore. The faculty are quite often having to separate little fights and busts up, so giving them the permission to beat the shit out of each other (in a controlled environment, of course) is perfect for them. It also provides them with excellent extra skills for their mosh training every other Tuesday.

The girls can learn economics from a fellow economics student that was in Molly's class at University, and we have seven different feminist and political leaders teaching them a variety of views and opinions every Sunday. That's our religion: *female empowerment.* Kitty Burkhart still runs 'The Magnolia Society,' through the school. They meet every Thursday night in a different part of the school and go into different schools, clubs, pubs and cafes on the weekends to spread their feminist agenda.

And our chapel is run by Suzie. My beautiful Suzie, who is there to talk religion if any of the girls want, but is primarily the school's guidance and support counsellor; dealing with anything and everything from girls falling out, to existential crises about the impending doom of the death of the album.

We also do a short spy course every April, where a different intelligence agent comes and teaches the girls how to be a spy for a month. *May* is always very interesting. I'm typically called about six times in May to come and reprimand 6 different girls who all put their spy skills into practice. The girls tend to listen to me when I'm in my pyjama's screaming about how fucking annoyed I am they've woken me up at 2am to drive here to tell them they shouldn't have done something they know they shouldn't have done.

I tend to never see those girls again.

Except for the one girl who planted a listening device in Kitty's office after our April Espionage class and recorded Kitty slagging of the neighbouring farm for having orange tailed cockerels that kept escaping. I did my usual and drove in the middle of the night to the school to meet the young girl who smirked the entire time I wailed about how tired I was, and how I was going to miss my son's birthday morning for this.

She said she wouldn't do it again, but a week later I got a call from the very same girl threatening to release my latest song I'd just recorded that week.

She planted a listening device on me, the brazen bastard! Unfortunately, she was expelled, and I took no joy in doing it, as I liked the blatant behaviour in her. That blatant and shameless behaviour was 'Stick It To The Man' class 101. But unfortunately, we don't advocate criminal behaviour (*as such*), so she had to go and the espionage month was derailed for a year to teach the girls the privilege of it.

Each girl's timetable is different at the Academy. When they arrive, we spend an hour with each girl taking through precisely what they want and need to be the best they can be. If a lyricist comes in and says: 'I can write lyrics, but I can't sing, I want a singer with a blues voice,' we make that happen. If a girl comes in saying: 'I'm incredibly interested in engineering and have this idea to make the quality of sound from trumpets better, but don't have the means or money to experiment and make it happen,' we make it happen.

We'd give the girl trumpet lessons and bring in a professional sound engineer to work on her idea. Her schedule would be 80% her project, 10% helping other girls in the school, and 10% her time to learn something new. The school works on girls supporting and helping other girls.

The lyricist without a band, the singer without a lyricist, the diva without a manager, the producer without an artist. All the girls work together to make their dream come true.

It's beautiful to watch. They're all free. They arrange their time themselves, we pride ourselves in creating totally independent and liberated women. If they don't put in the work, they're cut. Their progress is reviewed every three months. We understand on individual specific projects progression takes time, but if we've seen no commitment to their aspiration, they're either derailed to another project or cut loose.

We're cutthroat too. The school has to be. There are hundreds and thousands of girls that apply each year. Everyone's replaceable, just like the industry.

I founded a charity alongside the school, in the name of Molly, named: 'The Molly Jagger Innovation Organisation'. We fundraise vigorously and tirelessly for funds for other female empowerment groups and clubs that help, educate or empower women. The charity is a big part of the school, and most of our fundraising is achieved from the girls. Every year, every single girl is asked to find a newspaper or magazine article that slanders women.

They write a very cohesive letter, citing how disgusted they are and even offer a friendlier version of the report alongside a photograph of them giving the media the middle finger because we can. 'Slander Week,' is a busy and popular week. We gather all the 200 odd letters from the girls and send them off on the anniversary date of Molly's death. It feels like some form of retribution towards the medias accountability of her depression and death.

Mostly, I feel it's of paramount importance to teach the girls that being slandered in the press, is not ok. Being vilified as a woman is not ok. Men being held at a higher pedestal than women is not ok. We teach them to use their voice and speak up against the vilification of women. We teach them that they can right a wrong and can support other women if they're wrongfully criticised. We teach the girls to stand up for themselves and their opinions despite what others may say and think. Newspapers and Magazines are starting to listen, and 'The Star Express,' designated us a weekly column where we nominate a different girl each week to write about whatever they like.

We raise money for girls in disadvantaged countries for necessary sanitary products or access to an education too. We recently launched, what the girls wanted to nickname the; 'Bleeding Pad Scheme,' which is a recruitment of 10 graduates to send to Namibia for 6 months. The 10 graduates teach a handful of girls over there. They teach them basic literacy and numeracy skills, alongside music and its importance on liberation and mental wellbeing. Our girls will teach them a bit of everything they've learnt at the academy to the best of their ability, as well as providing the girls with the products we raised funds for.

The charity is incredibly important to me. 'The Molly Jagger Innovation Organisation,' is the very heart of the school. The very ethos of its core.

Helping other women; teaching female empowerment; advocacy for the safety and wellbeing of women and freedom, is what the academy is all about. I founded the school and charity because my best friend died. My best friend died because she was smeared by other women. 'Stick It To The Man' is a place where women can be themselves, without scrutiny. It's a place where they can be inspired by other women and not belittled or jealous. A safe, loving and inspiring environment where the talent and love of a woman can boom. Not just blossom, but boom. Boom from the Earth like a great oak in the sky.

About ten years ago, headmistress Kitty Burkhart wrote the 'Stick It To The Man book of sins,' which is a 50-page book on the school; its history, lessons and how to make the most of your education. In the opening page, it reads:

'*The woman who previously lived in these halls once shagged a butcher for a gig that never happened. Do not take this education for granted. The ghost of the shagged butcher haunts these halls; piss him off, and you'll be pissing in pub sinks like our Penny Jones. Do her proud, be a woman.*'

CHAPTER
TWENTY SIX
MODERN WOMAN

I'm a modern woman now. I masturbate myself silly. If you can't find me highlighting a book on feminism while refusing to shave my armpits and giving every sweating, eager-eyed bald man the middle finger: I'll be masturbating!

I masturbate in bed, in the bath, in the kitchen, in every cue, on every bus. In the bookshop, toy shop, health shop, supermarket, flower market, my office, *his* office. Tourist destinations, the beach (that's always a messy one), changing rooms, toilets, hospitals (a controversial one), in the car, on the stairs, in the lift and sometimes (most times) at the dinner table.

What can I say, I'm a *modern woman*!

I actually find it quite insulting that female masturbation is now a *trend,* as I've been doing it since 1962! If I talked about my masturbation techniques at the dinner table back then; I might've been sanctioned as mentally insane, or at the very least, sent to a Catholic school and refused a lock on my door.

I found masturbation a little dirty when I was young and not the good kind of dirty. I felt a lot of pressure on myself to make myself come. I thought that; 'if I can't make myself come, how could I expect anyone else to?' Me and Molly Jagger would talk all the time about sex and masturbation. We were very open with our sexuality in all aspects, and Molly was an avid masturbator. She had a lot of bad sex with a lot of bad men, so she felt it was her own responsibility to pleasure herself rather than rely upon or expect a man to do it.

The idea that women had a sex life when I was growing up was barbaric, never mind a *self-loving* life. I've always loved talking about sex. I partly love talking about sex because I know how uncomfortable it makes people (mostly men). But also, because I find talking about sex equally as arousing as partaking in any kind of sexual intercourse. And masturbation is my favourite sex thing to talk about because it's such a taboo; especially among women, but we all do it. And if you're turning up your nose thinking; '*I don't do that disgusting thing you animal,*' we all know you've slipped a finger in at some point.

I'm an *invisible* modern woman now. Which I guess is fantastic when I want a quickie, and dreadful when I want a job. When you're a young woman, you fight tirelessly to be seen and heard and watched. Now the fight seems so tiresome and futile when the world doesn't see you as a human, never mind a woman.

When society doesn't put older women on the big screen or give them the career opportunities they deserve in offices and restaurants across the globe; men take their place.

If there's ever an absence of a woman, a man will fall in the slot. It happens as naturally as the cycle of life. An older woman 'ages out,' a man falls in line like a soldier called to duty. Only, it is not a man's duty to replace an older woman. It is not *anyone's* duty to replace an older woman because older women do not need replacing.

I feel as though I have conquered my personal battle with sexism. It has not been an easy journey, but I'm successful. I've faced adversity and come through the other side, a successful woman. But, as if years' worth of sexism isn't enough; women are hit with ageism right between their waning eyes and decorative crow's feet.

I now face an entirely different kind of adversity; a wholly different monster. The sexism monster is a big blue monkey that chucks its shit at you every time you part your lips to speak. The ageism monster is a spritely fly that continuously orbits your head like the sun on smack. The two monsters together are quite the performance.

Typically, the upbringing of children can also derail the speed of your career from a mediocre racehorse winning the grand national, to a fat man with heart disease on a hobby horse running the same race. Being a mother can put your career on halt, stop it entirely or potentially derail it towards demotion and mediocracy. Not that there's anything wrong with mediocracy, having settled for that now in my 60s. Fortunately for me, my motherhood did not derail my career, and I battled the big blue monkey for another decade or so before the fly has occupied my head space like a poorly made science fair project of the planets.

I'm successful. I've earnt more than enough money to have happily retired in my forties. I own three properties. I own a music school and a charity. I've sold millions of records and have had dozens of number-one singles.

I have a beautiful baby boy and a devoted husband. I own two cats. I drink expensive wine and don't look at the prices when I eat at a restaurant.

I'm successful.

Probably *too* successful for a woman.

I struggled, but I prospered. Even if I didn't. Even if I never got a single number one album. Even if I never so much as graced the BBC front building steps; I still would've prospered.

Staying alive and continuing forward as a woman in a man's world *is* success.

That is a successful woman.

A woman stood in court, convicting her rapist: is a *successful woman.*

A woman raising her child alone: is a *successful woman.*

A woman singing her heart out to an empty room: is a *successful woman.*

Any woman persisting for what she loves or believes is successful. Because, sometimes, sexism leaves women no choice but to persist, and when she does, she'll likely *always* prosper because women are incredible.

I'm successful because I worked hard and never gave up. *That's it.*

You got to believe that you'll do it. That the Earth would have to kneel at your feet before you dare even think about giving up. That there is no other option. Befriend desperation. Hold it close and squeeze every ounce of hope you have into your dream. Create a life where blackness is the only other option. An abyss. A fucking terrifying, lonely abyss. Put every foot forward to your dream. *Every fucking foot.*

I don't want women believing they can't be successful because they're women. I want to show these girls at the academy that being a woman does not directly mean you can't be successful. Being a woman can mean you'll face adversity and tribulations. You can have a lifetime worth of fighting and difficulty, and still, be successful. I fought my way here. I'm a product of hardship. Being a woman can be indescribably painful. It can be fighting for your legitimate rights and needs for years on end. It can be degrading yourself for a society that doesn't favour the bold. It can be tiring and pathetic, fighting day in and out, arguing about what you rightfully deserve.

Sexism is the world's biggest nuclear weapon. An imbalance of the sexes is a chemical reaction imploding permanently. A chemical it seems, only the skin of a woman is scorned by.
So many of us are gagged by our femininity. We're gagged by our knickers. Strangled with the pill; beheaded with our expensive lipsticks and told to remain silent during the ordeal. Well, I won't be silenced. You're not going to get silence out of me. I can't keep quiet.

I won't be the pretty girl. The girl all the boys want. The girl with pink lips. The girl who knows the best techniques. The girl with the biggest arse. The girl with no head.

I'll be the girl who kicks your damn ass for touching mine. The girl who spits fire. The girl with no hair. The girl with more whit than a fucking encyclopedia and I'll be this girl without ever saying sorry to our beloved patriarchy for not succeeding their standards.

Because, you know what, *fuck you.*

Fuck your oppressive hands around my neck. Fuck your shackles on my ankles. Fuck your pedestal you shove underneath my feet every time I try to run. Fuck your fingernails clawing at my womb. Fuck your fingers tugging me down as you climb all over me to reach the top. Fuck your standards resting on my shoulders, and fuck your fucking sexism.

Fuck you!

I ain't gonna be oppressed. I ain't gonna be allowed to feel weak or scared or vulnerable, even when I do; because I ain't gonna allow you to make me feel anything other than *angry.*

Pissed off, at the fact you have more control over my own body than I do. *Fuming,* that there's a whole system fighting against my rights. *Fucking raging,* that you dare deprive my sisters and me an education, or a fucking safe street to walk down. Because I have to be labelled: '*successful,*' to be taken seriously.

I have to define and quantify my success, in the same way, I must define my worth, for a society that will never accept my success as something worth sensationalising, because of my *talent* and not my *gender.*

I will always be fighting a battle—the battle against sexism, against ageism, against inequality. There will always be women *fighting.* That is what we do best: f*ight.* And fight so tirelessly, we put the men just joining the combat, to *shame.* Fight so fiercely, they will change the pronoun she, to *lion.* Fight so vigorously, we *become* the fight.

It's been tough, but I am made to believe that the life of any woman is.

I *have* success because I'm a fighter.

I *am* successful because I'm a woman.

I feel very strange talking about modernity and my place in the modern world as a woman because I still feel as though I'm getting used to it and finding my feet. I don't get much of the trends nowadays, which makes me feel incredibly old. I don't get involved much either. It's not my place anymore. The world ain't my city to riot any longer. The towns, the bars, the bands, the clubs; they're for the youth. They're for the girls at the academy and my son. They're for the new wave of artists wanting to stamp their feet.

I only tend to stick my nose up at the state the music industry is in. It's in dire need of a shakeup, isn't it?

I mean, where did the album go? When did the album die?

I will most certainly still be making albums whether people have the attention span to listen to more than one song for 3 minutes or not!

Albums are the greatest invention, *ever.* I loved making album after album and telling story after story. The whole process of putting together an album; from concept to finishing product. The order of the songs, the story of them together, the artwork, picking the single, the outros and the intros, the whole thing piecing together to create a living thing.

A good album is a living thing. It has its own heartbeat, its own history and its own personality. Just like a person, *just like you and me.* Which is why I've always found it kind of silly how albums have *monetised* values.

Society doesn't agree with the (profitable) monetisation of people; despite there being a whole industry for it, it is generally disrespected and regarded as a dirty and unethical profession and source of income.

Hence my conclusion rock n roll is prostitution. A soul is sold alongside that LP you bought for £19.99; a rather cheap deal if you knew the suffering you get along with it.

Tucked in the sleeve, amongst the wreckage of lyrics, is an ounce of regret, a lifetime worth of agony and likely a dead relative or two. *All for twenty fucking quid.*

The world went from it being cheap to kill yourself at two quid a pop to a cheap industry for heartbroken teens: *Cheap souls, cheap vinyl, cheap agony.* Nowadays, music is about the same price as a packet of cigarettes; which is where the world went wrong.

You put the choice of death and music at the same price, on the same shelf, in the same glossed up store, in the same country, and because music is so expensive; it makes death *cheap.* If you don't have music, you don't have a reason to live and therefore (whatever the price) *death is cheap.*

As a child, I had no idea that I could be paid for what I loved. I saw money as a factor of graft in traditional physical formats. I thought money was given to those (men) who operated heavy machinery, working on construction sites or in factories. I often even wondered where my mother and father got their money from; I naively just assumed they got pity paid for their more *mentally* challenging work. I didn't think you could love your job and get paid for it. I thought you were paid as retribution for your demise and pain. The more you hated your job, the more you got paid in recompense.

Growing up, I knew that money didn't matter to me. Maybe it was because I didn't see myself ever earning much based on the skills I had, or the reliability of my creativity funding a career. I'm humbled I held onto the appreciation that money means less than things like love.

I've always been the kid happy doing what they enjoy; I never needed gratification that I was doing the right thing. Painting the rainbow, the right colours; or building the house out of sand the right way.

When it comes to women in music, it's not just about the numbers. We got to fairly represent and equally treat the female numbers we already got. Then they can be spotlights for women in music, and they can set the rules and standards. Because, you just know if we suddenly surge more numbers into the mix, they'll still be managed by men with the kind of expectations and preconceptions we're trying to change.

Record labels will rarely recognise you as a woman. You're just another *pretty, petty cash source*, whose income will go towards the staff Xmas party. Meaning that they're ignorant of the kinds, and *levels*, of abuse that you face. Unless, of course, you do what I did, and earn enough money they can't help but notice you're a woman because they're shocked at their *pretty, petty cash* fund overflowing with dollar and compliments. You must be bold. People won't look or listen unless you *make* them look and listen.

Plus, women need to look out for one another. I would've died without my Molly Jagger. No exaggeration. She saved my life in so many ways, so many times.

I wish I could've been braver to return the favour.

Regarding technology, well that fucked everything up didn't it. Technology and our current reality has estranged people from their morals. This makes it just as easy to steal music than to pay for it. As a customer and a customer of *anything*, you buy things because you have the *choice* to buy them. It is your choice whether you buy an album or not. Nowadays, people have the *choice* of whether to buy an album *rightfully* or steal it.

I wish I could highlight exactly just how much work, love, tears, time, effort, money and passion goes into making one album and how heartbreaking it is when it's stolen. My albums were made freely. I made the albums with no intention of profit or money. I hoped for self-respect, and that's it. I made and still make music because I must. It's a primal instinct burning daily inside of me. I'd still make the music whether I sold a single record because it's beyond habitual and instinctive to me. Yet, there's a difference between not directly intending on making money, and *losing* money because of schemers.

People can choose to buy my record, or they can choose to stream it online or illegally download it. It's their *choice*. Modernity has given people an opportunity. Music piracy is an odd kind of sea. My record company have rather extreme views on music piracy, and they do all they can to stop it, while I don't care too deeply. The money just doesn't mean enough to me for me to care. The money isn't great now music has been digitalised: It's something stupid like £7.50 for 1000 streams. Music piracy is wrong, and it breaks copyright laws, but I look at it like this.

Modernity has given people a choice with how they stream and buy music, a choice we never had. I know for a fact I can't confirm I would've bought every single album legally if I were given an option when I was younger. I didn't have enough money for food some days, never mind the latest music to hit London. I used to shove records down my pants as a kid and steal the physical copies, which is no different to modern music piracy. If there were an option for me to stream it without paying for it, of course, I would've chosen that option. While it stings myself and my record label, and while I wholeheartedly don't approve of music piracy; it is this generations cassette that fits into their streamlined cassette holder in their heads. Plus, how is a kid with no money going to find themselves if they can't steal music?

Music piracy isn't the only way to break an artist; there are hundreds of methods of breaking an artist; nowadays, more than ever. When I was becoming an artist, the most prominent form of damage was not getting rightfully paid. People in the industry will do anything to get out of paying you with *money.*

You'll notice they'll spend half their time belittling you enough to want their payment in respect and worship. The industry will make you believe that money means nothing when you can be worshipped like a God. There's a small amount of truth in that; money is not everything, and being respected does have value.

But being respected at the cost of your fair share of the money is not right or ethical: it's *exploitation.* It falls back to the fact the industry will do absolutely anything not to pay the right people and keep a hold of your money. Techniques might include degrading your self worth enough you believe you're not worthy of what you rightfully earned, or merely attempting to patronise you into thinking the money simply doesn't exist in the first place.

This definitely hits women harder. The men I knew would at least pocket a bit of cash at the end of the show, as well as being drowned in compliments. Myself and other women would be told that the gig didn't pay, but it was still a great opportunity as a whole seven people pretended to listen. Some managers would pay a crowd of men in beer to pretend to listen to '*humour*' female artists but refuse to pay their female artists for doing their job.

It's properly fucked up, and it's not hard. The solution doesn't require years' worth of research or trails in a lab. It merely requires men to fucking pay women the money they deserve.

It makes me feel sick that artists nowadays don't just have that battle, but the fight to earn enough money to make a living in the first place. I guess what I want to stress is the importance of buying albums, *rightfully* and supporting your favourite artists in this ever-changing and harsh environment.
It's crucial that art isn't lost to modernity.

Modernity has killed innocence, and modernity will go on to kill the innocent too. I hate modernity, it's made people *famous* because they're *people* and not because they're *talented*. When I was young, all I cared about was my place in the world and how it would make it better. I cared about what precious time I had. We were raised to want to be; doctors, firefighters, police officers, secretary's, pilots, soldiers; all noble pursuits. Now, children are raised to want to be *famous*, and while it is reasonable to go in search for fame; it is merely a search for self-appreciation and the want to be needed; which modernity has made us all need due to lack of empathy and human interaction because of the digitalisation of the modern world.

While I am fascinated by the dawn of the internet, it terrifies me more than it excites me. I don't know how I could have ever self-reinvented while in an age where my previous personas were forever digitalised and plastered over the internet for anyone to see. How I could've grown into and grown accustomed to my growing body during puberty; while being scrutinised by people oceans away that I've never met before in my life. A considerable portion of my career was the de-mystification of myself and my identity, which simply couldn't be achieved nowadays.

People, *children in particular*, are accustomed to having access to anything and anything they want almost *instantaneously*. It's created children with very short attention spans and a deeply rooted requisite for *more*. MORE, MORE, MORE! When I was growing up, music was subversive and a rebellion. Music felt like the thing that would change things. Music seemed to be the one thing that brought joy to an otherwise, dismal time.

Music was a matter of *importance*.

Now, music is just another thing that comes with the compulsory computer in a child's hand. And it has that '*easy access*', which makes it less impactful and rebellious.

The internet has now become what music once was. Since the internet and the world of social media has created underdeveloped individuals with self-esteem issues; it is not about the power or the monopolies anymore; it's about the *people*.

We live in an egotistical world; everything is about the *people*.

There's no longer any form of mystification between the audience and the artist because the internet has 100 cameras on one artist at all times. While I embrace the fact, it is a new form of art in itself and has created extreme and powerful fan cultures that have kept the music and other such art forms alive. It seems a shame that it is the internet that has taken on our pursuit of rebellion.

Music is now about the community and the fandom and where exactly you belong within the audience. Because belonging is the most essential thing in modern culture. The audience is now obsessive because they have access to such a massive part of their favourite artists' lives. It's no longer devotion and appreciation between the artist and the audience; it's an *obsession*.

The digitalisation of music opened our doors to a much wider audience. It meant more people could hear music from across the globe. It was, however, also the death of music cults, the death of the importance of albums and the end of intros and outros.

There are no longer any defining acts of a decade, only genres or the occasional subgroups. There are no longer any movements for people to be a part of. There's nothing for these poor people to belong to because music isn't about the artist anymore; it's all about the audience.

There wouldn't be any point in having someone define an era or lead the rebellion anyway, because the vocabulary of rock is too overused and overfamiliar. While it still rings true; they are only words, not indications for revolution. The words of rock n roll; not devoid of meaning, are perhaps devoid of *power* in this modern age. The *internet* has taken on the role of rebellion; a reasonably terrifying thought.

I believe that the internet would've appealed to me majorly as a young artist as the potential of content would've been overwhelming and unfathomable. I would've had hundreds and thousands of more tools to express myself creatively, and that is a massive thing for young people to have, yet I fear it could be the final bullet to kill the art world.

There are now so many tools of creativity, and so many mediums for outplay, the priority of realism is long gone. It is near impossible to tell what is real and what is fake anymore; that's where the internet shot art right in the fucking head.

While art may express the imaginary; it is of the utmost importance that the artist is, in fact, real and not only real in the flesh, but real to themselves as much as they know themselves to be.

CHAPTER TWENTY SEVEN
THE EARTH ISN'T QUITE
READY TO LET YOU GO

I was diagnosed with breast cancer on my sons 35th birthday.

I was very afraid. I'm not embarrassed to say that I was petrified. I had such a strong ache in my chest, and my eyes stung for days. I instantly couldn't stand the thought of Albie not having a mother and my Tommy not having a wife. It broke me inside, continues to break me. The shock was initially the hard part, then the immediate grief and acceptance and then the consuming wave of fear and the unknown that I'm still riding now.

All creators are terrified, *constantly*. I confess I spent my entire life terrified. I was terrified to grow up, terrified to leave town. Terrified to grow into myself, terrified I'd hate who I'd become. Terrified to leave, terrified to stay. Terrified, I wouldn't live enough, terrified to die. I still am a little terrified about it all; despite believing I've done it all. I've lived, I've lied, I've cried, I've (nearly) died, and I've done it all in sequins. But this fear that I feel now is like no other fear I've ever experienced. It doesn't compare to the fear of losing your child; the fear of falling in or out of love; the fear of overdosing; the fear of being pregnant; the fear of failing. This fear is terrified of itself. I'm afraid to feel this fear and for this fear to consume me. It's its own being with its own heartbeat and soul. It has its own emotions. It gets angry when you neglect it for a minute; it gets excited when it spends an entire day with you; it is unforgiving towards your happiness. This fear is jealous of love and life.

It is intoxicated with darkness and terrified by the daylight. This fear consumes me. It consumes me in a way that love never has. It sticks to my bones like honey and glues them to one another, so I am paralysed in fright. The fear fractures my limbs enough to numb its ache. It tears shreds at my mind and puts them back together all wrong, I am irrational. The fear sleeps in my stomach, weighing it down like a hammock to my toes that can't rest for the mites the fear has nested there. It has bred inside of me; I have an entire city of terror just playing out inside of my chest. There's a library, and a swimming pool and the bakers make incredible bread.

It quakes *relentlessly.*

I can't go a second without being reminded of how afraid I am. Which is *entirely.* I am *entirely* afraid, relentlessly terrified.

Things are coming to an end, although I wish for them to move on. Endings have never satisfied me the same as beginnings have. So, take this as the start of something new. I take my end as the beginning. I hope my end is the beginning for the girls at the academy. I hope another woman fills my place and inspires more women to do the same.

In a world where death is our every end, I pray that revolution can be our every beginning.

I always thought I wouldn't be afraid of death. I've faced it multiple times throughout my life, but as I lie in bed at night and try to slip off to sleep; the fear paralyses me at the thought of never waking up. It's the ultimate unknown that I wish not to surrender to; *just yet.*

I'm mostly scared for my kid and Tommy. Albie is more than old enough to understand, he's an age that means he's more than capable and likely to arrange my funeral, and that hurts. I never thought those sweet blue eyes would see such cruel things, *but here we are.*

Cancer has done marvellous things to my music. I live in fear of not knowing which performance will be my last; so, I try to give my absolute all at every performance hall across the globe, to not leave a single man, woman, or other, disappointed. I savour every second I have on that stage. Every person crying, every couple kissing, every little girl wearing a t-shirt with my face on, every grown man yelling my lyrics to the high heavens.

I laugh if I mess up; I cry when I remember the emotions behind the lyrics; I smile between songs; I cry again at the end when I see the blank space at the bottom of the setlist and know I must leave the stage. I hate that part. I hate leaving the stage. After watching hundreds and thousands of souls surrender themselves to you; it doesn't feel right to leave them, so they can get in their car and drive home to their beds to sleep. I want to stay there all night until each of our feet are bleeding and our eyes are dropping from the exhaustion of being alive so intensely.

I make a home out of each stage I perform. I have all my family there; all my favourite people and things. I carry a notebook on me at all times, so I'm occupied and comforted.

It feels just like a home.

How badly I wanted those kinds of stages to be my home and how hard I fought to make them a home. The rough nights, the fighting, the sleeping around, the lying, the drugs, the mistakes; the *lot*. Each time I stand on that stage of a night, and look out at those eyes staring back up at me; I am reminded of the fight I have pursued to attain my place front and centre on the worlds' stage. Every little bit of hurt doesn't hurt that much when you've got thousands of kids singing your songs back to you.

It makes sense to me that I'm healed by music at this time. Those people in the crowds are relieved of their own heartbreak by my music; I am healed by theirs. I love their laughter and their cries. Their screams and their whispers. Their exasperated breathes; their shaking lips.

I savour the moments I can feel their emotions radiating from their sweat; there's no better feeling. You can taste their hunger for a remedy in the air.

You can feel their agony, but it doesn't feel like hurt on my chest; it's more like a shaking. I'm shook at the realisation; I instinctively act with my voice. You can smell their desire, it's right next to the cigarette smoke. They all wear woe so well, their yearning to escape is the least bit pitiful.

I worry about these people. These kids with their mothers and fathers. I worry they'll want something to remember me by and fail to remember my music. I think they'll think of me as a dead mother leaving so much behind. A fallen angel who never put a toe out of line, leaving a poor son and widower. They're not wrong, I leave behind a family I consider a whole world, yet I also leave my music and I hope they turn to it. I hope my words can once again heal the broken as I break. I can't offer anything else, I'm afraid. Maybe for the first time, I have nothing but my music to give. That is healing to me. That is what I surrendered *everything* for. The knowledge that all I am able to give from my soul is my music.

That is how I wish to be remembered.

I dream about being a child a lot. I can taste the air. Air seems to taste sweeter when you think you'll taste it forever.

I dream about the little things children do. The relentless stream of questions; the blubbering tears with scraped knees; the unbridled belief in the unknown; the toys; the novelty shaped food; the joy of running; the faith in flying.

I think about how much I loved to sit in solitude, doing nothing but dreaming. How powerful that felt, to *dream* as a child. It wasn't called *dreaming* back then. When you're a kid; dreaming is not an imaginary hallucination, it's a reel of future images: it's *hope*. They're castaway lands and wholesome people, saying small nothings and sweet touching's. They're a cue of surrendering disbeliefs for the sanity of our Everworld.

390

I dream about what I'd name my fairies, such a tedious procedure. I rally through the small number of people I know and name my fairies after *things*, rather than people. I name one Table, one Orange and I name the twins: Salt and Pepper. I decide they are all slaves to the doll's house I keep them captive in. I feed them of a morning and night, letting them socialise with one another in the afternoon. The twins don't like Orange much; they think she's a bitch.

In my dreams, the leaves have character. They have a soul; it hurts to tread on them. The trees talk to me; they tell me of their history and all the things they've seen.
One has hung a witch for her craft. All things seem magical in these dreams; like childhood itself.
Discovering the joy of snow for the first time; the innocence of a whisper; the depth of darkness when the lights are out; the hypnotism of a flame; the heat of the sun and the revitalisation of rain.
Standing by knees, wrapping your anxiety around your parent's ankles. The feelings with no explanations, no words or definitions. The terror of an empty bed. The wide, open spaces. The ceiling of the world seems so high, the ground so close. Fumbling feet, fuzzy heads, growling stomachs; a constant quench for more.

I'd never missed being a kid until now. I didn't even want to be a kid when I was one. I was so quick to grow up. I wanted to see the world from a taller height too quickly. I wore heels too young and swore too early. I fell in love too quickly and deeply. I gave up my innocence too soon. I surrendered to fear and to disbelief far too young. I gave up my youth for the ultimate trick. I thought adulthood was the most magical dream I had. Turns out the dream I was living, is *the dream* after all.

I want my child to stay young for as long as possible, despite already being an adult. I wish all children to never grow up. Stay furtive and innocent. Keep harbouring hope and fertility. Believe in the things you shouldn't and love the things you should. Surrender to absolutely nothing but yourself. Forget sanity, it will weigh you down.
Hold delusion dearly, it will keep you warm when the chill of reality nips your tongue. Love endlessly and fearlessly: then love some more. Forgive yourself, forgive your mother. Talk to people, hear what they have to say, hear everything and soak it in as though your life depended on it because your *culture* certainly does. Don't be afraid to look people in the eye and break your own heart for their amusement; as it will make that cavity deeper for even more love. Write letters, sing songs, dance with bleeding feet. Wear the clothes you shouldn't. Sleep with the people who make you tingle and kiss those that make you feel alive.

Go in pursuit of happiness, but do not let it be your only pursuit. Pursue sadness and consume it like a bad dream. Wreak havoc. Spread ecstasy, but don't take it. Take from strangers, what you'd give to the world. Fight for what you believe and fight fearlessly and tirelessly.

Do not rest too easy. Wear the red lipstick. Do not speak politely to impolite bastards. Be aggressive, it'll likely suit you. Learn a language you won't speak. Watch the movies as though you wish to be in them. Say 'Fuck you,' more and with less regret. Don't cross your legs when you sit down. Learn every crevasse of your body. Do not attain a religion in search of direction; look to yourself for guidance, you know the way. If you must get a sexually transmitted infection, at least make it a good one. And *finally*; if you must die, do so with such grace, the Earth isn't quite ready to let you go.

If I must die, I wish to do so with love. I wish to leave the world as I came. I enjoy the roundness, the full circle; it's a small amount of satisfaction. I want to leave a little confused, like how I arrived. I want to leave, not knowing where I'm going, but trusting it'll be alright. Believing it'll be okay because I have nothing else to trust and nowhere else to go. I can't crawl back into the womb of life and wish for a revival. I don't think I'd make the most of my resurrection anyhow, which is enough to satisfy dying.

I think death might be another form of reinvention for me. I can only hope my followers will revive me if I must die. I like thinking about how they'll keep my legacy alive.

It makes me feel warm, in a very *cold* world.

I talk quite bluntly with my son about my diagnosis. He hates it, but I know he'd also hate it if I pussy-footed around the subject. I once tried to pussy-foot around the fact I'd ran out of condoms and rooted through his sock draw to find his stash when he was 16. He got that agitated at me repeatedly saying: '*sex is a completely natural thing,*' he went upstairs, handed me a fresh packet and told me to 'never, *ever,* ever put the image of us having sex in his head ever again.' He threatened to move out, it was all very dramatic. So, after that, I vowed to be blunt with him.

I'd always assumed I'd have a lifetime to tell Albie all the things I've wanted to teach him and show him all the beautiful places in the world I've had the pleasure of seeing. Not knowing how long I have left to do those things, has meant I've written a lot of letters and spent a lot of long evenings crying and talking with him. I try not to cry, but I can never help it. It's those blue eyes of his, they're just like his fathers.

Tommy tries to tell me how much he loves me; then he starts crying and has to go take a shower. He's promised me he'll stay clean when I die, but I'm uncertain the grief will be that kind to him. Tommy doesn't deserve this.

I wish him the kind of love that breaks the realms of reality. We have that now, but I don't know what will happen. I sit here unsure for our future, both separately and as husband and wife. He will become a widower; it won't suit him. He'll absorb the title and likely spit it back out again. I don't doubt he'll blab about never loving another woman again, but for everyone's sake, I hope he bloody does. He's a fucking whiny bastard, he'll only be a Debbie downer if he doesn't move on.

My grandchild is on its way, which is very bittersweet. I'm hoping it's a girl so she can look after my Albie when she's all grown up. Albie's already told me they're going to name the child Penny if it's a girl. It seems such a sweet sentiment, but I don't want the kid to grow up with such a permanent reminder that her Grandma is dead. I'm hoping to meet my first grandchild before I go. I'm praying life is at least kind enough to do that.

I've thought about my mother and father a lot recently; although long gone, I think about how they'd feel knowing their baby girl was dying. It hurts a lot, as a mother, it makes the whole ordeal a lot tougher to swallow. I think we forget we're someone's daughter or son, from time to time. I think we forget we're not just wives, husbands, sisters, brothers, friends, uncles, aunts. *We're someone's kid.* We're not supposed to die.

Now, loneliness tints the air a pale shade of blue. Floors lie flat and cushioned, with little ambition. There's no sound in the air, but the air is not still. It hums like the wings of a hummingbird and drops an octave like a bike changes gears. Desperation joins the sea of loneliness, in a swash of regret. I am swallowed into the void of its own fear.

Curtains close themselves. Absolute darkness would be a shade too light for how every room feels. The Earth now reeks of death, like it never smelt of life. *Death is the new milk.*

Death is what binds me and you, you and her, me and life, us and the Earth. I don't need to talk about death in metaphors or even in words. I simply need only say the word, and you're scared. *Death.* That's the power of it. The abruptness, like an unfinished

THE REVOLUTION STARTS NOW.

KITTY RIGGS
IS A 20 YEAR OLD, COWBOY BOOT WEARIN', BOWIE **OBSESSED** AUTHOR FROM MANCHESTER, ENGLAND. SHE WROTE HER FIRST NOVEL AGE 12 AND THIS, HER FIRST PUBLISHED NOVEL, IS HER 20TH BOOK.

INSTAGRAM: @KITTYRIGGS_

Acknowledgments.

Firstly, I'd like to thank my wonderful Daddy for saying the words: 'What If Bowie Were A Woman,' and changing my life forever. I owe him, and my beautiful Mummy everything. Thank you both for being so patient, understanding and loving.
I don't have the words for how much I love you. It's more than jelly tots, that's for sure.

I'd also like to thank Kel, for being the other half of my creative being, therapist and best friend. The K to my J. Your belief, lust and passion for all things creative is so wholesome to experience. I don't ever want you to feel like you're not enough as a woman. Penny is for you- thank you K.

Special thanks to my friend of 18 years, Charlie, for forever and *always* being there. *I Love you.*

Thank you to Alex, for his creative vision and his unbridled belief in mine. *Tuesday 4 o'clock.*

Thank you to *my Molly*; all that is good about Molly Jagger is you.

Special thanks to Charlotte Moore who's support I will always cherish.

I'd like to add thanks to my wonderful best friends: Alice, Betty, Maddy, Abbie and Hannah for all their love and support.

Thanks to Neil, Rach and Max for believing in me.

My family and my wonderful Wawa who embodies all of Penny's fiery spirit.

And I'd like to add thanks to my three wonderful cheerleading coaches: Kelli, Bethan and Julie, alongside every single Pixie: past, present and future; for shaping the woman I am today.

This book is all about the great lengths a woman will go to for herself, her career and her passions. I add extra thanks to all the women before and to be; who prevail, persist and prosper.

And lastly, the man who made this all possible.
Mr David Robert Jones.
For him, I owe my life.

Thank you, the reader, for believing in these words until the *end.*

Printed in Great Britain
by Amazon